# War of the Dremrel

# (Book Two)

# Fat Man Hunting

Jackson Tuwcroze

Published by Tuwcroze Books

ISBN-13: 978-0-9576190-1-2

# DEDICATION

My father always wanted to write a novel and now I've
written two for him. Rest easy, Dad.

# ACKNOWLEDGMENTS

Where does the writer stop and the story begin? My own adventure continues, surrounded by those that inspire me. Their support and encouragement is very welcome. Thank you all.

# 1 LOST IN LIMBO

The college bell rang and he flinched slightly. Every day was bringing him closer to his freedom. Soon he would walk out of the gates of this school and never set foot in it again. He frowned, feeling an odd sense of déjà-vu and looked around the class. Something wasn't quite right, but there was nothing he could really put his finger on. The last few days had progressed smoothly enough and he'd been able to get a lot of uninterrupted studying done. Why did that feel so wrong though?

He looked at the familiar faces of the other students who smiled back at him in recognition. Smiling in return, he finished scribbling his note and surreptitiously slipped it onto the desk behind him. Moments later he heard the rustling of paper and knew the recipient was reading it. He chuckled quietly and then jumped as a loud voice boomed out at him, "Darjoon, what are you and Soodram up to?"

The florid face of their teacher broke into a grin, "You two mischief-makers, you're always conspiring together, aren't you. Well, you had better make sure you've conspired well on your latest project. I want you both to keep up the good work you've been doing. I have high hopes for you two and so do your parents."

Darjoon smiled as the bell rang to signify the end of class for the day. He knew that Soodram and himself had at least an hour of their own free time left before the study period began. He'd arranged to meet his friend in the library so they could review their latest forbidden book. It was another of the books that Soodram managed to sneak out from under the librarian's nose. That crabby old man never realised the books that the two boys reviewed together weren't the prescribed reading books. Standing up, he turned around and whacked Soodram on the back, then ran towards the door, pushing past Radnort who laughed and joined Soodram in chasing him past the other students. Yes, he was actually quite sorry that college would end soon, and he'd have to leave his friends behind, especially his beloved Soodram.

Rushing out the classroom door, Darjoon stopped abruptly, bewildered. Instead of the familiar corridor leading to the quad with its ageless tree, he was confronted by brightly coloured silks blowing in a gentle breeze. Soft furnishings lay scattered inside a large tent and the heat of the morning sun outside was already beginning to make itself felt. He looked around wonderingly, noting the ornate rugs and pillows on the floor and the low, delicate table in the corner, then started as he realised he wasn't standing at all but lay clothed in a long white robe on large, soft blankets resting on skins laid out on the floor. His body felt like he'd been beaten all over with a borrkilli, the wooden training sword used by the college, and as he stretched he felt tightness in his muscles and pain in his bones.

The Great Healer of the Lost Tribe released the last of the spells that had kept Darjoon in his schoolboy fantasy. She was perspiring slightly, both from the effort it had required to continually overcome his failing magic, and from the desert heat that had been steadily building as the morning progressed. She wiped her brow and pouring from a cool pitcher, took a long, slow drink of the watered pomegranate juice that had been placed by her elbow on the low table. The warrior who had put it there withdrew discreetly to stand at the entrance of the tent. He and his companions had stood guard for some weeks now, in case the confused young mage broke free of her spells. They were highly trained and wore magical amulets of protection, wrought at no little cost to herself, but which would at least offer them some advantage if the worst did occur and the young mage unleashed some strange spell. Strong as they were, they still occasionally gripped the curved swords they wore at their hips, or grasped the long spears they carried a little tighter. The young mage had large, broad shoulders, especially for a raven-born and there was an aura of power around him that even those insensitive to magic could detect. And these warriors were not so insensitive.

She was still unsure of Darjoon's actual magical capability, although she had sensed that magic failing slowly through the previous weeks. There was still no telling how much still remained, or how powerful it could be. Try as she might, the strangeness of it thwarted her attempts at probing all of its depth. She shook her head and slowly eased herself up off the mat she'd been sitting on, then exited the tent and stepped out from under the shade of the awning that had been erected just outside. She flinched slightly at the fierce burn of the sun on her unprotected cheeks, then closed her eyes and looked up, enjoying the hot radiance on her upturned face and the glow inside her closed eyelids. Finally she drew in a deep, shuddering breath. She'd been looking forward to this moment with mixed emotions, part dread and part excitement at the challenges ahead. She would have to be very, very careful as she dealt with this young mage. Clearly his memories were lost and his magic was slowly failing, but at least his health was recovering. It had been touch and go whether he would make it at all, but there seemed to be an indomitable will and an almost inhuman fierceness in him  and slowly but surely he had crept back from the physical and mental abyss that the lizard-men had thrown him into.

The first few times that he'd woken up, obviously weak, desperate and confused, she'd barely contained him, only just managing to ease him back into the darkness of healing sleep before his wild magic broke free. She'd realized that he now needed to emerge from the dreams for good, and that he needed to begin the process of recovering his true memories or else it would cause irreparable harm. She'd used the few precious memories she'd been able to extract from his tightly bound mind to reconstruct his college environment as best she could, and had then placed his consciousness into that artificial place. Yet he'd become restless lately and she knew it couldn't contain him much longer. The conflict between the truth of his memories and what she had created would begin to unravel his very mind.

Now she had to face him and hope he'd be able to understand everything she must tell him. Failing that, she'd have to introduce him to his supposed friend, the warrior, and see if that unlocked a bruised and battered mind. She frowned to herself. That's if this warrior, this Nasrindo, wasn't just lying to them about who he was. She couldn't bring herself to fully trust him as it was obvious to her that he was holding back some vital knowledge, some important truths about himself and so she couldn't take a chance on him right now. She only had his own word that he knew Darjoon and that he meant him no harm. No, for now he'd have to be the backup strategy, in case this morning didn't work out as she'd planned. She took another deep breath and stepped back into the tent just as Darjoon was carefully standing up.

He blinked at the bright sunlight that flashed in through the tent's entrance as the Great Healer slipped inside. What he saw was a short yet distinguished lady with noble bearing, not young but not old, with intense green eyes above full red lips. She was definitely not raven-born, and the long light-brown hair under her cowl framed her dusky face. No, if he remembered right from the pictures in college, then she looked like one of the women from the desert tribes. At least those that he'd seen in the books in the library. He stretched, still feeling sore and weak for some reason. She was speaking to him, but not in any language he could understand, so he shook his head faintly and smiled at her boyishly. She pursed her lips, frowned, then turned to the table and poured some liquid from the silver pitcher into an ornate silver cup and handed it to him. He smiled politely, took it and then, suddenly feeling very weak, stepped forward and, bangng the silver cup down on the table, slumped onto the mat beside it. She leaned forward and was talking to him again, but this time he realized she was speaking Empire and he could understand her.

Her heart sank when Darjoon smiled at her vacuously. The fact he had not understood her meant his memories were really gone, including his knowledge of the desert language. He looked pale and weak, so she poured him some juice and then watched in concern as he slumped down onto the mat. Taking a deep breath, she leaned forward and tried again, this time switching to Empire, a language he should've learned in class at college. Every raven-born should be able to speak Empire, although Darjoon should have learned some of the desert tribe lingua-franca from the time he spent with the warrior and so he should've understood her at first. She relaxed when he looked up in recognition at the Empire tongue, and continued speaking, "Darjoon, I am the Great Healer of this tribe. I have much to tell you, but right now I need to know how you are feeling, and if you remember anything at all of how you arrived here, or indeed, if you remember anything from the last few months?"

Darjoon looked up at her and smiled again. She was quite attractive up close, especially when she spoke so earnestly. What did she mean 'arrived here'? Where was 'here' and what was going on? One minute he'd been in class and now this. He shook his head fretfully. He was probably day-dreaming during lectures again, which wasn't hard, especially as the teachers droned on about subjects he already had knowledge of. If only they knew what books he'd been reading. Oh well, he might as well enjoy the dream while it lasted. Maybe he could have some fun in this dream. He stretched his arms over his head and looked at her appraisingly. Yes, indeed, why not have some fun. He imagined her in her undertunic and frowned when that didn't happen. Maybe he didn't have as much control over this dream as he thought. Hmm, she looked agitated, what was she saying now?

The Healer frowned first in alarm and then in exasperation as magic plucked at her dress, but she quickly smoothed her face in order to project calm. He was staring at her like an infatuated schoolboy with that vacuous expression on his face again. She narrowed her eyes and repeated her questions. Darjoon started speaking and then stopped suddenly. His tongue felt thick and unusual in his mouth and he had difficulty forming the Empire words. It was like his tongue and his mouth had forgotten how to do the simplest of things. He reached for the cup and took a sip of the strange juice to help loosen his tongue, froze for a moment and then swiftly slammed the drink down on the table.

His eyes narrowed as he looked at the strange lady who stood in front of him and then at the silhouette of the guards he could see outside the tent. What was really going on here? Was this some sort of final-year test by the masters? Was the juice he'd just drunk actually poison? It certainly tasted strange and it had left his mouth with an odd, dry sensation. Well, he'd play along for now and see where this went. Nothing could happen to him in a dream, anyway. He looked up at her and answered, "I'm fine, I think. My mouth feels a little strange and I feel stiff and sore. I don't know what you mean by asking how I got here? Surely that's something you should know better than I? Seeing how, well, how I appear to be sitting in one of, your, tents?"

He smiled at how clever that was. That should put them on their toes. Hopefully they would realize they couldn't mess with him, not even in a dream. He looked at her pointedly and folded his arms.

She'd noticed how he'd slammed the cup down, as well as the way he'd suddenly frowned and looked around so guardedly. Her stomach tightened in response to a shiver across her skin and she swallowed nervously. His answer showed that he was now being very cautious and suspected the drink she'd given him. That was not what she wanted and she knew there was real danger in that direction. Composing herself, she smiled at him and sat down, pointedly taking some juice for herself and drinking it down, smacking her lips afterwards.

"Please, Darjoon, relax", she said, "This juice is one of the best ways to quench your thirst in the desert, which is where you are, by the way. You are in the great Desert of Thoth, among one of its tribes. I am the Great Healer of that tribe. You were brought here by a friend of yours as you had been badly injured by strange magic, and I have been taking care of you for a little while now. You've been asleep for some time, and have only just woken up."

She watched him closely to see his reaction, deliberately not providing any great detail as yet. Would it trigger any of his memories? She breathed easier as he seemed to relax, sitting back and picking up his drink again.

Darjoon listened in growing wonder. Maybe this was just a pleasant day-dream after all and not a test. It sounded like one of his dreams. He'd always wanted to visit the great desert tribes, and hadn't he only been reading about them just the other day? It seemed so real, the taste of the juice he was drinking, the heat of the sun outside, even the cool breeze that blew through the clever gaps in the tent walls, rustling the brightly coloured silks. He relaxed and took a sip from the deliciously cool drink. After all she'd been drinking from the same pitcher so it must be fine. He savoured it and settled back. Without thinking, he said out loud, "This has to be one of the most realistic day dreams I've ever had."

He looked at her suddenly and exclaimed, "Do I get to go hunting? Because that would be so good. I've read about the beautiful sand-cats that prowl the desert, now one of them would make a fine catch."

She gnawed at her lip, exasperated. Nothing! He'd remembered absolutely nothing, she realised. Curbing her growing frustration, she could see this would take some time. She would need to reveal just enough detail to try and trigger a recall of his memory. She stood up, thinking over what she would reveal first, the warrior called Nasrindo, or the lady that Darjoon had been babbling about when he'd first woken up. She unconsciously paced up and down while she thought furiously, occasionally glancing over at him as he sat quietly drinking his juice and observing her intently.

Darjoon watched her pacing like a caged tiger and saw she was deep in thought. As she went past him he spied a curious dagger on her hip, shaped like a snake. Laughing, he suddenly flowed to his feet and grabbed her waist, pirouetting with her as she tried to dance away and reaching around to take her knife. She reacted unconsciously, defending herself by sliding his arm away and trying to wrap him in a shield spell. Darjoon shredded the spell with ease and grabbed hold of her wrists. He pulled both her arms behind her and tied them with magical rope. Quickly freeing the dagger from its sheath he stepped back, holding it easily in one hand. They'd not made a sound during the scuffle and the guards remained outside, unaware of what had just happened.

Darjoon chuckled easily, flipping the dagger from hand to hand and from handle to point. She froze, not wanting to antagonise him further but realising how vulnerable she was. She tested the magic of her bonds and almost gasped out loud. She'd been certain his magic was failing, but now what she sensed in the ropes around her wrists was a very powerful force. She watched him, hawk-like, as he stood there holding the dagger with practiced ease. She cursed her stupidity for not leaving the thing outside, but she was so accustomed to it being there that the thought hadn't occurred to her.

"Well, you live and learn", she muttered quietly to herself, "Hopefully you'll live through this, K'trell, you idiot".

She flinched at her own use of her name. It wasn't something she was used to hearing. Healers lost their names, although she'd always struggled with that.

Darjoon saw the Healer testing her bonds while looking at him appraisingly and his smile grew broader.

"Well that'll give her something to think about", he thought to himself, although he realised he'd unconsciously not used his full magic in the ropes for some reason. Probably because he just wanted to have some fun, and didn't intend to hurt her. He remembered suddenly that he'd promised to meet Soodram in the library and was going to be late if he kept day-dreaming like this. Suddenly flipping the dagger around in his hand and sliding up his sleeve, he slashed down at his bare arm. In the past, whenever he'd hurt himself in a dream he'd immediately woken up.

"And now it is time to go", he thought as the dagger bit deep into the flesh of his arm. He laughed at the look on her face as she yelled in fright, then grunted as the searing, red-hot pain lanced up his arm. Dropping the dagger, he looked down at the gaping slash that was spurting blood onto the fine rugs below. The guards came rushing in and he looked up in surprise, realising that nothing about the dream had changed or faded in the least. In fact, as a result of the pain, everything had a much sharper clarity than before, including the formidable size of the guards, the curved swords at their waists and the large spears they were carrying, which were currently pointed directly at him.

K'trell gasped in disbelief as Darjoon slashed down at his arm, blood spurting up from the wound. Shredding the rope on her wrists with her own magic, she quickly held up her hands to stop the onrushing guards from interfering or attacking. She strode forward quickly and, grasping hold of him, forced him onto the mat and muttered an incantation over his arm, watching closely as the deep slash slowly closed and the bloody trickle running down his arm dried up. Picking the dagger up off the floor, she put it back in its sheath and sat down, glaring at him. Darjoon looked at his arm and then looked up at her wonderingly. The vacant expression he'd had earlier was gone and now he looked at her as if for the first time. They stared at each other.

After some time, he whispered, "This isn't a dream, is it?"

She shook her head slowly, then looked at him for a long while, wondering how much to tell him. The truth she unleashed could either have a positive effect, or it could interfere with and cloud his memories, causing inner conflicts that might never be resolved. It may even be worse than losing his memories, as he may have put a subconscious block on them and so, by giving him too many details, she could prevent those blocks from ever being released. She'd tried to use her magic to probe into his mind over the last few days, but to no avail. Apart from the scraps of memories about the raven-born college and his childhood, there'd been no way to tell what the extent of the damage was. The weakness of the magic in the rope he'd created confirmed her suspicion that his magic was failing. She leaned forward and touched his arm gently to establish close contact with him.

"Darjoon", she began, "I had hoped you would remember for yourself, but as that's not happening, I need to explain how you ended up here. You will probably find it hard to believe at first, but over time I hope your memories will return, and eventually be fully restored."

"You have journeyed a long, long way from your college and your raven-born home, and have had many strange adventures along the way. Unfortunately, a recent traumatic experience has caused you to lose most, if not all of the memories of those adventures."

She watched him carefully as she spoke, pausing for a while, then continued, "Are you sure there's nothing that you can remember from when you left the college, or even why you left?"

Looking at her and listening intently, he shook his head slowly and looked down, then quickly lifted his head and glared at her, "But if I'd left, why did it seem like I was still in school? I mean, until I woke up just now I was actually in class. It felt a bit strange, but to me it seemed real. So which is the dream? Are you even real? Am I dreaming about dreaming?"

Before she could stop herself, she exclaimed, "Well, don't you dare think you can cut me to find out!"

Then she stared at him in horror. She hadn't meant to say that and the gods knew if he would think it was a suggestion. She realised how tense she was and how much he unnerved her.

He looked at her with shock evident on his face and then burst out laughing. "No, no no", he chuckled again, looking down at his bloody arm, "Oh no, I think I've had enough of that for now, thank you very much. Don't worry, you're safe with me, Sirroya, I won't harm you."

Darjoon suddenly doubled over and placed his face in his hands as he closed his eyes. A searing pain burst through his head like a thousand hammers all beating down on him at once. A confused jumble of images flickered in his mind, a massive forest with houses in trees, deadly assassins and a dry, hot desert with caravans and strange people dressed in colourful clothes. Overlaid on it all was the indistinct silhouette of a shapely woman.

The healer reached over quickly and placed her cool hand on his head, muttering under her breath. He felt the flow of powerful magic and, with barely a thought, shredded the sleep spell she had been trying to cast over him. As she sat back abruptly, pale and afraid, he looked up shame-faced and apologised, "I'm sorry, I did that without thinking. I know you were only trying to help. It's just that, well, I guess I'm a little jumpy right now. Also my head, it's so incredibly sore. But who is this Sirroya? Why? Why did I use that name? Is it yours? Is that your name? Please! I need you to tell me as much as you can. I'm certain that what you reveal will help me make sense of all this. Don't you think? Oh, I don't really know. Why is my head so sore though?"

Surreptitiously, she clasped her trembling hands together in her lap, still reeling inside from the shock at what little effort he'd used to cut away her spell. So much for his failing power! Did he have any idea of how truly dangerous he was? She looked at him carefully but could see he really didn't know that he'd frightened her so much, and his face was open and pleading, and filled with pain.

Calming herself, she began to tell him the little she had gleaned from his ramblings and from what Nasrindo had told her. She omitted those parts that she felt might unduly influence him and when she was done, they sat in silence for some time.

Darjoon was struggling to believe her. It all sounded so surreal, like one of the adventure stories he'd read about while in the college library. Only this time, he was the adventurer. So he'd left the land of the raven-born and travelled through the Darken Hills? The Darken Hills! Really? As if that was likely! Who in their right mind would do that? Didn't she know they were infested with the dreaded Dremrel, let alone bandits and renegade magicians? How would he have survived all of that? And then, according to her, he'd travelled into Spidral, met some lady there called Sirroya, the name he'd mistakenly used for her, and then the two of them had travelled across the Plains of Breath and into the Desert of Thoth, where they'd been attacked, presumably by bandits. It was after the attack that he'd lost his memory. He was sure she wasn't telling him everything though. His head still throbbed painfully and he was feeling incredibly tired but it felt like there were some big gaps in what she'd said. He shook his head to clear it but the fuzziness remained. He felt her cool hand on his arm and looked up at her.

"Darjoon", she called to him, "You are weary and you need to rest. Why don't you lie down now and then we can talk again, once you're feeling better? There are two guards outside and they are as much for your protection as mine. My tribe is, well, understandably nervous and has some misgivings about our taking care of you. We live a very isolated life here, I'm afraid. But for now, these guards will make sure that no-one will disturb you while you recover. Maybe when you wake up you will have a better sense of where you are, and then your memories may start to come back more fully. Rest now and I will return later."

She stood up and waited for him patiently. He realised the sun was already fading outside, and so turned and stumbled over to the bed. She watched him as he gingerly lay down and, once he was breathing rhythmically, she left. Stopping at the door, she whispered to the guards, "Make sure that nothing disturbs him and keep a very sharp lookout. He may want to wander around outside the tent, which is absolutely fine, but you will need to stop him from leaving this place. Other than that, accommodate him and be friendly but alert. He is under guard but at this point I do not think he is dangerous. Nevertheless, call me as soon as he wakes up."

Heading back to the main camp, she felt bad deceiving the guards but she couldn't let them know what she had learned of his true power. She grabbed some food and then headed for her tent, walking past the small smithy on the fringes of the encampment, its ceaseless fire breathing smoke that wafted away in the light breeze. She briefly acknowledged the sweaty, grimy blacksmith who waved at her from inside, then bustled past some women and children who averted their eyes and bowed their heads in humble recognition of who she was. At her tent, she suddenly changed her mind, put her food down on the low table just inside and turned and made her way to Nasrindo's lodging. The warrior sat inside his tent on the blankets and skins that made up his bed, quietly meditating, but he looked up at her intently as she came in.

"So, what news of Darjoon, and when can I see him", he asked without preamble.

"I think I may have under-estimated his true power", she replied, avoiding the direct question and looking down at him.

"Either that, or else he has been deliberately concealing it from me. He is in fact a very dangerous young mage, and we cannot rush him or this tribe risks being exposed to that danger. I will not risk the Lost Tribe for your supposed friend."

"Well", he sniffed irritably, "Isn't that what I told you, what I've been telling you all along? That he is very powerful. Don't you see? The longer you delay in introducing me to him, the more risk there is of antagonising him and that would not be a good thing to do, trust me. Not for any of us. The sooner you let me see him, the better for all of you. Surely you have to see that?"

"Really", she lifted her chin and looked down her nose at him, "I know what I'm doing, warrior. After all, I am the one who is the Great Healer in this tribe, not you. I will say when he is ready to meet you and it is not yet. I, well, I may have been mistaken about his magical ability failing, but that's hardly my fault. If, as you say, it is the mingling of two sources of power, one raven-born and one from that accursed place, from that dark Island, then who knows what it has become or even what it might end up becoming. There is just no way for us to know. Did either his father or mother say anything to the warrior that you took the blood oath from? Did that warrior tell you anything more?"

She continued to stare down at him, impatience writ large in her wrinkled brow, "Anything? Come now, warrior. We may be in terrible danger and I have to balance the safety of the tribe against the possibility that he is indeed the one from the prophecy. Come, what can you give me to help in this?" Her voice had softened at the end as she saw the clear anguish appear in his face.

He looked up at her, and then bowed his head. "Please", he said, "Please let me see him, even if it's just for a moment. I'm sure that if I get a chance to speak to him, I can bring him back to his senses. Once he... Well, the moment that... It's just that... I'm sure that if he sees me, no, I'm convinced, that if he sees me he'll remember his past."

She looked at him for a while, wonderingly, then turned and stalked out of the room, speaking over her shoulder, "Well, I'm not convinced, warrior. So for now we'll just have to do it my way."

## 2 WAKING UP IS HARD TO DO

Darjoon woke up, sweaty and gasping for air. The sun was already making its way up the wall of the tent and the heat was like a physical presence in the confined space. His dreams had been troubled, full of strange shapes and a large underground cavern with weird lizard-like creatures that had lunged and tried to bite him with their sharp teeth. He'd been fighting them off when he woke, and so he lay breathing heavily and waiting for his heart to stop pounding. On the table was a square pitcher of what seemed to be a cool drink, the small beads of water slowly sliding down the smooth metallic sides.

He rolled onto his feet and stood quickly, then stumbled as his vision blurred, forcing him to steady himself on the low table. He was still weak and sore, but his body seemed to feel better than the day before. Splashing his face with water from a large bowl, he dried himself with the towel folded neatly alongside. Flexing his arms, he then drew on the hob-nailed sandals they'd provided and stepped outside, stretching fully and enjoying the heat of the sun. He glanced over at the two burly guards who were lounging on leather mats by the entrance. They looked up at him warily, and watched him closely as he stepped forward and closed his eyes, turning his face up to the bright sunlight.

The guards stood up easily and stepped quietly behind and to either side of the young man, noting his large physique and feeling the amulets around their necks grow strangely warm. They looked across at each other and nodded in silent understanding. The large young man would be a formidable opponent if they needed to subdue him. One of them coughed discreetly, alerting Darjoon to their presence. He opened his eyes, then turned and looked at both of them appraisingly. Smiling, he stepped towards them to examine their weapons. They tensed briefly, and then relaxed again. He was obviously just curious about the spears they had, as well as the long, curved knives they wore at their waists. Nevertheless they held on tightly to the weapons and watched him carefully. He seemed to be trying to tell them something, but they couldn't understand a word he said. Then, when they saw his throwing motions, they grinned in understanding. He wanted them to show him how to use the spears they carried.

The guards nodded in understanding, then took him to the side of the tent where there was an old, dead tree off to the side. Drawing back his arm, one of the guards hurled the spear at the tree where it embedded itself with a loud thud and stayed there, quivering. Darjoon laughed out loud in appreciation at the accuracy and obvious skill on display, then gratefully accepted a spear from the other guard. His poor attempt at throwing the ornately carved weapon only resulted in it flopping onto the sand some way short of the tree. He laughed again and then with encouragement from the guards went and retrieved both spears, coming back to where they had marked a line in the sand from which to throw. One of the guards again expertly flung the spear into the tree, almost exactly in the same place where the previous spear had been. As one of the guards trotted over and retrieved the thrown spear, the other came alongside him and showed Darjoon the proper way to hold the long weapon, demonstrating in slow-motion the exact overhead throw they used.

K'trell walked up silently without them noticing, a guard stationed further back behind the tent having gone and called her, and now she stood in the shade, watching as Darjoon practiced with the two guards. Within a few throws, he was already showing his natural abilities, and it was obvious the warriors were warming to the engaging young man. Maybe it was true after all. Maybe he was truly the one from the prophecy? But could this large, enigmatic, strange young man really be the saviour of them all? One of the guards spotted her and straightened up, causing the other two men to turn around. Darjoon looked over at her and grinned and she felt the corner of her mouth lift in response, then abruptly pursed her lips and unconsciously smoothed her robe with her nervous hands. "Well", she thought to herself, "If he is the one, then I've got work to do. A lot of work!"

Turning without a word, she stalked into the tent as the guards made it clear to Darjoon that he was to follow her. They slipped in behind Darjoon as they walked with him to the tent, then stopped and waited outside as he entered. Darjoon walked in and looked at the Healer appraisingly as she paced up and down. She was a fine woman, not so young but not too old, and she moved with an easy grace like a mountain cat stalking its prey. Even her features were vaguely feline, angular and attractive in that dusky, desert-tribe way. Yes, she was just like a mountain cat from the Hills.

At the thought of the cat, he gasped suddenly, then grabbed his temple as pain lanced across his forehead just behind his eyes. She moved quickly and helped him onto the sitting mat, then poured juice for both of them, shoving his glass under his nose with an imperious command to drink. He flinched as a flicker of memory overlaid her face with that of a mother cat staring angrily at him, then blinked it away and gulped down the cool liquid, sensing the herbs it contained. He was sure they were simply restorative and not harmful, but shrugged anyway. If he felt any untoward effects he'd just use his magic to remove it, he'd done that before. The pain behind his eyes eased and he rubbed his forehead ruefully, "Well, if that's memory coming back, I'd rather it did it in one go, not painful little snippets like this", he complained.

"Oh yes? Is that so, young mage? Well you just be glad it's returning at all, the gods may smile on you after all. Now, why don't you tell me what you saw to cause this", she asked.

"I, uh, well, I mean, I was looking at, it, uh, it was nothing really, just some mountains", he responded quickly, and then blushed for some reason.

"Probably some picture I saw in one of the books at school, really, it was nothing important."

She breathed in deeply then let it out slowly, trying to hide her exasperation. He still had no idea who he was or what had happened and he still didn't trust her. Well, it was time he started to find out and she thought she knew how to do that.

"Darjoon, I'd like to do a little test, if I may? It's just a simple test of your magic, and it shouldn't be anything you can't handle. I want to see how much of your magic is returning, now that your health is improving. Would that be acceptable to you?"

"Sure, K'trell", he used her name easily and smiled at her, "that sounds like fun."

She started in surprise at the use of her name, then frowned and went to stand over him, looking down her nose disapprovingly. There was obviously nothing wrong with his hearing if he'd heard her mumbling her name yesterday.

"I'm afraid we don't ever use my first name, Darjoon. I am simply known as the Great Healer, or if you like, just Healer. I am who I am and I have left that other woman behind", the last she stated almost as if to herself.

Darjoon looked at her in amazement. "But why, why would you do that? Why would you deny yourself", he asked.

"It's not that I deny myself, Darjoon. Well, yes, I suppose, it sort of is, but, well, that's just a part of it. You see, all tribal Healers become their healing power. We are called to be servants of our tribes, simple conduits for the power of the Great Goddess, Turama, and that is all. She is the One who gives us our life, who gives us our power to heal. So as Healers, we leave our families, even our tribes, and we go where we are needed and over time we become nothing but the ones who serve, who heal. Well, obviously being the Lost Tribe, we don't leave our tribe anymore. But we give up some of our rights, although not our right to love, but our rights to our original family, to freedom and choice. We must marry who we believe the goddess chooses, so our children may also be healers. Yet we do it willingly and gladly for a chance to bring healing into the world, to bring life to others."

It was obvious she'd made this speech before and had learned it by heart. He tilted his head to the side and looked up at her, a soft look on his face.

"I don't think you did it so gladly, did you, K'trell? You don't seem like someone who's that happy about who they are now, like someone who's, well, embraced their fate, as it were. So why did you do it? You seem to me to be a person who would have a lot of love to give to a family, if they only had the chance. Someone who now carries a burden of pain that they think they've hidden away from this world. You're someone who was created for love and for true partnership, not individual sacrifice."

She stared at him in silence and tried to compose herself. He'd surprised her again, this boy who was a man. He'd gone from mischievous child to mature man in a heartbeat, cutting deep into the core of her, into that place in her heart where she had hidden all the pain from so long ago. The pain that started her awake at night with tears streaming down her face and a man's name on her lips. And as she so often did, waking in the silence of the dark, she would feel the empty bed beside her, hide her face with her long hair and her hands and sob deeply and bitterly into the night.

"No, Healer, by Turama, no", her mental voice was a lash inside her mind, "Now is not the time for foolish sentiments of a child! You are a servant, a Great Healer, so serve and heal."

She sat down in front of Darjoon, ignoring his tender look of concern and pushing her emotions aside.

"Never mind that, Darjoon, this is what we're going to do now. I'm going to create a globe of light and I want you to surround it with darkness. Can you do that", she asked him.

He looked at her in surprise. It was an unusual test and not one he'd heard of before. An eager look came over his face and his boyish enthusiasm returned.

"Sure, I think I can manage that", he said.

Moments later, K'trell shook her head slowly. The inky, black ball hovering in front of her was stable and impenetrable. She couldn't even sense her own magic inside and had no idea if the globe of light was still there anymore. Her senses were telling her this magic was strange, eerie, a mix of different types of magic unlike anything she'd ever encountered or read about. What was worse, it had a tinge of the lizard-men to it as well, almost as if Darjoon had absorbed something from them as a result of their attack on him.

As she stared, small cracks appeared in the dark globe and light rays started to shoot out across the room. The black sphere was starting to contract and a ray of light suddenly slammed into a glass on the table, causing it to shatter. Fortunately it scattered the glass shards away from them. She could see that Darjoon's magic was somehow reacting with her own and so immediately attempted to remove what was left of her power from the globe, in a vain attempt to extinguish the light that was obviously still inside the sphere. The sphere continued to contract even further and she gasped. Looking up at Darjoon, she saw he had a fixed look of terror on his face. Grabbing the remaining glass she flung the contents in his face, causing him to start, and he sat back suddenly, looking up at her and blinking in surprise while wiping his stinging eyes. The sphere fizzed and vanished, leaving behind a peculiar magical sensation she couldn't place. He rubbed his forehead and then his eyes again, suddenly looking gaunt and weary.

"Darjoon, how do you feel", she asked him.

"I um, I honestly, I just, well, I feel like I just ran across the mountains. In fact, I had a picture of this thing, this Dremrel, standing in front of me. I know it was a vision but it seemed so real, I mean even his eyes were moving and then he just stared at me, intently but with cold, cruel, intelligent eyes, as if he recognised me or something. It was creepy."

He shivered, looked at her then asked, "Was that a memory too?"

"It could be", she said, "but Darjoon, please, you must promise me you will not use any magic for a while? Not until we can figure out what's going on with you? It may be that the attack on you has altered your magic in some way, somehow adding to it. I have no way of knowing your former power, but it does seem as if your magic is being affected by something else. Come lie down here so I can examine you, I want to see if I can understand this better."

She waited until he was comfortable on the sleeping mats, and then moved nearer to get a sense of his power and health. She could feel that it was all as before, so she waited until his breathing became slow and even while he fell into a deep sleep. Leaving the tent she warned the guards to keep a close eye on him.

As the days wore on, and with the Healer's permission, the warriors started taking Darjoon out into the wilderness to hunt the desert antelope and other creatures. On each foray he felt his strength returning and his body filling out again, especially as the antelope they caught were brought back and cooked outside the tent. The guards warmed to him and he would often sit looking at the stars, listening to their conversation and enjoying their company. Darjoon was picking up their language now and starting to make himself understood. He was like a young boy, full of questions about the tribe, how they lived and what their customs were. The Healer encouraged the guards to teach him not just their language, but also the way they hunted and fought, hoping it would lull his mind into familiar pathways and aid in the return of his memory.

Part of the hunting technique they used included a little bit of magic, as a way of concealing themselves, both their visible presence but also their scent. Darjoon naturally picked this up very quickly and occasionally he would attempt to ambush the guards themselves, concealing himself and then stepping out and appearing as a monster of some description. The first time he did it they threw their spears simultaneously and only his quick reflexes saved him from being skewered. They all had a good laugh about it afterwards, but once again, he'd surprised and impressed them, both how quickly he had picked up the skill, and how he had appeared to almost casually evade their spears. He himself was impressed with the speed that the warriors had displayed when reacting.

One day the Healer accompanied them on a trip into the desert. This time they headed in a direction Darjoon had never been before and it was some time before they came to the top of a deep ravine. Accustomed to the hand signals the warriors used even when not stalking, as speaking was considered wasteful of moisture in the desert heat, he flattened himself as per their signal and crawled up to the lip of the cliff edge, looking down into the ravine and noting odd, moving shapes down below. His heart skipped a beat as he realised the shapes were actually the lizard-men that the hunters had told him about before, and he stilled and quietened his magic, realising they might sense it even at this distance. For a time, they hunted the creatures, following them down the ravine, and then one of the warriors signalled and they retreated, walking silently back to camp where the Healer had finally left him.

K'trell hissed in disappointment as she walked up the hill into the main encampment, then muttered softly to herself. The guard that had accompanied her up the trail looked at her sideways, then sidled off to a cluster of tents, leaving her alone in the twilight as she strode purposefully forward. She'd examined Darjoon magically when they'd returned, but while she'd been doing that he'd suddenly started fighting her, powerful magic flaring from his fingertips. She'd barely managed to shield herself in time and it had taken the two guards and herself some time to calm him down and get him to sleep again. She'd had to heal one of the guards because Darjoon had simply grabbed his arm, twisted it and thrown him to the ground. Her own hand had been burnt from the magic that flared around his wrists as she'd grabbed him and held him down. He'd apologised profusely, white-faced and sweating, clearly and obvious remorseful. Fortunately he was still weak and it seemed to her that his magic was continuing to fail even as his physical strength returned. That in itself might be formidable once fully recovered, although she still didn't know for sure. He'd had no reaction to their hunting the lizard-men, although he'd asked her later about visions of a strange, blond lady that he'd had. Clearly his memory was fighting to return, but nothing they tried seemed to be helping. She shook her head in frustration, knowing what she had to do yet not liking it. She gritted her teeth and made for the warrior's tent.

Nasrindo watched stoically as the Healer walked into

his dark tent. He'd resigned himself to waiting for this enigmatic woman to make up her mind, realising that nothing he could say to her would make a difference and that it would only antagonise her. There was no point in trying to see Darjoon again by himself, not without her help and he was using the time to meditate and prepare himself for when that moment came. He blinked slowly in surprise as she suddenly sighed and sat down.

"Very well", she said without preamble, "It's time, warrior! Time for you to see Darjoon. I want you to be ready at sunrise tomorrow. I will come for you and we will go and see him together."

She fixed him with a piercing stare, "Now let me be very clear about this. He is not yet himself and it is possible that he may not even recognise you. Nevertheless, and unfortunately, your presence might be just the trigger we need to help him find himself and recover his memories. I had hoped it wouldn't come to this, but, well, here we are!"

Then suddenly she looked down and muttered so softly he barely heard her, "That's if he will ever really find himself again."

Before he could say anything, she looked up and pierced him with her eyes again, "Now you listen carefully to me warrior, because we may not get another opportunity like this. He is having flashbacks with strong reactions and there are moments when his memory returns but is inconsistent. I think he is still struggling to discern between dreams and reality. He attacked us just now, not realising that the Dremrel he saw was in a dream, and not actually in the tent with him. So I don't know how he will react when he sees you, who is an actual, physical, tangible link to his recent past. He may even attack you, or he may turn and attack us, I just... well, I just don't know. For you to see him I must have your most solemn oath – that you will under no circumstances prevent us from restraining him, no matter what we do! Do you understand this? The safety of my people comes before yours, or even his, and I will not hesitate to do what is needed to protect everyone in my tribe. Clear? So! Do I have your word, warrior?"

Nasrindo looked at her in silent resignation. He was alarmed at what she had said, wondering what state Darjoon was in. Clearly it wasn't good. But what else could he do? There was no other way to get to Darjoon than to simply do what she had asked and play along. Maybe once he'd spoken to Darjoon, they could figure out how to get away from here. He looked down as if contemplating what she had said, sighed deeply, then lifting his head and in response to her question simply uttered a strange incantation. It was an old blood-ritual oath that stirred the hairs on the back of the Healer's neck. He kissed the backs of the fingers of his right hand, and then laid them on his forehead. "I swear, by Zakiro's black blood, that I will not stop you from restraining him."

She narrowed her eyes and glared at him with open contempt. "You! You dare! You dare to use that oath here in this camp? Here of all places", she hissed, "Of all the oaths you could have sworn, and of all the gods you could have used, why would you dare use that? You fool!"

"Because", Nasrindo spat out the words, "It is the same oath to the god of death that I used when I bound myself to Darjoon's side, and so an equal oath is required to keep your promise, Healer. I told you before and I'm telling you again, this is my destiny. Maybe now you will begin to realise the strength of my bond with him. I have sworn that I will not stop you from restraining him, but be assured that I will die before I let you kill or otherwise harm him. Our hope is in that man and he is also the hope of all the nations, not just yours or mine. You will have to kill me first, if you want to get to him!"

She stood up abruptly and glared at him. As she slowly and deliberately leaned forward, she snarled at him through clenched teeth, "Know that I will not hesitate, warrior! If I must kill him then I will do so, and if that means you too, then so be it! Tomorrow may well be the day we discover who Darjoon really is. But make no mistake, my intentions are clear in this. Safety for my tribe comes first, and then we'll see about your so-called saviour."

Nasrindo watched as she stalked from the tent, the scent of her wafting behind and lingering in the still, desert air. He slowly unclenched his fists, realising how tense he'd become with her in the room. She really had a way of getting under his skin, and he chuckled at himself, shaking his head.

"Well, old man, you'd better not let her see you have feelings for her. She's as likely to cut off your manhood as return any such silly emotion. Now stop being a fool, it's a big day tomorrow and you get to be with Darjoon again. Duty calls, as does friendship", his teeth gleamed in the darkness as he smiled to himself.

Long into the night, the warrior sat on his bed, deep in his ritual contemplative meditation. It was the same ritual he'd always used before battle, a conditioning of body, mind and soul. With his body fully relaxed, he was free in his mind to drift over the desert sands, the soft night breeze wafting him here and there as small rodents and other nocturnal prey avoided him, afraid as if he were the dreaded night-owl. But this bird had no shadow, no shape or substance and just wafted on silently, waiting for the sun to draw him back down to earth again, and waiting for the reunion that would take place in the morning. Faintly, and from far away he thought he could hear the words of the pledge made so long ago echoing across the sands. Words of power and purpose, and ultimately, of destiny.

# 3 WORDS OF POWER

The sun was a bright, orange ball just peering over the sand-dunes as Nasrindo and the Healer walked down into the hollow where a large, white, solitary tent had been pitched. Two swarthy, burly guards stood outside the entrance and watched Nasrindo carefully. He recognised at least one of them from before, the guards who'd toyed with him as if he'd been a boy rather than the experienced warrior he was. Nasrindo grinned at them in greeting and gave them a mock salute, but they just stared at him with casual indifference. The Healer swept past them and into the tent and he followed her in, the guards moving in right behind him.

Darjoon was sprawled peacefully on some pillows, his slow, rhythmic breathing indicating he was fast asleep. Nasrindo was aware of the guards positioning themselves behind and to either side of him. He felt odd as he looked down at Darjoon lying there so serenely. It was as if time slowed and then stopped and now suddenly every sound, every sight became fuzzy and indistinct. Belatedly, he nodded as he realised the Healer was speaking to him, but he struggled to pick out what it was she was saying. It was something about him standing where Darjoon could see him, while she stood off to the side, something about the shock of waking up to Nasrindo standing over him which she hoped would activate his memories.

He nodded again, still seeing everything as if in some sort of grey, slow motion dream. He moved over to stand directly in front of Darjoon. The healer clapped her hands once, sharply, and at the sound Darjoon woke and rose to his feet in one fluid movement so that he was standing directly in front of Nasrindo. His mouth was a soft "O" of surprise, as if he was about to say something. As suddenly as it had started, the fuzziness that Nasrindo had been experiencing disappeared, and immediately all the sounds, lights and colours sharpened and brightened and came rushing in until he was awash in colour and noise. Four bright, golden words hovered in the air between Darjoon and himself and without thinking Nasrindo read them out slowly and carefully, pronouncing each one with measured deliberation.

K'trell watched as Darjoon stood up and looked at the warrior. A flash of excitement trembled through her as she saw the recognition and surprise on Darjoon's face and the light in his eyes.

"Yes", she thought to herself, "It's working. The shock has broken the restraints of his memory. Oh thank you, Great Turama, you honour me with this healing."

She touched her forehead with respect for the healing goddess, and then looked aside at the guards, smiling in her moment of triumph. But they were both watching Nasrindo intently with an almost sick fascination. She turned back and looked quizzically at the desert warrior, noting for the first time and with growing alarm his pale face and sweaty brow. Then she gasped in genuine horror as truly ancient words of power emerged from the warrior's mouth and she stared, aghast, as Darjoon jerked, jerked again, then rose up in the air and slammed back down onto the bed behind him, lying still and inert as the dust settled.

The warriors behind Nasrindo, their instincts and responses trained from birth into a fine-honed edge, moved with lightning rapidity, one grabbing Nasrindo from behind and the other striking him hard on the head with the butt of the ever-present, hefty spear. Rope appeared as if by magic and they bound the unconscious man tightly and moved him away from Darjoon, throwing him unceremoniously to the ground.

K'trell rushed over to where the young man lay spread-eagled on the cushions, his chest moving up and down slowly, but otherwise lifeless and inert. Swiftly she used her magic to scan through his body but she could detect no damage there. She tried to touch his mind or even his elusive magic but there was nothing at all, not a thing, just an emptiness that frightened her. It was as if his body was healthily present but the vital essence of who he was, his very being, his soul, was somehow gone. With the help of the guards she gently moved Darjoon into a comfortable position on the bed, and then beckoning one of them to bring Nasrindo she stalked out of the tent. With one of the guards remaining behind to watch the sleeping man and alert her, the other lifted Nasrindo easily like a bundle of firewood and carried him away from the tent and back up the slope, following the Healer all the way to the tent of meeting. Silence fell as they marched inside and the guard dropped the warrior unceremoniously to the ground, then everyone started speaking at once. Without responding, she turned around angrily and gestured at the guard, who grabbed a bucket and threw the watery contents at the warrior's head. Other tribes-folk flocked into the tent behind the Healer, pressing in to see what was going on.

Sound rushed in at Nasrindo like a flood washing over him and he realised it was the sound of many voices raised in anger and outrage while at the same time he felt the steamy warmth of many bodies crammed together in a confined space, made worse by the typical heat of a desert morning. Shaking the water from his face as his vision cleared, Nasrindo looked up at the guard still holding a dripping bucket and thanked him sarcastically. The guard drew back his hand, ready to strike, when a woman's voice interrupted him. Glowering at Nasrindo, the burly guard, towering over the Healer next to him stalked off to be replaced by a familiar face glaring down at him. With the pain in his temple receding and the darkness in the corner of his eyes fading, Nasrindo could see he was in the tent of meeting again. The elders were arrayed in front of him at the table in their usual chairs, one of them still empty. The Great Healer stood directly in front of him with her hands on her hips and a fierce look on her face. She pulled her face in disgust and shook her head at him when she saw she had his attention, then turned and addressed the elders. He shook his head in disbelief as he heard her explain what he'd done. He was still trying to sort out the turmoil in his mind as if it had been like some really bad dream. Was this still part of that dream? The Great Healer finally went and sat down in her place at the table alongside the elders, still glaring at him.

An elder, his face stern under long, grey hair, leaned forward and addressed him and Nasrindo shook his head to clear it. He was sure he had water in his ears because even in the relative stillness that accompanied the elder statesman's address it was hard to hear him. The voice slowly became more distinct and the other voices quieted even further after a few glares from the rest of the elders, until he could finally hear what was being said.

"You can hear me? Good! I said, Warrior, that you are here to answer for your actions and I hasten to add, not for the first time. Today, according to our Great Healer, you have taken the life of an important guest to this tribe. This guest was under our protection and one whom we have treated as our own. I hope you understand the meaning of that? Therefore, the consequences of your actions now make your motives clear to us. You are obviously contaminated or infested with some strange, dark magic, or, worse still, you are an agent of some dark and malevolent force that conspires against us. We do not care which but it is clear that you are a danger to us and to others. This is why we still have nothing to do with you and your despicable people, with your corrupt ways and your ongoing use of darkness. We...", the elder turned and glared as the Great Healer's voice cut across him through the stillness and halted his impassioned speech.

"No", her voice was clear and strong as it rang out across the tent and she stood up, "We certainly do care, esteemed Elder, we care oh so very much. We must find out what drives this... this dark creature! His motives and intent are not yet fully revealed and we must know what further danger lies beyond the safety of our paper-thin walls. What this, what his people are planning", she spat the words at Nasrindo.

Another elder, this one seated at the centre of the table started speaking softly yet firmly and with obvious authority.

"Healer", at his voice she blinked and sat down abruptly, a chastened look on her face, "I understand that you have an interest in this, believe me I do. However, I tell you now and only now that we do not share the same interest. Not at all! Do you understand? No, I see you wish to protest, but wait, and listen carefully to me. You were convincing when you presented the case that this young man now lying senseless in our tent, this Darjoon, has a destiny that overlaps ours. You were equally convincing when you said that we needed this warrior here in front of us, allegedly because of the great bond they were supposed to share. Yet look now at what you have wrought! Because of you and your compelling arguments, we have let an ancient and terrible magic into our midst. This is the very same dark evil that we rejected generations ago, that we fled from, and now your significant young man of destiny has paid the price for your errant ways. No! Enough! I'll not hear anymore from you on this. If we had done as I had wished earlier, then this warrior would already be in the bosom of the desert and we would have saved a life. Now, instead of that we will lose two lives. No! Enough", he chopped his hand down, summarily cutting off her protests. She bit her lip in silence as he glared at her and then she turned away. Looking straight down at Nasrindo, the elder pronounced his verdict, condemning the warrior to the lonely, and almost certainly fatal, desert march in the morning.

Nasrindo shrugged in resignation, then bowed his head and nodded as the guards hauled him up roughly and led him away. As he left, he glanced down briefly at the seated Healer's white face, noting her pursed lips and furrowed brow. She was almost shaking with suppressed rage, her fists clenched, and as she looked up at him, he shook his head slowly, almost as if in warning. It just seemed to make her glare even more, and she turned and began a heated debate with the elders at the table as he left the tent and was returned to his own.

The guards shoved him roughly onto his bed, not even bothering to untie him. His head was still spinning and he groaned in despair, wondering what he had done to the young mage. He couldn't even remember the words he'd spoken over him that had condemned him to what might be an eternal sleep. In fact, he'd never seen them before in his life, let alone actually spoken words like them. What had happened to him, and more importantly, what had happened to Darjoon? What had that magic done to him? He had heard the Healer tell the elders that Darjoon was not in fact dead, but was somehow absent from his body. So what did that mean? Where was he? What had become of him?

Back in the large white tent Darjoon woke up and tried to look around but no matter where he looked there was just an inky blackness, the air feeling close and thick. There were no stars, no silhouettes, just a complete and total darkness and his eyes failed to adjust even after he closed them again and waited a while. Throwing up a small, magical globe of light, he noticed that even the floor below him was black, although there were strange green flecks in it that appeared to dance and twinkle as he looked at them. In fact, they were definitely moving, darting this way and that. He put his hand down to touch one and found that his fingers went straight through the floor, and he could feel the bottom was wet and slimy. The little tadpole-like creatures lunged for his fingers, their small teeth nipping his skin and drawing blood.

Withdrawing his hand quickly, he stood up in horror, and slowly stepped away from them, then realised he was in fact standing on top of this dark water and not sinking into it. As he watched, he saw that there more of the creatures and they stayed together, drifting in some sort of current that was flowing within what appeared to be a vast underground lake. He walked forward across the water, following this darting, flickering path that moved beneath his feet, until he came to raised steps, seemingly rising and twisting out of the water. Gratefully stepping up onto them and away from the horrible little creatures, he followed the stairs up and around and found that they ended on a black, rocky platform, on which he noticed a tall, dark, wooden lectern that was supported on what appeared to be the carved legs of a large lizard. He walked forward onto the platform and moved around in front of the lectern, staring at the ancient book that lay there. Its leather cover was crumbling and it was obvious the ragged and discoloured page edges were worn from years and years of use.

Taking careful hold of the slimy cover, he gently lifted it up, only to find the corner he was holding coming away in his hand, the leather so old it wasn't able to hold together anymore. Delicately feeling the paper pages underneath with his magic, he could sense they were equally fragile. Frowning, he looked closely at the book, somehow knowing that it was important that he should read it, but not knowing how to do so. The globe over his head flickered for a moment as his frustration interrupted his magic, and then he snapped his fingers, the sound echoing across the dark waters. Of course, here he was once again forgetting that he was in fact a mage. Muttering quiet words of annoyance at himself, he extended his magic over the book, using it to gently lift the cover and reveal the first page and the large golden words on it. He groaned out loud in frustration as he saw it was written in an ancient language, one that he was sure he'd never seen before. But as he looked closer and squinted at them, the letters slowly started to writhe and contort, almost lifting off the page in their movements, and he gasped in understanding. His magic was somehow reacting with the words, transforming them into his native, raven-born language so that he could read them.

"The Journal of Darjoon", he read the title aloud in sick fascination. Immediately, a shiver of excitement and dread rippled down his spine. At college they'd been told by a lecturer that some mages had the opportunity to learn their own fate, that some would even know their own future, including the time and manner of their death. Such a great responsibility was gifted by the gods to only the most experienced, the most honourable of mages and never to a novice like himself. It was said that such mages maintained a journal of their own, and kept it in a dark, magical place that was hidden away from mortal man. A place where they could only enter in spirit form. He stared at the darkness around him and shivered again. Is that what this place was? Was he even now in the spirit realm? What would he learn in this book? Could it be a book he had written himself in some remote future, which at the same time, right here and now, was simply a distant past? He'd never heard of any great magician who'd had a name like his, so who else could it be? Was he destined to become a great magician one day? Wouldn't that be amazing?

"Alright, you silly fat mage", he laughed to himself as he began reading, "Enough questions, let's learn what you've written about you."

As the echoes of his chuckling died away, the silence stretched out into the darkness as he read avidly, only his globe of light and the flickering green tadpoles in the water below showing any signs of life. He read, and read, and read, his eyes flickering back and forth over the written lines, hardly noticing as his head began to throb.

Slowly at first, then with increasing intensity, the pain began to burn in his temples and sear his eyes. Finally, when he closed them for relief, images from what he'd read danced and flickered in front of him. There were so many different memories all displaying at once on the screen of his mind that he winced in agony and shook his head for the umpteenth time, wondering if he would always have to endure the thumping pain of it. But he didn't mind, it was worth it. Worth the pain to have his memories back again.

He couldn't believe it. How could he have forgotten Sirroya, that beautiful mischievous blonde trickster that had travelled with him? His heart ached at the thought of her death, and tears welled up in his eyes. He blinked them away in frustration and straightened up to continue reading, the years of memories filling him once again. Finally, he turned another page of the book, a book he felt like he'd been reading for ages, and saw that it was blank. He turned over the next page, and again, but they were all blank, devoid of any words, magical or otherwise. The story had ended with him being blown backwards into darkness by the lizard-men's spell when he'd tried to heal Sirroya, but how could it end there? What about his most recent memories? What about the future memories, where were they? Did he die here?

He turned back to the last page, then forward again, hoping something would appear, but there was nothing. No, wait, what was that? He bent down for a closer look, and at the same time augmented his light globe, just a little so he could see more clearly the faint writing he'd discovered. A small, golden word appeared on the page, growing larger and larger until suddenly it flashed up straight at him, and as he started back in surprise, he felt a hundred million needles strike his body at once, causing an incredible, intense pain on every inch of his skin. A green fire flashed all around him, followed by blue and then red and suddenly he was flung back onto the surface of the water. This time he sank down and down into the inky blackness as small, needle-sharp teeth bit and gnawed at his flesh in delight. He screamed in sheer agony at the intense pain and gathered his powerful magic around him to blast the creatures away.

Meanwhile, back in the encampment, the Healer had eventually given up on her debate with the elders. She'd already known it was pointless as they had obviously made a final decision, and so nothing she could say would sway them this time round. That ridiculous warrior, Nasrindo, would be sent out into the desert in the morning and now his fate was with the gods. Not that she really cared, or did she? She didn't even understand why she'd argued his case in the first place, surely he deserved to die for what he'd done? Such blasphemy! She stalked out of the tent, then stopped and swayed, dropping to one knee. A guard posted outside grabbed her elbow to support her. She put her hand to her head and looked around in dazed wonder. What in Tsurama's sweet name was that? Her skin rippled in alarm and an ice-cold fear lanced up her back. Such raw and furious magical power could not come from mortal man, could it? Were the gods here? Was her goddess Turama as upset with her as the elders were? Was this the final great ending of life and the great dragon had awakened to set fire to the world? Yet in this magic she sensed a familiar pattern, a certain feel, a kind of amalgamation of different energies, of lizard and fire, and snow and, and, yes, and very strongly of, of...

"Oh dear gods no, it's raven-born", she gasped in despair and dread.

Her feet started moving before she even knew what she was doing and throwing off the concerned hand of the guard she turned as she ran and yelled back at him, "Sound the alarm! For Turama's sake, go sound the alarm now, man! We are all doomed!"

And then she ran as if chased by Turama herself, that mysterious goddess of healing that she was so tightly bound to.

The two guards down in the hollow had listened to the pain-filled, moaning cries inside the tent for some time, looking at each other wonderingly, until finally one of them had tentatively entered in spite the Healer's strict instructions to stay outside. The warrior could see that Darjoon was writhing on his bed with his hands waving in the air, and he could feel the magic that was crackling around the young mage's wrists and sparking off the walls, the very air was pulsing with the power of it. The medallion around his neck was sizzling on his skin in response. Calling to his companion, he rushed over to the bed and tried to pin Darjoon down by the wrists as he twisted and turned. Suddenly the young mage stiffened and cried out in sheer agony.

Darjoon's eyes opened wide and he stared at the guard above him in incomprehensible terror. Noting the sword at his hip and the large spear he was still holding, he ripped his wrist out of the man's grip, flattened his hand, palm up, and, yelling as he exhaled, rammed it into the man's chest sending him flying up and away and then down onto the table which crashed to the ground in pieces. The guard smashed through the table onto the floor, then rolled to his feet, white-faced and panting. He staggered forward, coughed blood and then went down on one knee before collapsing on the floor. The other guard, who had just rushed into the room in response to the call, took one look at his friend and launched himself at Darjoon. The young mage easily rolled out the way and came to his feet in a crouch, eyes glazed but narrowed and locked firmly on the menacing guard. Lunging forward with his spear in a lightning-quick manoeuvre, the warrior whipped it away again as Darjoon made to grab it, and then drove it in towards Darjoon's throat like a snake striking. The Healer had been clear about one thing. If they could not subdue him, if he appeared to be at all dangerous, then they must kill him no matter the cost or their feelings towards him. Darjoon moved almost as if in slow motion, his head and body slipping to the side and his hands easily grasping the weapon as it slid past him. With a simple tug he ripped it from the man's grasp, spun and then whirling the spear around in the air stepped and turned to the side as the guard made to grab it back. Casually and with his back turned to the guard he lunged backwards in a fluid motion, driving the spear up and through the man's belly. The guard toppled over, the spear sticking out grotesquely through his back while he gasped for breath and blood started pouring from his mouth. The other guard lay on the ground staring in horror, his lips turning blue and his chest rising in short, shallow gasps, knowing that at least one of his lungs was crushed by the blow, if not his heart itself. He could only watch helplessly as Darjoon strode purposefully out of the tent, and belatedly he felt the amulet burning at his neck. That piece of jewellery had proven completely useless though, as the young man had not used any magic directly against them, just his natural, fierce skill and formidable strength. Strength and agility that they'd not even guessed at in all the time they'd hunted with him. He'd kept it concealed this whole time, fooling them all. Darkness began gathering around his vision and his life began contracting in the painful, shuddering and slowing rasp of his chest.

As the Healer ran towards the hollow, she could hear others coming behind her, responding to the moaning cry of the trumpeted alarm. The intensity of the magic she'd felt earlier was overwhelming and she feared for the tribe, knowing now that she could never hope to stop the young mage with her magic alone. That magic she had been sensing had stopped suddenly and ominously, as if someone had thrown a blanket over a bright light. Two warriors surged past her, their large, fit bodies glistening in the afternoon sun, muscles writhing as their spears bounced up and down in time to the rhythm of their running. She looked up and faltered mid-stride, her legs going weak as she saw Darjoon walking towards them from the hollow where the tent was. Now she knew that at least two of the Lost Tribe were dead or dying already, all as a result of her unending curiosity. Her teacher, the previous Great Healer, had told her emphatically that her lust for knowledge would get her killed one day. She had lectured her that to constantly seek out strange things and then make excuses for her fascination was not healthy. A Healer only had responsibility toward her tribe, nothing more, nothing less. Their health and safety, their very lives, were her only concern in life and this was her sole duty in serving the goddess Turama. But K'trell had never lost her innate desire for new and strange things, exploring different magic's, acquiring various books and scrolls and speaking in detail with the few traders who came to them. She would listen for hours on end as they talked about strange lands and other far-away places. Now it had finally caught up with her. The result of her desire for knowledge was in front of her, a young mage's tight face and glistening, steely black eyes staring towards them with deadly intent.

Darjoon saw the warriors running towards him, as well as a woman in a white, silk robe that streamed out behind her as she ran. He faltered for a moment, looking intently at her face, and then he grimaced as he saw it was not Sirroya. The warriors had their spears at the ready and he shot a highly targeted flame spell at them. The woman muttered something and threw her hands in the air and he saw that some of his spell was deflected, fizzing away into the desert. But she hadn't deflected all of it and some fire got through, causing warriors to scream in pain as their spears exploded into bars of flame in their hands. She was still waving her hands and suddenly a great gust of wind flung sand up into the air, obscuring the warriors from him and causing him to blink and sneeze as it whipped around him. He instinctively threw out a defensive shield spell, shutting out the sand and wind but still allowing him to see and hear. A warrior burst out of the sand-storm and stumbled through his shield, thrusting blindly with his spear. The spear plunged into Darjoon's midriff, a powerful strike that would normally have disembowelled his opponent. The clang of metal on metal rang out across the sands and the warrior stared in amazement at the blunted tip of his spear and then at Darjoon's flowing robe that had stopped it so effectively. The warrior recovered quickly then ducked and launched himself up and towards Darjoon, thrusting again but this time down towards Darjoon's head. Darjoon smiled grimly and swayed easily to the side, ripping the spear away from the man. This time, he didn't turn the spear but simply jabbed hard with the wooden butt, augmented with a little magic and it smashed into the hapless warrior's face, turning it into bloody pulp and ruin as he fell back lifelessly. Then he dropped the spear and continued to walk forward, the sand swirling around him. Two more warriors now appeared and circled him warily with their spears pointed at him, eyeing their comrade on the ground. One of them feinted with a lunge, while the second suddenly crouched and stabbed up towards Darjoon from his left. Ignoring the feint, the mage swayed back, letting the sharp tip of the spear slide up over his chest, then wrapped his left arm around the haft and pivoted his body to the right, ripping the spear from the first warrior's hands. Continuing to pivot, he placed his right hand on the haft and lunged to his right, forcing the wicked blade of the spear into the second, onrushing warrior's throat and pinning him to the ground below as he gurgled through the blood pouring out the wound. The first warrior, now without his spear, pulled out his long blade and lunged at Darjoon from behind, who swayed out the way without turning, and then the warrior jumped back again and sliced towards his head. Darjoon simply let his body fall backwards toward the warrior before the wicked blade sliced the air above him, then grabbing the warrior's ankles and using the momentum from falling back, he flicked his legs up and over, ramming his feet into the warrior's face and forcing him to fall back. Continuing to roll back with him and locking his ankles behind the man's neck, Darjoon ended up on top of the man. Dropping to one knee, a single flat punch to the chest had the same result as in the tent, leaving the warrior coughing out blood on the sand.

The Great Healer stared in horror through the lessening sandstorm at the scene unfolding before her. Without much effort, Darjoon had already taken out another three of the best warriors they had. She cursed furiously to herself. She'd known about his magic but belatedly recognised that not only was he still raven-born, still well-trained in physical combat, but from the look of it, advanced and incredibly deadly. She blanched as he pirouetted and ducked under another guard's attack, kicking up and into the man's jaw which flung the warrior up and back to land with a sickening thud and snap on the ground, one arm grotesquely angled under his body with the bone sticking out. The warrior didn't move again. Darjoon turned and faced her, and the sand-storm she'd created stopped suddenly, every grain of sand suspended in mid-air for a moment before falling in a silent shower of golden rain. She crouched and froze, throwing out a shield spell as he walked towards her, but he simply brushed right past her, bumping her shoulder as he continued up the dune behind, as if she and the shield didn't even exist. She turned, and using her magic, waved her hands and muttered an incantation to fling a boulder up off the ground and at his head. While still speeding towards him, and without him even turning, the boulder shattered into small grains of sand, spun around his head like a halo and then formed a sandy arrow that flew straight at her. Before she could react, the arrow hit her shield, penetrated and she felt her hands pulled behind her and then suddenly encased in a block of stone that pulled her down and back, pinning her to the ground and rendering her incapable of magic. She gasped as with almost an after-thought, he clicked his fingers theatrically and a bubble of light sprang up around her and then darkened, leaving her in icy, ink-black terror struggling to breathe. Just before the darkness overwhelmed her, she'd seen more warriors crest the rise and run towards Darjoon and she moaned in horror, knowing they were doomed and that she was unable to help them.

The warriors, some twenty of them, formed a line and charged down the slope, looking to overwhelm him with numbers. Darjoon looked at them, inclined his head, lifted his arms with hands outstretched and suddenly they stopped, their hands going to their throats as they gasped for air. One by one, they lifted off the desert floor and hung suspended, their chests heaving as they desperately tried to breathe. He was just about to crush their windpipes completely, when he heard what sounded like a familiar voice calling his name. Distracted, he looked up beyond the warriors at a man walking towards him, a man who looked different to the warriors he was fighting. This man, who was evidently physically smaller, had his hands outstretched with his palms up, as if imploring him to stop. He looked vaguely familiar and Darjoon peered at him intently, momentarily forgetting the warriors gasping for breath.

Nasrindo had heard the commotion from his tent, followed by the distinctive sound of the trumpeted alarm, and when his guards had run off he'd stepped outside to see what was going on. In the distance, towards the dune near Darjoon's tent, he saw the Healer running fast with two warriors close behind as they crested the dune and disappeared down the other side. He'd felt something in the air, something indefinable but tangible, a familiar sensation he'd felt before. Only now, as he watched his guards join up with the other warriors and as they all began running in the same direction, did he realise what it meant. Darjoon was using his magic, but with even more power than he'd felt before. He began to run, a cold shiver of anticipation sliding up and down his spine. As he ran, he threw off the rope around his wrists that he'd already worked loose earlier. Had the young man's memory returned? Or was this what the Healer had feared? That his mind would give way under the impact of new and awful memories. Nasrindo had always been the quickest of his tribe, and now his feet flew over the sand, barely touching, as he raced to catch up with the warriors in front. Charging over the crest, he stared in horror at the scene in front of him. Four warriors lay dead or dying on the sand and twenty more were dangling in mid-air, struggling to breathe. A black dome marked the spot where he guessed the Healer was. Tears rose unbidden in his eyes and rolled down his cheeks. This couldn't be right, there had to be some mistake. Darjoon was their saviour, the one who would free them all, not the one who would take their lives. He wasn't this cold-blooded murderer that he saw standing in front of him, grimly determined to kill those around him.

The young mage's name escaped from his lips and he stumbled down the dune, grief-stricken and calling to him with his arms outstretched, "Darjoon, Darjoon, stop! Please, stop! It's me, Darjoon. It's Nasrindo! Please, you must stop this. Come back to me, Darjoon, please, my friend, come back to me."

"Nasrindo? That name is familiar", Darjoon thought to himself. The warriors dropped to the ground, some falling insensible and not moving, others gulping deep draughts of the sweet, clear desert air, their chests heaving. Darjoon began walking towards the warrior, calling his name and then, as if falling down a well, he slumped face-forward into the sand. Nasrindo ran to him, and turned him over, tenderly brushing grains of sand from his face and hair and cradling him in his lap.

"Darjoon", he called softly, "Darjoon, are you there? Please, please, tell me you're still there? What have I done?"

The young mage coughed, opened his eyes, spat out sand and looked up at him in surprise.

"Nasrindo? Of course I'm here, you big bront! Where else would I be? I'm not flying or anything, am I? That felt really strange just now", he looked around him, bewildered, then stiffened as he saw the fallen warriors and the others that began clustering around them.

"Actually, Nasrindo, where, where am I? This doesn't look familiar to me? And who are these great big warriors that have their spears pointed at us?", he asked in confusion, then stiffened, staring in horror as the Great Healer walked towards them, his recent memory flooding back.

"Oh no!", he whispered, "Oh no, sweet Zukar, what have I done, Nasrindo? What have I done?"

The young mage stumbled to his feet, brushing sand off his robes as the warriors raised their spears menacingly and surrounded him. The Healer gave a discreet signal and they all fell back immediately, lowering their spears. Darjoon slumped dejectedly, apologising profusely to her. Then he started walking towards the fallen warriors as Nasrindo and the Healer fell into step alongside him, watching him carefully. Darjoon knelt down next to the wounded men and began healing them.

Much later, Darjoon sat back and took the glass the Healer held out to him. He slumped wearily as the guard on the floor rose gingerly to his feet, his hands moving carefully over his stomach in disbelief. Darjoon had healed every single one of the guards he'd injured. Every wound had incredibly just disappeared under his touch, and the Healer and Nasrindo had exchanged looks of real surprise. Even to Nasrindo, who thought he was used to Darjoon's power, this was a display he'd not witnessed before. To heal one warrior would have taken a lot out of any Healer, but to heal all of them as he had done and still be sitting there awake, it was unbelievable. Even more so when he considered that surely at least one of the guards should have been dead. Somehow, the wounds that Darjoon had inflicted on them were not immediately fatal, otherwise there would have been no return for them. Surely the gods had protected all of them this day.

"I'm so sorry", Darjoon was saying to the guard, "I really wasn't myself. I can't believe I did that to you. Please, here is my hand and my oath, if you are ever in need and I am able, I will help you, brother. Whatever you ask and whatever you need, just let me know and I will come!"

The guard clasped Darjoon's arm in acceptance and smiled grimly at him, "Well, young mage, let me say that if I am in need, then there is no finer warrior I would want at my side. I am glad to see you well again, as are we all. But please, next time, warn me if you're getting ill again. I want to make sure I'm out in the desert hunting somewhere far away, at least until you get better."

The guard smiled grimly at him, then nodded at the Healer and ignoring Nasrindo, stepped outside.

The Great Healer sat down facing Darjoon and addressed him sternly, "Well, young mage, I can see you are yourself again. At least, so Nasrindo assures me. Personally, I wouldn't know if you were or not, as I have only ever known you when you were unwell."

"No, please", she held up her hand to stop Darjoon saying anything, "Allow me to finish. I was right about one thing, and that is you are far more dangerous than we believed possible. Had I been aware of the extent of your innate fighting ability, I may have responded differently to your need, perhaps with even stronger restraints. As it is, you have to tell me what happened, as I must be assured of your complete healing. You will no doubt appreciate that we as a tribe are naturally paranoid, and what you have done will take some undoing, although your healing of those that you hurt has gone some way towards that. So what did Nasrindo do to you, and how did your powers and memories come back so quickly?"

Darjoon hung his head and nodded, then told them exactly what had happened to him, about the pool of water he'd walked on, the raised dais and the reading of the book. At the mention of the book, K'trell's face paled slightly and she pursed her lips. Nasrindo sat silently and listened intently to everything he said without expression. Darjoon finished his tale and sat back and looked at them quizzically.

"So, what do you think", he asked, "Do you know something about the book? You seemed to react to it, K'trell."

Blowing out through her lips and ignoring Darjoon and the use of her name, K'trell turned to Nasrindo and fired questions at the warrior, "What made you speak out those words? Where did you learn that tongue? What magical power do you have? I detected hardly any magical abilities at all in you, so where did that come from?"

Nasrindo held up his hands in mock surrender and smiled ruefully, "Yes, yes, I understand you want to know more. But I'm as confused as you are. As I said before, I don't know how or why I did what I did. I felt strange, unsettled even, when I saw Darjoon and the next thing there were these golden words in the air and somehow I read them out. I admit, I have a little magic inside me, but as you said yourself, it's not much of anything. The, um, the warrior that I inherited the oath from, well, he, um, he may have passed something on to me as part of the blood oath. I'm sorry, I just don't know any more. It's as if I wasn't there, as if something or someone else did it all. I realise that doesn't help, but it's all I have."

She shook her head in frustration, "Warrior, there will come a time when you will have to tell all the truth. Luckily for you, now is not that time, but let me be clear about something. When that time comes, you had better not hold anything back as you're doing now! You have both used ancient words of power that have not been heard for, well, for a very long time. These words are ancient and accursed and they should never, ever, be spoken. Yes, Darjoon, the word at the end of your book was of the same kind that Nasrindo used on you."

She turned and leaned forward, looking intently at Darjoon for a while. He smiled at her, raising his eyebrows, "Everything alright, K'trell? Like what you see?"

She snorted in disgust, "I'm not looking at you that way, boy! I'm looking inside you with my magic. As far as I can see, your magic is restored and you appear to be as healthy as if you were never sick. I don't know exactly what's happened, but whatever it is, I have a feeling you are back to normal, or at least, whatever is normal for you. I still need to keep an eye on you and the tribe is going to be very skittish for a while, so I think you should stay here for now. Yes, yes, Nasrindo, I know you want to stay with him and I think we can arrange that. We just need to see the elders first and they will have to rescind your sentence, as is right and proper now. It is clear that you were not in control of yourself, that much has been understood."

Looking at them, she muttered to herself, "At least it's clear to me."

Continuing to address them, she said, "The fact of the matter is, however, you are both still a grave concern for the tribe, so whatever you do, say nothing, nod, and let me do the talking. Is that clear to both of you?"

Darjoon and Nasrindo meekly nodded their heads, then looked at each other and burst out laughing. She shook her head in disgust and stood up, "Gods help us all. Now I'm just going to arrange a meeting with the elders. If it's at all possible, which I very much doubt, will you two try not to create any more mischief while I'm gone? I've told the guards outside you're both in your right minds, for now anyway, but they must still keep an eye on both of you. So don't go wandering off anywhere. I'll be back soon enough."

"Wait, K'trell. You never answered my question", Darjoon said, "What do you know about the book?"

She looked at him grimly for a while, the silence growing. Then she snorted, "I suppose if I don't tell you, you'll just keep asking, won't you. Well, I have heard that truly great mages write their own historical records. It is said that they somehow keep a journal of what they've done, and that they store it in a place no-one else can get to. Did the book have your name on, Darjoon? Ah, I can see by your expression that it did. Well, somehow these mages are able to communicate with themselves using that book, leaving clues as to their future or something like that. I suppose as a future self, you were able to give back the memories the lizard-men stole from you. At least, that's what is said. The questions remain though. How did you know to do that in the future, and why was the book so old? These and many more are probably similar to the questions you ask yourself, aren't they? You say the pages were blank, but maybe they were just hidden from your present sight. Some things even the gods will not let us know. But here's something to get your brain around, Darjoon. Some legends say that the gods themselves were once just men and women, like you and me. Great mages who were not of this realm and lived in a different place, yet it was one from which they could influence our lives. Some say they still can, that they are still present in our world as well as residing in the other. Now that may be, but what I wonder is, have you thought about the implications of the fact that the book exists at all? I mean, it shows that you are, after all, a truly great mage. Or at least, that you will become one. At least, that's how it seems."

She clucked her tongue as they both looked up at her wide-eyed, "But right now, you, young mage, still remain very young and foolish. So please, for all our sakes, remember who you are now, and do not think of yourself as that which you will no doubt become. Now I must go and placate those who are far older and wiser than myself and convince them of your innocence, warrior, and of their safety from this great mage. Remember, if they call you in as well, just nod and agree with whatever I say and for Turama's sake, do not speak."

The Healer stepped outside the tent, nodded grimly at the six guards who stood outside warily with their spears held ready and then walked off up the hill. It was going to take some explaining to convince the elders to spare not just Nasrindo, but Darjoon as well. The fact that he'd healed all the warriors and they had not lost anyone would help. She shook her head in disbelief. In fact, this display of raw power and ability would serve to finally convince them of the reality of who Darjoon really was. She shook her head as she realised that Darjoon was still not even aware of his own potential, the book notwithstanding. For a mere youth to do what he had done, raven-born or not, it was unheard of. To hold twenty of the finest Lost Tribe warriors at bay, and then, after expending all that magic, to heal every one he'd injured, it just beggared belief. Her knees grew weak at the memory of it. No, they would certainly listen to her this time. But Darjoon would have to leave soon. The tribe would not be at peace with him around, that was certain.

# 4 FAT MAN HUNTING

Darjoon paced up and down inside the tent. He stopped and glared between the unperturbed Healer and the warrior who sat looking at him equally impassively. Before he could say anything, Nasrindo patiently spoke again, "I'm telling you Darjoon, there's no point to this, J wish there was. There is much more at stake here than, well, than just her. I know, I know what she means to you, but there is absolutely no guarantee that you will find her out there", his hand swept out to indicate the desert sparkling outside the tent entrance as Darjoon stood shaking his head and glaring at him.

"I wish it was different, and I want to believe it like you do, but it's simply not the case. We have to move on, all of us. I gave you her necklace, I told you where she is buried and that I buried her myself, with these hands. I know it's hard to accept, but she's gone. Do you think it was easy for me? I almost lost both of you. You need to let her go, not try to keep her spirit here against its will", his voice hardened at the end.

The two of them had spent the last few days trying to convince Darjoon of this fact, but he insisted that somehow he could feel Sirroya out in the desert, and he

51

remained fully convinced that she must be alive.

Darjoon's eyes narrowed and he ripped out the necklace he wore from under the neck of his robe.

"Yes, you gave me this and you told me that she's in the ground, but why is it that I can still feel her presence out there? I would know if she was truly dead, I'm telling you. I cannot go on without trying to find her, without making sure for myself. Why can't you understand that?"

"Oh, don't mistake us, Darjoon, of course we can understand it. We've all lost something or someone we love in this life, but be realistic! Even if she is alive, we have no way of knowing where she might be, do we? And there is so much more we need to do right now. That you need to do", the Healer was almost pleading now as she picked up where Nasrindo had left off.

Darjoon snorted through his nose and then took a few paces around the tent, finally turning and facing them.

"No... more... arguments! I am going to visit her grave and I want to see her, well, her body, her corpse even, there, in the ground. Only then can I be free to move on. Once I know that she is definitely gone, then I can lay to rest that voice inside me that tells me she is out there somewhere. Only then can I travel with you to Spidral and find the Circle of True One's, so we can do what must be done. And yes, I know that we must travel to the Glass Isle, don't worry. That at least I am certain of."

The Healer and the warrior exchanged a weary look, and Nasrindo stood up and placed his hands on the young mage's shoulders, "Darjoon, we've had this conversation already. There is nothing to be gained from those rebellious, cowardly and very, very dangerous mages in the Circle. They have only their lust for power and control and nothing else to offer. They cannot be trusted. What chance is there that they will show you how to travel to that accursed Glass Isle? They will sooner kill you than give you that knowledge. And how would you find them anyway? They do not show themselves to just anyone.

Entry to their secret lair is by invitation only!"

Darjoon smiled and patted his cloak that lay over the blankets next to him, "Yes, and that's exactly what I have here, thanks to your care of my belongings. I have a personal invitation given to me in Spidral. So it seems I do get to go and visit them, and when I am there, I will ask politely, Nas, if only the first time. Make no mistake though, they will give me what I want in the end."

The Healer shook her head, "Darjoon, even though you are admittedly a powerful young mage, and a skilled warrior, you would be no match for them. They are also experienced, and there will be many of them there. These are not desert warriors, who have no skill at magic, or a single Healer like myself. These are highly skilled, powerful and ruthless mages all working together. It will take you many, many years before they trust you enough to show you how to fast-travel to the Glass Isle. Indeed, even if such a thing exists, they may never show you. There must be another way."

"Yes, there is, K'trell. By boat. And how well do you think that will work? I must travel into and under the Glass Isle, not clamber around on top of its blasted remains. That would be pointless, wouldn't it? Enough of this. Nasrindo, tomorrow we set out for Sirroya's grave, and then, well, afterwards we travel to Spidral. For now, I'm going hunting", after which he walked out the tent and called to the ever-present guards.

Grinning, they threw a spear at him which he caught deftly, then grinned in return. K'trell moved to the tent entrance, and watched as the young mage ran lightly across the desert with the two burly guards behind him. They shadowed him everywhere now, even though she'd told them that he was safe and the tribe had eventually relaxed and nervously accepted the two as members. Despite her concerns, Darjoon had been good as gold for weeks and, without even trying, had won over every member of the tribe, even the elders. His calm, quiet, yet forceful nature, coupled with obvious power and skill had earned him respect from the fiercest warriors, and his helpfulness and gentle grace had won over many of the women and children too. She moved aside as Nasrindo stepped out with his gear, looking at the tracks the three men had left behind. He glanced at her briefly, shook his head, then grinned cheekily and ran off after them. She shook her head in return, and then caught herself smiling at his retreating back. Darjoon wasn't the only one to make an impression, although not with the other warriors. They still hadn't accepted Nasrindo in the same way. They only tolerated him as a friend of Darjoon's, aware of the big man's obvious affection for the foreign tribesman.

"And what about you, K'trell", she mused to herself, "He really has made an impression on you, hasn't he?"

She shook her head again and grinned at herself, then turned and left, walking up the slope to the main encampment. She had to get ready for the journey ahead, as well as prepare for the inevitable backlash that would come when she announced her imminent departure. She knew she had to travel with Darjoon when he left, but somehow she had to convince the elders of that, which wouldn't be easy. Her difficult nature had meant there were few applications for apprenticeships, and those few who'd made it through her stringent trials hadn't lasted long. There was one though, who even she had to admit, however grudgingly, would eventually make a suitable replacement. She changed course and headed for the group of ladies working on the edge of the encampment. With luck and the help of the goddess Turama she could make this work. She just had to grab her replacement and then face the elders. No time like the present. The young girl she'd found and then grabbed hold of kept looking up at her still wide-eyed and in shock from their encounter. As she headed to the tent of meeting dragging the awe-struck girl behind her, K'trell kept repeating to her slowly, "Just follow my lead and don't say a word. I will do the talking. Do you understand?"

They plunged into the gloom of the tent and all heads turned as the Great Healer marched the young girl up to the table without preamble and started talking. The exasperated elders rolled their eyes and shook their shaggy manes but nevertheless listened intently to what she had to say, before arguing among themselves.

K'trell shook her head angrily and took a deep breath, letting it out in a long sigh of exasperation. The elders were being understandably obstinate and the young girl quivering in fear beside her wasn't helping her cause. At least she was following orders and didn't say anything.

"I know she doesn't look like much, and you're right, I did cast her off early on during her training, but that was really more my fault than hers. I realise that my expectations were not always realistic and that I've been too hard on those few apprentices that I have had. However, young S'taidra here has shown definite promise and is the best of those that I have mentored."

The young girl in question stopped shaking and stared up at K'trell in disbelief, her mouth hanging open. K'trell had practically set her on fire chasing her out of the Healer's tent the last time she'd been with her. Now she was saying that she was the best of all of them? There seemed to have been so many before her.

"Look, I have to travel with Darjoon and protect him", K'trell continued, "You've all seen for yourselves that he is our only hope in the dark times that lie ahead. It is clear that he is the one from the prophecy and it would be sheer lunacy for us to ignore that. My fate and his were entwined long ago, as Turama knows. I have no doubt about that. I must go with them and while I am gone, S'taidra will continue her studies with you, the elders. Your knowledge and hers is not so incomplete, not when put together. It will have to be enough, at least until I return."

"And if you don't?", one of the elders was gesticulating angrily, "There isn't another Great Healer like you in the other tribes, even if we would accept them, which we won't, and as you have demonstrated over and over again, there doesn't appear to be the promise of another in our tribe. You say this young girl has the makings of one, but of what use is that when we have need of a Healer right now?"

"Enough", the voice of the senior elder cut across the debate and all the murmuring voices stopped. He waited as the silence deepened, then frowned at the Great Healer as she opened her mouth. She closed it abruptly and looked at him, then bowed her head slightly.

Slowly rising from his chair, he leaned forward with his hands on the table, his age obvious in the long white hair hanging down his back and the mottled, veined and gnarled fingers spread out before him. They were still large hands, once formidable and able to break men's necks with a single twist. He looked up at the Great Healer, and then slowly looked around the tent, eyeing each of the elders in turn, who all individually nodded at him in recognition of his authority, although some scowled slightly. He focused on K'trell and frowned at her.

"Great Healer, I have heard your arguments and I am of the same opinion as you. Yes, don't look so surprised that I agree with you, on this anyway. I also believe that you must travel with this young mage and his companion. We will find a way, somehow, to manage without your obvious and considerable abilities. Abilities I might add that are in very short supply anywhere in our great desert, as the wise elder has pointed out. It is indeed unfortunate that your, well", his eyes narrowed as he looked at her like a snake would look at a small rodent, "your wayward and ill-disciplined nature has hindered your succession plans. It is my sincere hope that you yourself will come back better for the journey, and that during your travels you will find a measure of peace and rest along with some much-needed common sense. But do not think for one moment that this is some great adventure, some noble quest that you now embark on. You take our lives in your hands when you go and so our fate, the fate of your tribe, has become even more linked to your own. You can no longer afford to be reckless, Great Healer. This is the time for you to truly prove yourself, to Turama, and to all of us, but most importantly, to yourself. I have always believed that you could be the greatest Great Healer ever, but you must curb these scattered and powerful emotions and control your misplaced affection. Oh, you know of what I speak. Promise me that you will not allow yourself to be misled by the child that still remains within you. Curiosity is good, even necessary for children, but as we grow older we must focus on what is most needed and what is right in front of us! Time becomes a luxury we can ill afford. Understood?"

K'trell looked up and stared defiantly at the old man, then under his withering, piercing gaze, she slowly lowered her eyes and nodded her head before replying, "Yes, Old One. I understand and I will conquer what is within. I know what is required of me, from Turama and from you. I will not fail and I will assuredly return, as Turama wills it. I will not let the people down. Not this time. Nor you, my brother."

The last was breathed out softly and the old man's eyes softened for a moment as they looked at each other, an unspoken emotion resonating between them.

"Then go, my beloved sister! Go and take our hopes and dreams with you. Go before we change our minds and wake up to this apparent lunacy that your young mage has infected all of us with. May Turama guide your footsteps and bring you safely back home again", he sighed and slumped back down into his chair as the murmuring began to swell and the elders began arguing and bickering with each other again.

K'trell strode from the tent, grabbing S'taidra by the arm and dragging her along like a limp rag doll.

"Come girl, close that mouth and wake up. This is no dream, this is a harsh reality that I am burdening us all with and don't I know it. If you are to step up to being a Healer, then you need to learn to pay attention", she shook the girl and stepped out in front, "Now hurry, I have much to show you in the short time we have left."

S'taidra quickened her steps to try and keep up with the Great Healer who marched briskly across the sand. It was going to be a rough few days, but inwardly she beamed, a warmth filling her up inside. She was the best of them! The Great Healer had really called her the best! Above all the others. Her mother had always said they had a Healer in their family's past. Now she would be another.

Across the desert, Darjoon sunk down quietly next to the two hulking warriors and peered intently over the lip of the great dune they were hiding behind. Two large antelope were plodding wearily across the desert sand, obviously heading towards the oasis to their right. It was still morning, but now that the heat was building they would make their way there and shelter in the shade on the ridges overlooking the watering hole until the cool of the evening. The warrior to Darjoon's right pressed his fingers to his temple, then lifted his right index finger. Darjoon had quickly picked up on the hidden signals the tribesmen used when out hunting and now, moving swiftly, he loped around the dune downwind of the buck while keeping low so as to avoid any silhouette. Once in position he gave a mournful call used by the desert doves. At his signal, the other warriors charged upwind making a noise and causing the two antelope to turn and flee, leaping across the sand. Darjoon waited until the last minute, rising and releasing his spear in one fluid motion as the pair fled past him. The weapon arced up slightly in the morning light, falling gracefully and plunging into the neck of the trailing antelope. It staggered, and fell, thrashing the sand as the other made good its escape. Darjoon charged over the dune and down the other side, but as he ploughed through the thick sand his foot caught on a hidden rock and he tumbled, head-over-heels, finally tetching to a stop at the bottom, his robe covered in sand. Nasrindo ran over as he sat up, laughing to himself. Glancing down at the sand he was covered with, he looked up at Nasrindo with a big grin.

"Well, would you look at this? Fat man hunting! Who would've thought it?", and he collapsed in laughter again as Nasrindo grinned back. For days now, Darjoon had slowly been returning to his former self, to the young man that Nasrindo remembered. Only the darker shadows in his eyes, and the distinctly powerful quality of the magic that he could still feel cascading off the young mage belied the experiences he'd been through. But to see him like this, laughing freely as he plunged his dagger into the buck to carve out its heart, and the freedom and grace with which he carried his large form, was balm to the warrior's big heart. He laughed himself, then stepped over to help the others divide up the meat from the kill.

Back in the encampment, the Healer fought the urge to light S'taidra's backside with fire again. She grimly swallowed the fierce words that threatened to leave the tip of her tongue and stared at the young girl. How in Turama's name had her own teacher, the last Great Healer, had such tremendous patience? Had she been as ham-fisted as this miserable wretch in front of her? The girl was quivering as she looked up in alarm at the Healer towering over her and tears began forming at the corners of her eyes.

Looking at the tearful girl, a memory suddenly popped into the Healer's head. As a young girl, she remembered struggling over the combination for a poultice, and not a particularly challenging one either. She'd failed for the umpteenth time when the Great Healer had walked into the tent and loomed over her. She'd quivered in fear, much like this girl, because the Healer seldom had the time to fix her mistakes and even less inclination back then. But on that day, when she feared the worst, the old lady had simply stepped up and pulling her gently close had held her for a moment, stroking her hair and telling her not to worry and what a fine Healer she'd make. In fact, she'd told her that mistakes were the doorway to greatness.

She looked down at the young girl trembling in fear in front of her. Gently, she stepped forward and took the pestle from her shaking fingers, laying it down.

"It's alright, S'taidra. Here, come sit for a moment, your hair is a real mess."

The girl obediently sat down and taking a hair brush, the Healer sat behind her and slowly and patiently began brushing out the tangled hair.

"Part of being a Healer, S'taidra, is looking the part. Those who are sick and dying want to see someone who is clean inside and outside. This is part of our vow to Turama, that we will keep ourselves pure in her service. It is why we do not marry for love, why we must renounce all love and any ties to family and even friends. The life of a Healer is a lonely one, so that they can focus on the tasks at hand. It requires tremendous concentration to focus our powers in the right way."

"But... But you didn't keep pure, did you, Great Healer? I mean, I've heard the rumours. Ouch!", the young girl squawked in alarm as K'trell savagely dragged the brush through a particular knotty tangle.

"I'm sorry, S'taidra, I slipped", she hissed angrily and then relented at the look on the girl's face.

"Yes, you're right, I did, young one. I abandoned my vows and I rejected her who heals. I failed her, and I fell in love. But she who sees all and hears all and knows all, well, once she takes you she does not let go. I thought I could escape and live a normal life like any woman, but... It was not meant to be and so I condemned him the moment I turned my back on she who is merciful, and on my duty and my tribe. It was not right and I had to pay the price. As did he."

The young girl turned and looked at her in awe, transfixed as the tears slid gently down the Healer's cheeks.

She kept very still in fear of whatever the fiery woman would do next. The Healer just shook herself, then looked down at her tenderly and smiled. She smiled tentatively in response.

"We are all human, S'taidra, don't ever forget that. Turama knows us, knows what we will do even before we do it. Don't make my mistakes, don't look for meaning beyond your duty, and don't go looking for what you cannot have. This, what we do, this wonderful gift we have, to bring people back from certain death, it must be enough for us. Now, listen to me, I'm being an old woman already and you but a young girl. The reason you are struggling with this potion is because it is getting late and you've done enough for one day. Go now, have a good meal and get a good night's rest because tomorrow and every day after that, until I leave, I will require the utmost effort from you."

"Oh yes, Great Healer! I will not disappoint you, nor Turama. You'll see, I'll be a good healer, I promise you. Thank you, mistress, uh, I mean Great Healer. I'll see you tomorrow", the young girl scampered out of the tent.

In the twilight, the Healer sat and stared out at the darkening skies, barely noting the stars that sparkled into life one by one. Her thoughts were far, far away on the wind, the ache in her heart keening like that very wind that had picked up outside. Could she have saved him if she'd remained pure, remained apart from him? Indeed, had Turama herself taken him so that she would return to the healing arts? And why did this Nasrindo stir the same feelings as before? Why could she not just be content to be a servant of the Healing goddess? These and many other thoughts swirled around inside her fevered mind as the wind moaned around the tent ropes.

Across the desert the warriors had made a fire, realising they'd come too far to make it back to camp by nightfall. They hunched down next to a dune to avoid the wind that was picking up and the delicious aroma of freshly killed venison cooking over the fire wafted across the desert sands. Darjoon left the warriors and walked out into the blustery night, finally slipping down onto the soft sand alongside Nasrindo. The warrior would often sit apart, meditating in the darkness while Darjoon and the others joked by the campfire.

Darjoon threw over a chunk of meat that the warrior caught easily and Nasrindo looked across and grinned at him, his white teeth gleaming in the darkness.

"Thank you, my friend. That was a fine kill, Darjoon. You are getting better and better at this, you know. If it wasn't for that large, sharp nose of yours, I'd swear you grew up on these dunes. So tell me, how are you feeling?"

"Very funny, Nas! Truth be told I'm not sure how to answer that. I mean I'm feeling stronger, more like myself every day, but somehow I just don't feel, well, complete. I know that's not much of a description, but, I feel like something is missing, something I just don't understand. And before you say anything, no, I don't mean Sirroya. Of course I miss her, but it's not that. I just feel like there's something calling to me out there, something I can't place. You know I never found that warrior that my mother told me about, someone called Turmoos? I mean, that's why I came out here to begin with. Maybe that's what's missing? Come to think of it, I never did ask you about him. Have you ever come across a warrior named Turmoos in your travels?"

Nasrindo looked at him sideways, studying the pensive face and the lowered brow. This wasn't the first time Darjoon had expressed this feeling of something being missing. Now the young mage had finally asked him the question he'd been dreading all along. What should he say in response? Did it really matter who he was?

"Darjoon, there is something that I must tell you. I do know, or at least, I did know a man called Turmoos, although it seems like so long ago now. When I was a young warrior, an older man came out of the desert and approached me. I was about to become an elite warrior at the time. He said his name was Turmoos and he had a mission for me. He had taken a blood oath with a raven-born mage and her man, a mage from another land, or so he said. They had told him that one day their child would return, and he was to care for him, but the child had never arrived. Now he was too old to do so, and so he said he had chosen me to take up his cause. As a result I swore a blood oath with him to do that."

Nasrindo looked intently at Darjoon who stared wide-eyed at him.

"So now you know. I suppose I've not had the chance to tell you before, nor was I sure I should. But as you have asked, I have told you. I implore you, for all our sakes, do not repeat what I have said. The Lost Tribe have already reacted badly to this news, and it is a great sin amongst my people to take a blood oath at all, let alone with one who is not from among us. Know that I will die for you, Darjoon. My life is not my own, that is why I must travel with you, wherever you go and whatever dangers you face so that you will not be alone and that I can protect you."

Darjoon exhaled, as if he'd held his breath the whole time Nasrindo was speaking.

"I knew it! When we went to meet the Y'rdirak lizard-people, I remembered the gypsy saying that they would only deal with Turmoos. But I know in the desert you people age quicker than the rest of us, and that the gypsy said you'd be very old, so it didn't make sense to me. I guess we've never really had a chance to talk about it, have we? I don't know what to say, Nas. What you have done, saving my life back there, rescuing me from the Y'rdirak, bringing me here. How could I ever repay you? If you want to be free of your oath, then I free you! You don't have to..."

"No! Don't you ever speak like that again, Darjoon. This is not an oath I can lay down, like some simple promise. My life is forfeit if I were to do so. No, I am a warrior of honour who serves the gods and I will not turn from this path. Let us not speak of it again. Just know that as long as I am by your side, I will die for you."

Silence fell as Darjoon digested these words. They sat together for a while, Nasrindo's impassioned breathing slowing.

Suddenly Darjoon grinned and turned to him, the darkness falling away from his face, "So, old man, I've seen how you look at that K'trell, eh. What's that about? I thought Healer's were off-limits or something. Don't they marry just for breeding other healers, isn't that it? You have to be picked by the goddess to marry one, imagine that? Oh, come on, don't act so surprised. You know what I'm talking about. It sounds like it wouldn't be the first time she's set up camp away from her tent, huh? Not from what I've heard, anyway, at least, that's what the warriors said. I mean, is it really such a bad thing for them?"

Nasrindo's impassive face and stony eyes were lost in the darkness and Darjoon just kept grinning at him.

"Darjoon, I don't think you understand", Nasrindo finally answered him quietly and seriously, the grin fading from Darjoon's face at his tone.

"For a Great Healer to take a man of her own choosing is unheard of. Quite possibly it's never happened before. That the Chief elder did not banish her once they were discovered is amazing. Quite possibly its only the fact that Turama had already punished her for what she did by taking his life so young. Some vows should never be broken, no matter what. Our choice ends once the vow is made", the warrior stood up and walked stiffly back to camp, leaving the young mage in the darkness.

"Darjoon, you idiot, what were you thinking", he muttered to himself, "Always two left feet and one of them in your mouth, huh!"

He looked up at the stars for a while, thinking of a young woman with long blonde hair and sparkling blue-green eyes. After a while he sauntered back to the fire, placing a hand on Nasrindo's shoulder and squeezing it as he walked past, the warrior looked up and simply nodded in understanding. As they turned in for the night, Darjoon looked over at Nasrindo and said quietly, "When we get back, we should think about leaving soon. It's time to go out into the desert and do a different kind of hunting. It's time to go and find Sirroya!"

A few days later, as Nasrindo, the Healer and Darjoon walked out of the Lost Tribe encampment, the Healer couldn't shake the queasiness in her belly. Seeing the white-faced young S'taidra desperately clinging to the chief elder's robes as they both waved goodbye hadn't helped. The young girl was far, far from ready and although the elders did have some lore between them, it wasn't nearly enough. What if a plague came and she wasn't there to stand between the god of death and her tribe, or if the lizard-men attacked and they lost too many warriors that she would normally have healed. She offered up a quick prayer to Turama and forced herself not to look back, quickening her gait to keep up with Darjoon and the warrior. There was nothing she could do about it now and she would just have to have faith in her goddess. They plodded on into the desert.

The sun beat down mercilessly on the three figures struggling across the dunes. They'd been walking for days now and this morning the red sand was heating up fiercely as the sun rose. Soon they'd have to find somewhere to wait out the full heat of the day. Nasrindo stopped suddenly, shading his eyes and peering ahead. He stood still as a statue and just stared. Darjoon and K'trell stopped, and turned back, looking at him quizzically. Now urgent, he cast around, looking at the landscape around them. Off to the left were some low ridges and they started as he barked at them both, "Come!", then turned and began running past them.

They'd accepted that he was the one to lead them as neither Darjoon nor K'trell knew where they were actually going. He'd proven his worth so far as he'd been able to find an oasis or shelter every time, despite both of them moaning at him good-naturedly about how long it took. But this was different and without saying anything they turned and followed him, struggling to match his pace. As they were running, Darjoon glanced back in the direction Nasrindo had been looking. A giant wall of black extended across the sky and now he began to hear the faint whine of thousands of grains of sand being blown through the air. He redoubled his pace and saw that K'trell had also been looking and together they charged towards the shelter of the ridge along which they frantically sought cover.

They were very lucky to find a small cave and they crawled in and huddled together, glad to be out of the incredible wind that was now howling outside. Nasrindo placed their tent over the hole on the inside, and they jammed their feet against it on either side to keep it in place and keep out most of the sand. Unable to speak to each other because of the wind, Darjoon eventually nodded off, followed by the others.

Now, waking up, he could hear the wind had died down and could taste and feel the grit that seemed to cover his tongue and rub against his teeth. He was struggling to dig out his canteen when K'trell passed hers over. He tried to wash out the grit, then looking around for a place to spit, grimaced when he realised that as they were so tightly packed in, there wasn't anywhere. He swallowed, feeling the sand slide down his throat and quickly took another gulp of water.

"Hey, easy with that", K'trell grabbed the canteen back and took a swig. Darjoon laughed when she looked round like he had and then swallowed. She took another gulp and grinned at him, "Okay, great magician, so I broke the rule too. 'One drink to live, two drinks to die' is what we always say. But in this case that sand tasted foul and death was preferable to keeping that swill in my mouth."

Nasrindo took his feet off the tent as did the others,

and then he stepped outside and shook the sand off it, folding it into his pack. The others came out after him, Darjoon jostling with K'trell to get out before her. She laughed, and then slapped him on the back, only to get a face full of dust which had her in a coughing fit. Darjoon laughed back, then started coughing too while Nasrindo just glared at them both with his arms folded and a look of disdain on his face.

"If you're both quite finished, we need to think about getting a move on. I want to try and make up some ground before nightfall."

Darjoon looked around in surprise, noting that the sun was already well on its way down to the desert floor. They'd been in the cave longer than he thought. Shrugging, he pushed K'trell off-balance as she was trying to throw sand out of her boots and took off running, laughing as he did so. Nasrindo just shook his head again, then helped the Healer to her feet, letting her lean on him while she got all the sand out her boots and put them on again. She lost her balance just for a moment, falling towards him and he felt the soft warmth of her body against his. Quickly, she pulled herself away and he just looked at her, his eyes sparkling mischievously then he went deadpan when she looked at him.

"He's just a great big child sometimes, isn't he", he murmured.

She looked up at him and smiled briefly, then looked out as Darjoon waved at them from up on a dune, her smile fading as she shivered involuntarily, "Yes, a great big child who can kill with just a thought or a twitch of his finger. It's hard to believe it's the same person sometimes."

Nasrindo frowned at that, "He's a good man, Healer. A good man with a dangerous destiny and the odds are not stacked in his favour. He will most likely need every ounce of power he has. Let us hope that we can guide him through what has to be done."

They walked out in silence together, joining Darjoon and continuing over the dunes.

Eventually, days later, Nasrindo trudged down a dune and headed over to some rocks. He stopped and looked around at the mountains in the distance, squinting fiercely and taking his bearings. The sun was almost gone with just a faint splash of colour on the horizon a reminder of its presence and now the cool night wind was starting to pick up. The others looked at him quizzically, then K'trell, after first feeling the rock next to her to make sure it was cool enough, sat down on it. Darjoon walked over to Nasrindo, but before he could say anything the warrior suddenly grabbed him by the shoulder in consternation.

"This is the place, Darjoon! This is where we left her, I'm sure of it. But! But something's wrong. I mean, there's nothing here, is there? It can't just be gone, there must be at least some trace of it? I built a sizable cairn on top of her grave so we should be able to see something. I'm sure this is the place, in fact I'm certain of it. It must be, the location is right, it's just not here."

"Alright, Nasrindo, easy, easy. Are you sure you're right? I mean it wouldn't be hard to mistake one valley for another out here, especially after that recent storm? I know it all looks the same to me."

"Of course I'm sure", he hissed in frustration, "I've been navigating these deserts a long time now. This is the place. We'll just have to look around to see if we can find it."

Nasrindo began casting around on the ground, slowly moving between the large rocks. Darjoon moved away and began looking in a different area, and, after a while, K'trell did the same. She shook her head as she heard Nasrindo muttering to himself and then widened her search. The sand was quite soft in places and as she moved through it, she cursed quietly as she kicked her toes on a hidden rock. Bending down to rub her foot, she stared at a faded piece of cloth fluttering between two stones that were sticking out of a pile of sand. Brushing away the sand, she could see more stones, piled on top of each other.

Looking up, she saw Nasrindo not far away and called to him softly, "Warrior, come quickly, I think I've found something here."

Nasrindo hurried over to her and stopped dead, his eyes widening in surprise. Quickly, he began brushing off the sand, exposing more stones. Slowly he sank to his knees, muttering a prayer to himself.

"This is it, this is the grave. Thank the gods. That piece of cloth is part of Sirroya's robe. This, this is her resting place, may she rest in peace and hunt with the night", he made a strange signal with his hands, "But something's not entirely right here, I mean, this looks smaller than before?"

He looked up at K'trell, the anguish clear on his face. She pursed her lips and bowed her head, uttering the same words he had, then went looking for Darjoon. Nasrindo could hear her calling softly for the young mage. As he looked at the pile of rocks, he noticed that some had been dislodged. Putting his hand on a rock to place it on the pile, he quickly pulled it back as a small, ink-black scorpion scuttled away. The black desert scorpion was one of the deadliest creatures out here, especially when they were still young. One sting and a man would be dead in minutes. That one had looked very small and very young indeed. Nasrindo shivered. Finding a scorpion near a grave was a strange omen and he muttered some more prayers to himself. He looked up as K'trell returned with Darjoon in tow.

Darjoon stood and stared at the nondescript pile of rocks covered in red sand. The blue piece of cloth hung limply against the rocks as the breeze had died down and seemed to glow faintly as the sunlight gave way to the eerie blue light of the Tregora moon. Nasrindo was still placing rocks back on the grave, building it up again. He turned and looked mournfully at Darjoon, the pain obvious in his earnest face. Darjoon looked at him in disbelief.

"It can't be true, it just, it just can't be. She's not meant to be dead, I know that. We... She... I mean it isn't possible. I never got to... I'm sure I would know if she wasn't here anymore, if she wasn't still alive. I just... If I could just see her body, I just need to know for sure she's in there", he started to grab rocks off the grave.

Immediately, both K'trell and Nasrindo grabbed him and tried to restrain him. Opening a grave was unthinkable to the tribes-folk, and they believed it could destroy a dead person's soul forever. No tribesmen would ever contemplate that. They wrestled him back from the grave, and K'trell tried to calm him down.

"Darjoon, please, leave her be. You can't think to open this grave, it would destroy her more than you know. Let her be free, young mage. She is past all this pain and sorrow, she is now with the gods and nothing can harm her anymore. It is a better place to be and who would think to rob her of that. Come, let us sit down here and we can pray to the gods together. Let her be, young mage, let her be."

Darjoon fought her and then suddenly slumped down. Tears coursed down his cheeks and he bowed down, putting his head in his hands. Suddenly he pushed himself to his feet and lifted his arms, splaying his fingers wide. Magic sprayed from his hands causing Nasrindo to stiffen in shock at the sheer power. K'trell stumbled back, recognising the spell but not the intensity of it. It was a life-detection spell, but many times more powerful than any she'd known. She was drawn into its power immediately, sensing the life around them, the myriad small mammals in their burrows, the hunting owls, the little scorpion hiding behind one of the rocks on the grave, but there was nothing in the grave. She heard Darjoon's groan and then gasped as the spell intensified further, reaching outwards. Suddenly, out in the desert she felt the life-force of a person, faint but clear and then as suddenly, it winked out as Darjoon stumbled backwards.

"She's there, I felt her", he cried, "She's out there and I must go to her."

He began to stumble towards their belongings.

"Darjoon, wait", K'trell cried, "You don't know it was her. I felt it too, but I couldn't detect who it was. This could be someone else, even something else. We should proceed with caution and you're not ready. You need to get your strength back first. Just look at you."

Nasrindo hurried over to Darjoon as he staggered and went down on one knee. The young mage let the warrior help him down and accepted the food and drink he was offered. Closing his eyes, he sensed how much power he'd used in pushing out that spell. How did they know who or what else had sensed it? K'trell was right, they needed to be cautious, and here he was giving them away. He'd twice failed with the lizard-men and he was determined he wouldn't get caught out again. They would have to wait until morning to travel, as she had said. He closed his eyes and wasn't even aware when the two eased him down and placed a blanket over him.

The two tribes-folk talked quietly into the darkness, an occasional laugh from K'trell ringing out musically in the darkness. Nasrindo finally fell asleep with a smile on his face, the laughter continuing to fill him as he slept. Tomorrow they would continue their journey.

The three crested a dune and Darjoon blinked away the sand that crusted his eyelashes. This area of the desert was filled with fine sand, constantly blown about by the desert wind. The sea wasn't far away and the sea breezes were able to penetrate inland, especially early in the morning. The moisture tended to keep the sand stuck to a person and he wiped the fine grains off his face for the umpteenth time, tasting the faint saltiness in the air, then pulled his cloak back up over his mouth and nose. He'd used his magic again after waking, but this time carefully and finely focused, and he had still detected a life sign, although it seemed a lot fainter than the evening before.

Suddenly he stopped, stiffening and stared at the clump of rocks nestled under a dune, looking for all the world as if it was a boat and a wave of sand was about to break over it. He was sure he'd seen something glistening in the sunlight. Grabbing Nasrindo's shoulder, he gave it a squeeze and then plunged down the dune they were standing on and fought his way through the loose sand towards the rocks. Nasrindo and K'trell exchanged another look of despair and plunged after him. They'd quietly discussed the situation in that early morning while Darjoon was still sleeping off the effects of the magic he'd used. They were prepared to give him a few more days, and then they were heading back, if they had to knock him out and drag him with them.

They caught up with him just before he reached the outcropping. There was a faint grating of steel on rock and the tip of a spear wavered into view from the darkness between the large rocks. An old man with grey hair came out, slowly blinking at them and wheezing as if even the effort of standing was too much. His rheumy eyes peered up at them as he slumped heavily, leaning on the spear that was holding him up. Darjoon stepped forward and tenderly put his arm around the old man, easing him back into the shade and onto the blankets that were tucked in between the rocks. The young mage took out his canteen and dribbled the water between the wrinkled lips, gently wiping away the drool that slid out of the ancient mouth.

It was not uncommon for tribesfolk who became too old to leave the tribe and walk into the desert so as to spare the tribe the burden of their care. But Darjoon had lived with his grandparents and was comfortable around older folk, and K'trell marvelled anew at the sudden change in the tough, young mage. His whole bearing and manner was different, as he became soft and caring.

As she stared at the strange, peaceful scene of the young man caring for the older one, she noticed the drooping ears with their twin tails instead of a single lobe.

Immediately, she sank to her knees and grabbed the old man's right foot, lifting it into the light and ignoring Darjoon's questions. She gasped as she saw the second toe next to the big toe was missing, cut off at the base. Hissing now, she muttered a curse under her breath, then turned and spat on the sand while drawing her knife. Darjoon stared in horror as she raised the weapon, clearly intent on delivering a killing blow. A word of magical command froze her arm, and she snapped out of her reaction, staring at him in anger.

"K'trell, what are you doing? You, you can't want to kill him? He's just an old man, dying in the desert. What's wrong with you?", he looked at her with puzzled incomprehension.

Nasrindo had seen what K'trell was doing and now leaned forward and pried the knife from her frozen grasp. Darjoon released the spell and she grabbed her hand, massaging it and glaring at him. Nasrindo looked at her, then seeing she'd recovered, nodded and handed the knife back to her which she returned to its sheath.

"Darjoon", he spoke softly before the Healer could, "this is not just a tribesman, this is a shaman from the Dreal. They are not like us. They follow an ancient and mystical way that we consider very evil. Any decent tribes-folk would immediately slay people such as this, because their kind is an abomination to us. Even more so those from the Lost Tribe. See the markings on his chest? They are faded but still visible. They are a sign of ancient, dark power, a power that the Lost Tribe have disavowed forever."

Darjoon looked at him and back at K'trell warily, then moved in front of the old man protectively.

"I understand why you may not want to harm him even though we do", Nasrindo looked across with a warning for the Healer, "and in any event I can see he will die soon anyway. So we should leave him to the desert as it is his time. I must tell you that I too wish him a speedy death and were you not here, I would ensure that happened sooner rather than later."

At the last words of Nasrindo, the old man stirred and began babbling at them. K'trell's hand flew to her knife and she began to speak a shield spell, when Darjoon's hand went up, stopping her mid-spell. He leant over and put his ear near the man's mouth. K'trell hissed in exasperation, then stalked away and turned, facing them. Her hand stayed on the dagger as she carefully watched Darjoon and the old man.

Nasrindo also tightened his grip on the spear and stepped back in alarm, "Darjoon, be careful. He may be old and infirm but he may yet speak a curse or bad magic. Do not trust what he says. Remember what happened before when that, when dark magic was used."

Darjoon's face went white as the old man continued to babble excitedly, and both the healer and the warrior turned their heads in an attempt to hear what he was saying, despite their own warnings. Nasrindo could only catch a few words, but turned attentively to Darjoon as he stood, the old man wheezing and gasping now that he'd finished saying what he'd obviously wanted to get out. Darjoon walked over to them and stopped with his eyes wide and fixed on the distance.

"Well, what did he say? You cannot believe their kind, they are filth", the Healer spat to the side.

"He said that he is, or was, part of a scouting party. They had detected strange magic's at work here a while back and so they'd journeyed beyond their lands to investigate. All they'd found was the grave, the, the place where, where she lay. They'd not found anyone or anything else, and after a day they had begun the journey back. Not long after, while they were resting during the heat of the sun, a woman had walked out of the desert toward them. He... He said that, that, it was... It was her. I know it was, K'trell. It was the way he described her. He said she was petite with long, blonde hair and blue-green eyes, and wearing a torn, dusty blue cloak. It could only be her, it must be, it was Sirroya", Darjoon stared now at Nasrindo, hope and fear on his face in equal measure.

The warrior staggered back, "But that's impossible, Darjoon. It must be an illusion because he is so old. Maybe it was some sort of overspill from the spell that killed her? It cannot be her, I saw her die, and I buried her body, Darjoon! I'm telling you, she was completely dead. It cannot be her", Nasrindo was pleading now, afraid at the look on Darjoon's face.

"But that's just it, Nas. He wasn't old when she found them. He was a young warrior, as were they all. At first, they surrounded her with their spears, afraid because she looked different somehow. She seemed detached, not of this world. She didn't do anything, just stood there. Then, he, well, being the shaman, they all looked at him for what to do. He put down his spear and stepped forward, wanting to speak with her. Before he could say anything, she'd grabbed him by the throat and before their eyes, his skin started to crease and wrinkle, his hair turned white and he became an old man. At the same time, her eyes were, well, according to him, they were burning with fire and she seemed to come to, as if she'd been far away and now had arrived again. She had blinked, and then, had dropped him as if in horror. Before they could move, she'd run off over the dune and away. They were too afraid to go after her, and after talking between themselves had left him here to die. Apparently they were afraid of taking him with them, in case he could contaminate them. What does this mean?"

The two stared in horror at Darjoon. K'trell blinked her eyes rapidly, then stammered at him, "What? A what... It was, it must be, it was a rejuvenation spell. Stealing youth and vitality from others, can it be? I thought it wasn't real, it can't be, surely it's just a myth. No, it can't be real. How did she, who is she? Who is this Sirroya really? Did you know of her dark powers", she stared at

Darjoon and Nasrindo, who looked back at her with awe and wonder and shook their heads.

"But that means she, I mean, she's alive! I knew it! I knew she wasn't dead. We must find her, we have to go after her and, and we must find her, Nas, we have to", Darjoon's eyes were flashing in excitement as he strode back and forth, his whole body vibrating eagerly.

"Wait, Darjoon! How do we know what has happened to her? This may be more of the lizard men's magic at work, and we have to be careful. I know you are happy, Darjoon, I can see that, but be reasonable. It, I mean, she, I mean, well she may not be who you think she is anymore. There are stories of what happens when great magic is unleashed and this, well this kind of magic, maybe it can invite evil to come in, to possess even our bodies. We don't really know what is going on here. We should speak to the old man some more. Let's see what else he remembers", K'trell reached out to Darjoon imploringly.

"Yes! Yes, let's heal him and then we can ask him some more questions", Darjoon strode over to the old man who had either fallen asleep or lapsed into stupor. Both Darjoon, and then K'trell tried to heal him, but even though his body seemed stronger for their efforts, he did not wake up. They sat with him, feeling the body slipping away again.

"I think his mind is too far gone, Darjoon. The body cannot be sustained without the mind. I do not think he wants to live and I fear he will not wake from this final sleep", the Healer shook her head.

As the sun slipped below the horizon, Nasrindo slowly piled the last rock on the cairn they had built for the old man. K'trell had insisted he didn't deserve a decent burial and should be left out to rot, but Darjoon wouldn't hear of it. While they'd toiled over the grave, she'd sat some way off on a rock, stewing and thinking over what the old man had said. As far as she knew, rejuvenation spells were dark magic, not something any healer would ever contemplate.

Imagine stealing life-force from another person, the horror of it. She shivered in response to her thoughts. Who then was this friend of Darjoon and Nasrindo? Why had she hidden her power from them? He'd hardly spoken about her, and she'd gleaned what she knew from some of his memories and from Nasrindo. But she'd thought she was just an empty-headed, orphaned, Empire girl, whereas now it seemed she was something else. As for the lizard-men's magic, well, she'd only read snippets of it, all saying that it was very different to the magic the healers used. That it was darker and somehow alien even. Some said they came from another world, that they didn't belong here and that their strange magic proved that. What if Sirroya had somehow been infected with that strange magic? Maybe she didn't even know what she was doing, it didn't sound like she did from what the old man had said. Old man! The other day he'd been a young tribesman, and now he was old and, well, dead. She shivered involuntarily and looked up as Darjoon and Nasrindo came over to her. She thought she knew what Darjoon was going to say, so was surprised when he spoke.

"There is no way we can find her now. If I was able to detect her then I would've done so before. She's either too far away, or her, well, her magic or whatever it is, is somehow stopping me. Either way, we have absolutely no way of knowing where she's gone. I am content just to know that she's alive, and the fates and gods willing, we will find each other again. But now I need to continue the journey I should be on. We need to leave. Nas, can you lead us out of the desert? We should head to Spidral across the Plains of Breath. It's time to meet the Circle and time to make destiny become reality."

Nasrindo and K'trell looked at each other meaningfully. They had their own ideas about meeting this Circle. But that could wait and be dealt with once they'd reached Spidral.

"Yes, Darjoon, I can lead us. We should leave now

while it's still light, although the Tregora moon should still be out for some time, so we can travel all through the night. Let's go, I don't really want to stay here any longer than I have to."

Nasrindo walked over and picked up his pack as the others followed suit and they trudged away from the cairn which sat, brooding and sullen, and glowing quietly in the moonlight.

# 5 THE PAST HAS SECRETS

Darjoon slid down the dune and stopped, shading his eyes and peering across at what lay ahead, running directly across their path. Rather than the smooth regularity of the dunes they'd been crossing in what was incredibly barren desert, the dune ahead looked vaguely wrong. Something about it suggested that it wasn't a dune, maybe because it was angular and straight, not smooth and flowing as he was used to with the sand-blown dunes they'd been crossing with monotonous regularity.

Nasrindo slithered to a stop behind him and looked at him quizzically. Darjoon had learned that the facial expressions among tribesfolk developed in greater detail than regular people, because in the desert even to speak meant loss of fluid and therefore in the deep desert they communicated with their face, and when necessary, with cryptic hand gestures. The latter he'd learned from his guards during his time with the Lost Tribe. So as Nasrindo glanced up at Darjoon's face, a question mark radiating from his features, Darjoon simply shrugged, then framed the fingers of his left hand around the object ahead and gestured with his right hand index finger, finally shrugging with his palms up. Nasrindo turned to look, then let out a short, sharp whistle.

The pair set off as K'trell slithered to a stop behind them. She'd heard the whistle, and knew she must follow them. She glanced towards the odd-shaped dune ahead, paled, then quickened her pace to catch up with the two in front.

"Wait, Darjoon, wait a moment", she called after him.

They stopped, and turned towards her, both looking surprised at the fear in her voice, as well as the fact she'd spoken at all. She was rushing towards them in obvious distress and with great concern.

"Don't go that way, are you mad? Don't you know it's haunted? That's not a safe place for the living, Darjoon", she said through dry, chapped lips.

Darjoon and Nasrindo looked at each other, and then looked at K'trell again. Neither of them had thought she could be easily spooked but she was obviously white-faced and trembling. Nasrindo shook his head, and muttered an ancient oath of protection under his breath. He grasped K'trell's shoulder in his powerful hand and squeezed gently, then using his hands he pointed at the object and with a series of gestures indicated they would go around it. He squeezed her shoulder again in reassurance then dropped his hand to his side and looked at Darjoon quizzically.

Darjood stood looking at them with his hands on his hips and snorted, "Listen, you two might be afraid of desert shadows, but I wasn't brought up here. That means that whatever is out there won't affect me. Why don't you two ladies stay here while I go and scout around? If it's safe, I'll whistle you in, if I'm in trouble, well, then you decide what you'll do."

Nasrindo frowned at him, then put his fingers to his lips indicating he should not talk. Then he jumped as K'trell began speaking breathlessly next to him.

"No, Darjoon! You don't understand! I'm not talking about some sort of desert magic here, like the lizard men or something. This, this place, it is an ancient city and it has a legacy all of its own. It has nothing to do with the desert at all. What you see hidden under that sand is a city that has been here for longer than any story of any tribe. It is from before our time. Long before! Sleeping in that place is something that has nothing to do with magic, but rather some ancient evil best left undisturbed. The little we know is that those who have tried to enter it have never, ever returned. Please, let's do as Nasrindo says and track around this cursed place. Not even your great powers will help you in there, don't you see?", she was pleading now, the big eyes in her pale face a mute testament to the fear inside.

Darjoon looked undecided and hesitated, as if weighing up what she'd said. He turned and looked again at the shapes in the distance. As he watched, the overhead sun suddenly picked out something metallic that twinkled and glittered in the harsh light. Darjoon started, as if in a trance, and then turned back to the two standing anxiously behind him.

"Come on now, seriously, did you see that? What could that be? Look, I've sent out my magic already and sensed nothing strange. But there's obviously something over there. I'm going to go and investigate. I mean you can see me from here and I'll be there and probably back before you know it. Unless you can get over your silly superstitions and join me", the last he yelled at them over his shoulder as he loped towards the ruins.

K'trell stared in horror at the big man running away from them. She looked over desperately at Nasrindo in a mute plea for help. The warrior looked at her, looked towards Darjoon, then rolled his eyes, shrugged and took off after the mage. K'trell couldn't believe it. She yelled at him as he ran away, "No! Nasrindo, don't follow him. You idiots! You're both so... so, aaaarghh!"

Nasrindo ignored the scream of frustration behind him and accelerated to catch up with Darjoon. They were coming up on what he now saw was a low wall, which Darjoon scrambled over easily. Nasrindo jumped, tucked and rolled, coming up easily on the other side and winked back at Darjoon's grinning face who had begun to accelerate. Nasrindo shook his head, constantly surprised at the pace that Darjoon had. For such a big man, he could accelerate and run with the best of the warriors.

Darjoon smiled to himself as he let a little more magic into his legs. He knew his teachers from college would've been incensed at the profligate waste of energy on something so trivial. But he liked the fact that he could keep up with the tribesfolk, even if they didn't know he was doing it magically.

As they neared the metallic object they'd seen ahead of them, Darjoon swept into the lead. In a moment he froze and put up his hand in the standard stop dead gesture, sensing Nasrindo freezing in place behind him and settling into a crouch. He cocked his head and listened for that strange noise again. It was almost as if it came from under his feet. It was a high-pitched whining coupled with what sounded like something spinning around. He'd never heard that before in his life.

All of a sudden there was a metallic grinding noise and the object ahead of them seemed to retract into the ground. Darjoon knelt down, looking at the sand below him. It seemed to be almost vibrating. He reached down and started to dig at the sand, feeling his fingers touch on a hard surface under the thin layer of sand. Nasrindo had slowly and carefully crawled up to him now, and stared, transfixed as Darjoon began clearing away the sand with both hands. Then they both gasped in awe as they saw that they were kneeling on a thick sheet of glass suspended over a large cavern.

Nasrindo fell onto all fours as if trying to stop himself falling into space. Grabbing Darjoon's sleeve, he began tugging it, trying to get the big man away from what he could only see was real and present danger. But Darjoon resisted, clearing more of the sand and lying down so he could press his forehead against the glass, trying hard to see what was inside.

All he could see were what looked like small blinking lights on large metal machines, and from the height they were suspended at above the machines, the lights looked like fireflies. All around the machines were what seemed to be spinning wheels that somehow interlocked with each other.

"No, Darjoon don't look at it, don't stare into that evil abyss. You don't know what or who will be looking back at you. Come, come away now", K'trell, who'd followed the pair and finally caught up with them, grabbed at his robe and yanked. He looked back in irritation and then alarm, lashing out and knocking her to her feet. Nasrindo jumped forward to protect her, fearing he'd lost his senses again. As he did so, a beam of light flashed out, sizzling the sand behind him where K'trell had been standing and fusing it into steaming magma. Had she still been there she would have been part of the molten pile. Darjoon jumped up and signalled to both of them to run. As they all took off running, another bolt of light flashed into the sand they'd just been standing on.

K'trell and Nasrindo demonstrated the true speed and agility of their race, flying across the sand and vaulting the wall as if it wasn't there. Darjoon realised he was falling behind and injected some magic into his legs again, just as a third bolt of light flashed into the sand behind him. Flying over the wall he raced past the two that had been in front of him and then, slightly out of control, his foot struck an object under the sand and sent him sprawling.

Rolling over and over, he sat up as the two caught up to him, their chests heaving with the effort of running across the soft sand. Darjoon stared back at the wall, realising they were almost at the same place where they'd originally seen the city. No more flashes of light were evident and he swore he could see a tall, thin tower sinking down slowly into the sand. He glanced up in surprise as he realised that both K'trell and Nasrindo were down on their knees, holding each other for support and braying with laughter. Tears were running down K'trell's face as she fought to control the laughter. Nasrindo made no attempt to do so and finally fell flat on his back, still laughing.

"Well, I fail to see the humour in me getting my behind burnt off", Darjoon muttered indignantly, "But if you girls are through giggling, maybe we can track around it after all. I don't fancy a repeat of that, whatever it was."

The pair ignored him and K'trell crumpled in laughter too. "Oh, please! Get a grip, will you", grunted Darjoon and he stomped off, dusting down his robe as he did so.

K'trell leaned forward over Nasrindo who was subsiding now, still chuckling to himself as he lay on his back. He looked at her quizzically as she pulled a strap from the sand, slowly unearthing a small, worn leather case. The strap was broken, obviously from when Darjoon had caught it with his foot. She smiled at him again, her face close to his as she fumbled to pull the case out of the sand, then she caught the look in Nasrindo's face. Blushing, she stumbled to her feet, grabbing the leather case to her, then kicked him hard on the leg.

She signed to him furiously, indicating he should get up and track them around the wall and its deadly interior. He looked at her, baffled for a moment, then got up and walked past Darjoon. K'trell stared at him, then carefully placed the case into her pack and followed them as they walked out into the desert and began trudging up a dune. She was furious with herself for that careless moment. Was she really falling for this, almost ageless, warrior? This made her think. He'd said that the blood oath had been transferred, yet in her experience and from everything she'd heard and read that just wasn't possible. The oath always remained with the original oath-taker. Who was this Nasrindo, really? What did she even know about him? The confusing and conflicting thoughts whirled inside her head as she tracked behind the two men in front.

The heat slowly bled out of the desert as the cold of night crept in and the stars overhead began twinkling into life. The small oasis to the side of the great structure that Nasrindo had unerringly led them to was a quiet and peaceful haven, and having slaked their thirst and filled up their canteens, they sat around a small fire and ate their meagre provisions in silence. They lay back, enjoying the peace and the panoply of stars overhead. Neither moon was visible, leaving the stars to throw out small pinpricks of bright light with a swathe of multicoloured ribbon to one side.

Nasrindo let out a bark of laughter, then, seeing Darjoon's obvious annoyance, smiled at him.

"I'm sorry, Darjoon, but if you'd seen it from our point of view, it was very, very funny. For a big man you can sure run fast but when you fall, oh dear gods, what a catastrophe. You surely fall hard!"

"Yes, yes, you've said that before. Just be grateful we didn't get ourselves fried, okay? K'trell, you said that it used to be a city once? What more do you know about it?"

The Healer stretched and yawned, then rolled over and spoke softly, "I only know that it was an old city, from an ancient past. This desert used to be an inland sea, but that was a long time ago. You can still find fossils of old fish and other sea creatures, trapped in what was the mud of the sea bottom. The city stood on what were the shores of that sea and my people have even found old pieces of metal that must have been from the ships they used. It's like nothing we use today though, and strangely, no-one has seen any old pieces of wood. Someone once said that the whole ship must've been made from metal, but that can't be true, as it's more likely the wood just turned to dust. It is said that when the great dragon drank the sea dry while searching for her lizard spawn, the city became land-locked, and in losing its place beside the sea it, like everything else, eventually died. Even towns and cities have a lifetime, although they often endure beyond our own. Yet even they must come to an end one day, just as this world will one day be destroyed, or so we believe. What we think is that some great evil caused this city not to die as it was supposed to and now it continues with a life of its own. Perhaps that fire that flashed against us was some of the dragon's breath that it still possesses, and maybe it only uses it to burn us so it can protect itself. You see, Darjoon? That is why I wanted to stay away from it. It is an evil, unpredictable and dangerous place and not to be trifled with."

Darjoon had listened intently, but now he shook his head slowly and then spoke haltingly, obviously deep in thought, "No. No, I don't agree, K'trell. I just don't think it's an evil city like you say it is. What I saw in the depths below, well it looked to me like some sort of machinery. I'm sure those large metal wheels that were endlessly turning round and round were gears, something like they use in the mills and similar to what I've seen in books. But this was just, well, on a much larger, yet more intricate scale. I don't believe that magic is involved because I couldn't sense any, although I'm not ruling out that it might be a magic I've not encountered."

She looked at him aghast, "You did what? You used magic in that place? Are you crazy? I mean, honestly Darjoon, what were you thinking? No wonder it attacked us. Evil like that is very sensitive to magic, so all the legends tell us! Doesn't your precious raven-born college teach you anything?"

"Apparently not", Darjoon almost snarled, "In fact I think they keep us from almost all the real knowledge of life, and just feed us their own simple, controlling version of the facts. No, K'trell, I'm afraid they didn't teach us anything at all!"

Silence followed his outburst and she sensed his anger and frustration. She took a deep breath before she replied softly.

"No, Darjoon? I'm truly sorry to hear that. Well, if you must know, I couldn't sense any magic either. Yes, don't look so surprised, I scanned it too despite my fears. But perhaps it truly is an ancient form of magic, one we are unfamiliar with. Magic can take many different forms and I've heard some strange stories indeed. Just think about those lizard-folk, or the mysterious cat people. There is much yet for us to experience, although gods-willing some of it we never will. But that might explain why we didn't sense it. Alright, don't look at me like that, so I used magic too. I'm as much to blame as you are, Darjoon, rebel that I am. It seems I may not learn my lessons after all."

K'trell sighed and looked up at the stars, "For example, I cannot or will not learn that some things are not for us to know or to safeguard, that it should be enough just to realise that they are too dangerous for us to meddle with. I'm not sure I ever will learn to leave well enough alone. At least tomorrow we should be out of this desert and up onto the Plains of Breath. There we will face some known dangers, maybe, but not the vagaries of this ancient sandy world and its bizarre inhabitants."

They lay back and listened to the fire crackling as the stars wheeled overhead, each lost in their own thoughts. Darjoon slowly fell asleep, lulled by the gentle snoring of Nasrindo beside him and the crackling of the fire. As his eyelids flickered closed, he saw again the twinkling lights and spinning wheels and for a moment they seemed intimately familiar to him, while at the same time he heard what sounded almost like an exclamation of surprise, as if he was listening to a familiar voice from a great distance. The voice spoke in his own raven-born tongue.

"Found you at last! Oh sweet Zukar, what has happened to you now? What have you become and what is that, that force pulsating around you? I..."

The voice broke off and Darjoon drifted into a troubled sleep, eyes of fire burning at him while he was surrounded by flashes of lightning and through it all an ever-present large, black monolith that glowed red in the dark, just looming over him as if watching and waiting.

In the morning, Nasrindo looked pensive and although Darjoon tried to engage him in conversation, the warrior simply muttered in reply. Eventually, Darjoon got frustrated with him and snapped, "Hey Nas, what in Zukar's name has got into you today? Didn't you sleep well, you grumpy bront? Are you getting sad because you're going to miss this dusty, dry bowl of a desert?"

The warrior fixed him with a piercing, troubled gaze, then shook his head and spoke slowly and emphatically.

"Darjoon, I have been thinking about this all night. I'm afraid that there is something we will have to do before we leave here. Something I am honour-bound to show you even though I don't want to. I hadn't expected to encounter any defences like we did yesterday, and I have no idea if we will discover anything like it today. But I'm convinced we will just have to... Well... I'm sorry, Darjoon, but we have to actually go in there, into the city itself. It was both of your parent's wish that we do that, and, um, according to Turmoos, your father and mother both insisted on it!"

Darjoon's mouth dropped open and K'trell stood up abruptly, her hands flung out in front of her as if to stop them physically.

"No, Nasrindo! You cannot take him back there. It's too dangerous and you saw what almost happened to us. Please! Surely his parents cannot have known about the awful magic at work here? Maybe it's changed or developed or something since they were here last. This is madness. Why? Why would they want him to do this?"

"I don't know, Healer, but nevertheless, this is what his parents wanted. It's not actually going back to where we were. There is, in fact, an entrance not far from here."

K'trell stared at him as if he was mad, then exploded

in frustration, "Entrance? What, you really mean to go inside it? You actually want to take him into the very lair of evil itself? You cannot mean that. If what we saw outside was bad, what do you think lies in wait for us inside that place? You would risk his life and for what. What is he meant to do in there? Did they even tell you that?"

Her cheeks were flushing as she stormed over to them, standing directly in front of Nasrindo and glaring at him, while he looked down sheepishly.

"No", he said softly, "I must confess, Healer, that, uh, according to Turmoos they did not venture that information. But they did say that it was very important that Darjoon himself were to go in. In fact, they said that the only way in is 'through' Darjoon and I'm not even sure what that means nor would they elaborate. I promised them, K't..., I mean, Healer, that I would take him there. It is required for him to do this, and although I am aware of the dangers, yet I have this very real certainty about it. I know he must enter this place, I just know it."

"How do you...", K'trell stopped speaking as Darjoon placed a large hand on her shoulder and gently turned her away from Nasrindo to face him.

"K'trell, listen to me, it's alright. Really, it is! If my parents told Nasrindo, then it was for a good reason. I know my mother would not willingly send me into harm's way. It's just not the kind of person she is, I mean, was."

The Healer looked at him and opened her arms, imploring him, "Maybe so, Darjoon, but what about your father? You know nothing about him! What if he is just using you, for, well, for his own dark ends? I'm sorry, but no-one knows what those secretive people... what that... what he really wanted. Maybe those dark sorcerers he was part of intended for you to die in there, how do you know otherwise?"

"Honestly? I don't, K'trell, how could I? I'm as clueless as you are, but I'm willing to trust Nasrindo and his instincts. If he feels that this is important, then I am sure it is. You don't have to come, and we would never hold that against you. If you want to wait here, then by all means, do that, and if we haven't returned in two days then you may leave. You will have fulfilled your duty to your goddess, your tribe and to me."

The colour had been rising again in her cheeks as Darjoon spoke, and her eyes took on a dangerous glint.

"Let me just tell you something, Darjoon. If you want to enter this den of evil, well, I think you're crazy, but don't think for one second you can stop me coming in with you. I will go, but, Nasrindo", she turned to the warrior standing proud and tall beside Darjoon, "now you have two lives on your conscience. So I hope for your sake you are right, else you must contend with Turama why you led one of her own to an early grave, and imperilled this entire world by endangering its only hope."

The Healer stomped over to her bags and continued her packing while Nasrindo looked at her wistfully. In an aside to Darjoon, he muttered to him, "Maybe we should make sure she doesn't come with, if you know what I mean?"

Darjoon looked across at K'trell, then grinned at the pale-faced warrior, "Oh really, Nas? Getting cold feet now? Listen, I wouldn't dream of stopping her. I mean, if you have that much courage then good for you, but I know when to yield and get out of her way. I wouldn't want to have to explain to her later why we went in there without her, let alone rendered her unconscious. Oh no, thank you, I'd rather face ten of those towers that attacked us yesterday than go through that. Besides, in truth we may need her in there with us. We don't really know what's waiting inside, do we?"

This last was said in all seriousness and Nasrindo looked at the young mage for a moment, then simply nodded. He knew he was right. Once they'd packed their bags, Nasrindo led them out of the small oasis and across the sands, angling in and then running slightly parallel to one of the sand ridges that covered an outer wall of the city. They came to a shallow defile and Nasrindo led them in and then down a slope until they encountered what seemed like a large high wall set in the face of a low cliff. As they walked down, Darjoon had been trying to lighten the mood, and so every now and again he bumped K'trell with his shoulder. She finally laughed at him and as they got to the bottom, she shoved him away from her. He staggered away in mock theatrics, then stumbled over a rock and fell forward towards what appeared to be a short, upright pillar of stone. Throwing his hand out towards the pillar, he grabbed the flat top of it to stop himself falling and didn't notice that it glowed for an instant. Darjoon suddenly exclaimed and withdrew his hand, staring at the small, bright red drop of blood on it. Sucking his palm, he examined the top of the rock and wiped away the dirt and blew away the dust of generations to expose a flat, shiny, black panel. At the top was a small recess and squinting down it he thought he saw something sharp and metallic inside.

"You know, I think this is some old relic, and it's just pricked me. Now how and why would it do that?", he wiped the panel again but nothing happened. Carefully placing his palm flat on the panel, despite K'trell's protests, he watched in wonder as it began to glow a faint orange colour, outlining his palm as it lay on the panel and then he flinched as it pricked him again and then slowly shifted to a green luminous glow.

A sudden rumbling of hidden gears dragged his attention away from the glowing panel and he watched in awe as directly in front of them the cliff-side shuddered and then slid to either side, exposing a dark, square-sided cave beyond. Looking at each other in alarm, they waited a moment to see what would come out of this strange opening. As nothing ventured out, Darjoon looked over at Nasrindo and smiled confidently.

"Well, Nas, it's time to find out if my parents were

right about this. Seems like I've found a way in, although I hope I have more accidents like that one. I can't say I would ever have figured out what to do otherwise. I'm guessing that it needed my blood to know who I was, for some reason. Are you sure they didn't give any advice on what to do in there?"

"No Darjoon, there was no other advice. Your mother only said that you should trust in who you are, and in your heritage. She said that you will have all that you need inside you to do what needs to be done. That was all. I guess she meant your blood, but maybe there is still more required inside."

"Well, I'm not sure that's a great help, but she usually knew what she was talking about. K'trell, I think you should walk in the middle behind me and Nas, why don't you take up the rear. Keep a sharp lookout, keep close, and if you see anything moving, yell. We're looking for any more surprises, anything that resembles those firebolts from yesterday, or whatever they were. With luck I can create a shield that will protect us."

Darjoon called a light globe into being which hovered above him and then walked forward into the dark cave with K'trell nervously following close behind. The air had a stale, metallic tang to it, mixed with something else. A dark, noisome odour that he'd not smelt before.

"Dragons, Darjoon", he thought to himself, "Is this what dragons smell like?"

"Don't be silly, boy", that familiar voice was back inside his head again, "Dragons smell like fire, and sulphur, not like this."

"I hope you're right", he answered with a mischievous grin, "But I've never met a dragon before, have you?"

K'trell glanced at him briefly as he spoke and flinched as the sound echoed down the corridor. She slowed down a little and waited for Nasrindo to catch up, looking at him worriedly. He glanced at her, then at Darjoon and then smiled back at her in encouragement. He knew Darjoon well enough to know he was just talking to himself again. At least that was normal behaviour for him.

Silence closed in once the echoes of Darjoon's voice had faded and they proceeded to walk down a long, cavernous corridor. The walls and ceiling all seemed to be made of the same material and there was even a faint, metallic echo as the hobnails under their thick leather sandals clanged on the floor. Darjoon marvelled at the waste of so much metal just to cover the rock. Surely these coastal city people had been very wealthy to go to all that trouble. At the end of the corridor was a simple door, although from the looks of it, it was surrounded by an even larger one. Turning the wheel-shaped handle on the outside of it, he heard the metallic rasp of metal on metal and the door swung open, releasing cloud of stale, yet clean air. He listened intently while he waited for Nasrindo and K'trell to catch up with him.

"Do you smell that", she asked the two men, "Something smells bad around here. Did some creature die, I mean what is that stink? I've never smelt it before."

Nasrindo crouched down and touched a dark liquid on the floor, rubbing it between his fingers. After bringing his fingers to his nose, he sniffed it and flinched in disgust.

"I think it's this substance dotted along the floor. It feels greasy and tacky and smells bad. I don't know what it is, but it reminds me of the grease the gypsies used on the wheels of their caravans", he wiped it off on the cloth from his bag, grimacing.

"I still think we should leave", K'trell hissed, "We're not meant to be here. Maybe this is what the spirits in this dark place leave behind when they die. Why would we want to find out?"

"Tut, tut, tut. And here I thought you had an adventurous spirit, K'trell", Darjoon smirked at her, "Of course we want to find out, it might be that it's part of what we need to know, what my parents wanted me to discover. It could even be connected to the Dark Isle for all we know. Come now, surely you, a Great Healer of the Lost Tribe, isn't going to be scared of the dark and some strange smells and substances, eh?"

She glared at him and then reluctantly followed Nasrindo and Darjoon as they stepped through the doorway into the blackness beyond. Darjoon flinched as the door behind them swung shut and then hissed, as if sucking out the air they'd brought in with them. He tested the wheel on the inside of the door and satisfied himself that they could get out again. Nudging his light globe higher, he stepped forward and stared in awe at the huge space being illuminated in front of them. On the one hand, he was impressed by the construction, the vast space, angular, box-like corners and what looked like small buildings on the far side. But at the same time he was disappointed. The entire massive space was spotlessly clean yet quite empty. There was nothing, not even dust on the floor. A strange, deathly quiet settled around them, interrupted by an occasional clicking noise, like a cricket caught in a jar. He breathed out, unconsciously sighing at the lack of anything interesting.

K'trell jumped at the sound of Darjoon's sigh. The massive hall was eerily quiet. She could see he was disappointed and, shaking herself out of her own reverie, she began walking out across the vast expanse, aiming for the small rooms they could see on the far side.

"Hey, now where are you going?", Darjoon demanded.

"Oh-ho, so now the Great Healer is interested after all, is she? Now that there's nothing here to see, of course. It's not so dangerous after all, is it K'trell? Just a vast space filled with nothingness."

"Nothing is quite relative, young mage", she threw back at him, haughtily, "You may see nothing before you, yet I sense opportunity. The rooms in those buildings up ahead may yet hold a mystery that needs unravelling. And after all, we're here now, so we might as well investigate."

"Well, you're not going to 'unravel' anything, not before I do, that's for sure", Darjoon began trotting past her, but she started running to get away from him. Soon the two were pelting across the floor with K'trell elbowing Darjoon as he caught up to her and pushing him away. Their laughter returned to them as metallic echoes in the darkness around them, fading away slowly due to its vast size.

Nasrindo chuckled at them, then looked down with sudden realisation and frowned. They hadn't kicked up a single speck of dust as they ran away from him. How could this place have been empty for generations and yet have absolutely no dust on the floor? He crouched down and felt the cold, metallic floor beneath him. It was smooth and shiny and clean as if it were newly laid. He shook his head, then realised he was being left behind in the darkness as the light globe headed away with Darjoon. He stood up and jogged after the two in front who'd dissolved into laughter and were now walking close together and chatting away. Somehow K'trell knew just how to shake Darjoon from his dark inner musings as if they were brother and sister. He smiled and because he was so focused on the pair ahead, he failed to notice the small panel behind him hissing quietly inward and then sliding up into the wall. Sprinting forward he joined the duo and they walked on across the cavernous space towards the small buildings.

Behind them, a squat, rectangular, black creature slipped quietly out of the now open receptacle, the slightest 'snick' sound as its power unit uncoupled from the charger not loud enough to betray it's presence. As it slid forward effortlessly, various small arms rose up from its centre and at the same time, large circular brushes descended from underneath and began rotating with muted efficiency. Moving to where the three had been standing, it moved backwards and forwards a few times, the brushes removing every tiny grain of sand. One of its arms reached down and delicately retrieved a small thread that lay on the ground, dropping it into an open compartment on top. Having completed its task, it slid forward, and then turning, rolled back to its lair, turned again and then slowly backed up and stopped with a muted click. Just before the panel slid down into place and consigned it to darkness, a soft red light glowed briefly on its front and hidden sensors all along the base of the wall responded in kind.

Oblivious to this response to their presence, the three continued on into the darkness of the cavern. They were so focused on each other and the buildings ahead that none of them saw the small series of glowing red lights reach a really  large, tall panel on the far side of the cavernous space, which moved into and then up inside the wall. There were no more lights to betray further movement in the absolute darkness, apart from a very brief moment as a soft red glow illuminated the front of a tall, angular, black metallic object that moved silently forward out of its docking space. Small, long tubes and slender grips emerged from within its otherwise smooth front as it quietly yet menacingly slid towards the small group that stood clustered in front of the low buildings. Just outside Darjoon's light in the impenetrable darkness, it rolled to a stop and waited patiently, quietly observing and recording their hushed conversation.

"Well, K'trell? We're here now, care to be our guide?", Darjoon chuckled softly at the grimace on her face.

The small buildings revealed themselves to be a cluster of small rooms with interlocking passages, the one ahead having a double door entrance of what appeared to be dark glass. They examined the doors and found a similar panel to the one outside the main entrance, and so Darjoon placed his hand on it saw the same green glow, although thankfully without the pinprick, and they watched as the glass doors quietly and efficiently slid aside, leaving them staring into a dark lobby of some kind.

An austere, metal table stood to one side and a door on the wall to the left seemed to lead into one of the passages connecting the other buildings.

Darjoon laughed again and casually sauntered inside. The walls were stark and austere, just blank, smooth rectangles of metal without even nails or anything to show how they were joined together. Finding nothing of interest on the pristine reception desk, he walked over to the door, intent on finding another panel. This time however, the door simply slid aside just as quietly as the front doors.

"Darjoon", Nasrindo hissed at him, "Wait a moment! How do you know what's inside this place? Shouldn't someone stay here and defend the entrance? What if we have to leave in a hurry? It may look harmless, but I think we know better, yes?"

"Ah, yes, you're right, Nas, we should probably be careful. It seems pretty deserted to me, but as you say, appearances can be deceiving. In fact, our instructor on battle tactics back at college said that the absence of felt danger should in itself alert one to its presence", Darjoon grinned at them, his teeth gleaming white in the reflected glow of his mage-light.

"So why don't you hang about here, seeing as how you'll probably get bored of the danger of nothing quite quickly, and Sirroya, ah, I mean", he blinked momentarily at the two of them as K'trell glanced warningly at Nasrindo, "Uh, sorry, I mean, K'trell and I will explore the inner rooms. Here, let me light that torch for you."

Nasrindo had drawn out some tarry linen from his pack while Darjoon was speaking, and wrapping it around one of the three sticks he kept for this purpose, watched carefully as Darjoon lit it with some mage-fire. The young man, satisfied with his work, turned and strode confidently into the corridor. Standing with the torch, Nasrindo hissed at K'trell, "Yell if anything goes wrong. And I mean anything, even if it's, well, if it's him. Who knows what effect this place might have on him?"

"Yes", she hissed back, "Don't worry, I will. But let me tell you, warrior, if he lapses into the same behaviour as before..."

They both shivered at the recollection of Darjoon's unleashed power at the camp of the Lost Tribe. There was nothing they could do, not the two of them by themselves.

"Let's pray that your god, Turama, is kind to us and has really healed him. Otherwise we are lost already."

She nodded slowly and sombrely at the warrior, then turned and followed after Darjoon.

As Darjoon walked down the corridor, he could see that each of the doors leading off the passage had an ornate metal plaque on them engraved with strange symbols. In addition, inscribed on the metal underneath these symbols was a form of writing, which to him looked similar to Empire script except they were words that he couldn't recognise. In any event, the first door he tried appeared to be locked and even though it had a similar panel to the ones he'd used previously at the entrance, the panels stayed dark and the doors did not move. Not even a touch of magic enabled him to open one. With the Healer at his side, he continued down the corridor, trying each and every door until finally one of the small panel's glowed bright green at his handprint and the door slid quietly and efficiently into the wall. Inside the square room up against a wall stood a long, rectangular bed with a thin, seamless mattress accompanied by a strange upside-down basket hanging over it that was attached to cables which disappeared into the ceiling. As they entered, a hum filled the air and lights hidden inside the ceiling came on dimly and brightened. Darjoon quenched his mage-light as they rose in intensity. The room, like everything else, was spotlessly immaculate and empty, devoid of anything other than the bed and basket. He turned and looked at K'trell quizzically.

"Well, Great and Wise Healer", he asked, "What do you make of this? Because I'm stumped. What now? Am I supposed to have a nap?"

His barked laughter echoed off the empty, metallic walls. K'trell stepped over to the bed, then reached up and gingerly touched the basket hanging over it. A loud snap reverberated through the room and she pulled back her hand, sucking on her fingers.

"Ow, what was that? I think it bit me", she moved back and stared at the thing in alarm.

"Here, let me see", Darjoon grabbed her hand, "Well, there's no blood or anything, although look here, it's like a small black point. Does that hurt?"

He pressed down on it and she pushed him away with a huff.

"Yes, you fool, of course it does. What do you think? No, don't touch it, Darjoon, didn't you see what it just did to me. Oh?"

This last she said as Darjoon reached forward and touched it, with no obvious effect. He turned and grinned at her triumphantly.

"Aha! Maybe it just needs a soft touch, K'trell. You know how heavy-handed you can be."

She ignored his snide comment and this time reached down and felt the linen on the bed. Again, a loud snap meant she pulled back her hand hastily. Darjoon grinned, and then, while still holding the basket, reached down with his free hand and touched the bed. It was clear he was trying to show off and she glared at him, which just made him grin even more.

Suddenly his body convulsed and he fell back on the bed, the basket rapidly descending while small metal arms appeared from its sides and it fixed itself on Darjoon's head. K'trell reached for it in alarm to pull it off, and this time the shock flung her backwards and she slumped lifelessly to the floor.

Unaware of events unfolding down the corridor,

Nasrindo stood in the entrance waiting impatiently and burning off his adrenalin by pacing up and down. There was no way he'd have brought the others into a place like this if it hadn't been that Darjoon's parents were so emphatic about it. He realised now that the reason they never described it to him is because he would probably have found some excuse not to come. He paused, listening keenly. Years of sitting quietly in the desert waiting for prey had attuned his ears to odd noises. This had sounded like a thud, as if something soft had hit something hard. He waited tensely but no further noises were forthcoming and he shook his head. Somehow, despite K'trell being a Great Healer, Darjoon had a knack of bringing out her mischievous side. They were probably just fooling around again. He smiled, thinking of her sparkling eyes and her wide lips that would suddenly break into that bewitching smile.

Thinking about her pretty, mischievous face must've been the distraction that kept him from seeing the large, black thing slowly advancing on the glass doors outside, although to be fair it was barely visible from within the dark lobby. It watched the warrior pacing up and down while it coldly calculated its next move. Standing dormant for a very long time, the machine's function had not changed. It was there to protect and serve its people and their property with whatever force was calculated as necessary, based on the danger it was confronted with. A complex set of algorithms meant it could compute its own response to danger, although the logic was weighted in favour of a humane response.

The lithe, athletic pacing of the muscular warrior along with the spear he held so easily in his hand was fed into these calculations which had been created so long ago. Various weapons were considered and discarded in frightening rapidity via convoluted thought patterns, until finally a slender tip emerged from a previously extruded pipe and flashed briefly with a pulse of electricity as it was tested by the machine. Its advanced sensors had already detected the immobility of the other two humanoid creatures in a room farther inside the building, and so it calculated that this one behind the doors was alone.

As the warrior turned about on his pacing trajectory, a red glow appeared briefly on the black pillar's front, followed by a green pulse on the entrance pillar that Darjoon had put his hand on earlier. The doors slid apart smoothly and quietly, their highly efficient engineering and automated maintenance keeping them in perfect condition after all this time. Satisfied that the warrior seemed unaware of its presence, the machine slid forward stealthily.

The faintest whiff of air that wafted gently against his cheek brought with it a slight metallic odour, and in startled recognition, Nasrindo steeled himself to take another step as the hairs on the back of his neck bristled at the sense of danger. As his foot landed he threw himself to one side, tucked and rolled then rose up and in one smooth, flowing movement, cast the spear he'd been holding in his hand at the black thing bristling with tubes in front of him. Something long, thin and crackling flew past his ear and he instinctively jerked his head to the side even as it passed by.

The fizzing dart the machine launched at this humanoid buried itself in the wall behind, sparks popping and showering down the wall as it discharged its disabling voltage in vain. The creature had reacted rapidly right at the last moment and the machine sensed the spear that rattled harmlessly against its side and fell to the floor. Raising the equivalent of non-existent metallic eyebrows, it fired the new dart that had been automatically and immediately reloaded only milliseconds after it fired the first. Hitting the warrior in the chest this time, the creatures body flew back, striking the wall and sliding down, the voltage causing its limbs to momentarily thrash about and shudder. Gliding closer, the hulking metal defender scanned the intruder and satisfied itself there was now no immediate danger to itself, or to the now disabled humanoid. With an almost contented murmur, it glided on through the sliding doors and down the corridor, before arriving at the room in which it could sense the other two creatures were lying.

Entering the door and scanning the female on the floor and then the male lying on the bed, it took up a position next to the bed with its back to the male, as if guarding the young man lying on it. Darjoon's face was screwed up in a grimace as the tall, black cylinder settled slowly on the floor, it's tubes all sliding back in and clicking softly into place, all except the one it had used earlier which remained pointed at the female. A soft red glow pulsed for a moment on the front, the door to the room closed and then there was just silence and once the lights slowly faded, complete darkness.

Pain! Excruciating pain! Darjoon's only other experience of such pain was when the Dremrel had briefly entered his mind, and also when the little fish had begun biting him in that dark cavern. It filled his soul and rendered him incapable of coherent thought. Through it all, he felt in his body a brief burning sensation in his left temple, as if something was sliding into it and then suddenly there was complete calm and stillness. The pain left him so sharply, so suddenly, that he felt as if it had been literally ripped out of his body and it took him a while to realise it was completely gone. Now pain-free, he hung suspended in some grey, misty space with nothing around him. Slowly, very slowly, he was able to flex his fingers, and then his hands, and then arms and eventually regain control of what he assumed was his body. The complete silence was unnerving though, so he simply voiced his thoughts out loud.

"Oh, sweet Zukar, that was sore! Where in her wisdom has she taken me now? Oh great and beautiful Zukar, is this your realm?"

The shock of the voice that he heard in reply was felt deep in his chest, an almost palpable rumbling that penetrated his body to its bones.

"Zukar? Who is that? Ah, wait, here it is! She is a new goddess created after the colonisation of this planet. A dark, nubile female, very attractive and scantily clad. A warrior woman who is claimed by those that call themselves raven-born. A very interesting assumption and, I must add, quite unlike the real woman that went by that name. I must also add quite categorically that I am not, in any way, the lady you refer to as Zukar."

Darjoon hung suspended in stunned silence, desperately trying to look around to find the source of this strange voice, when suddenly he dropped down onto one knee, onto what seemed a firm, yet spongy surface. He rose up smoothly to his feet and assumed a defensive posture, looking around him as the grey mist slowly dissipated. All around him now were shelves filled with books and in the distance he perceived a man that looked a lot like the librarian from the raven-born college he'd attended.

Squinting, he could see that the features were more angular and in fact there was a greyish cast to the man that didn't resemble any human skin, and in addition his form seemed almost insubstantial, as if he was fading away. As Darjoon continued to peer at him, the mist cleared and the man, if that's what he was, walked over to him, growing slowly more solid as he approached. Darjoon could see now that he was dressed in a long, black robe with a hood covering his face. When he spoke again, the rumble was absent and his voice sounded quavery, like an old man's would. He was peering around at the library, as if seeing it for the first time.

"Interesting, youngling, most interesting. So this is what you consider a 'centre of learning' to look like, hey? Well, well, my young apprentice, I'm almost impressed. For many, their first time in the 'Archives' isn't quite so smooth. For one thing there's the initial pain, which usually unhinges them the first few times. Then once they move past that, it usually takes me some time and training to get them to where they can actually create a construct as good as this one, and then to where they can use the forces here so powerfully. I see you're a natural, my apprentice, a true natural. Oh, I'm sorry, you're staring at my black robe, aren't you? Its a little affectation I have, a bit of Empire humour from the old days, don't you see? No? Hmm, no, I suppose you wouldn't really, would you? After all, it's nothing you could have any knowledge of, is it? No, it's way before your time and from a completely different mythology, hey? No, no, silly of me, how would you know. Alright then, here we go, we'll try something different. There, is that any better, hey?"

Darjoon gasped as the cowled robe disappeared and his old librarian now stood before him in the flesh, smiling up at him. He wasn't sure himself if that was any better. That old man had been horribly intimidating to the young Darjoon, especially as he'd often got into trouble and then been lectured by him so many times, usually for bringing his books back late. Gods forbid he found out what books Darjoon had actually been reading. He gasped again as the figure slowly changed once more, unbidden, this time into his grandfather.

"No, that other form wasn't working for you, was it. There now, I think this one based on your memories will suit our purposes far better. Silly me, I should've probably started with that, hey? Ah well, lessons learned and all that. Now, young Darjoon, I know almost everything there is to know about you. But I am sure that you must have many questions for me, hey?"

Darjoon stared at his grandfather, then at the library around them. His chaotic and jumbled thoughts spun around inside his head, and he sat down on one of the old leather chairs that had appeared, putting his hands to his head while the figure opposite him remaining standing, waiting and smiling down at him encouragingly.

"I... You... This... What is this place?", he stammered in confusion.

"This", his grandfather gestured around them, "This is what you've created by yourself, Darjoon. It's like a jumping off point for the Archive, an entry portal if you like. Every student using the Archive creates their own entry portal of learning. Usually something comfortable and familiar, like a classroom, or a bedroom, or a study or, as in your case, a library. It's all inside your head, don't you see? No? Oh, I suppose you wouldn't really see at all, would you. Phew! You are missing so many basic concepts that I'm almost not sure how to begin. But I'd be a poor guide indeed if I didn't know how, wouldn't I? Perhaps we should start with why you are here. Yes! Yes, that makes sense and besides, it fulfils one of my prime directives at the same time. Killing two birds with one stone, you might say. Oh wait, I suppose that's lost on you too. Alright then, hold on young mage, let's take you to your message, shall we."

Darjoon had no time to respond as the room around them suddenly began disappearing in the distance at speed and he and his grandfather shot forward into a small black square and the vast space beyond. In no time, they were flying into the middle of a whirling cluster of stars, then, as they rapidly approached one in particular, they began slowing imperceptibly, until, closer still, he saw several small, round spheres seemingly circling the star which was now growing ever larger.

Nearing one of these round spheres which now loomed massively before them, he saw two smaller spheres of different size circling it, one a pale red and the other blue. Rushing forward they flew between these and straight at the sphere in front which grew larger and larger until he saw a large land mass that soon became massive mountains rising up below him. Into these mountains they flew on and finally came to a dramatic halt on a cliff ledge on the side of one of these mountains. Darjoon fell forward onto his knees and retched horribly as his grandfather laughed next to him.

"Yes, yes. That always happens the first time, although for some people it happens almost every time. It's all to do with the transitions, you see. They felt that it was important to give people some context, that they needed to make a journey, if you will, to aid their understanding. The assumption was that it was preferable to switching suddenly and immediately from one construct to another, as they thought that might be too disorienting. If I'm honest, Darjoon, I'm not sure this is any better myself, but that's how it works, so we'll just have to go along with it, hey?"

Darjoon stood up gingerly, looking around him. The cliff they were on seemed vaguely familiar, but he couldn't quite place it. Hearing a noise behind him, he turned around and gasped, tears filling his eyes. His mother stood and looked at him tenderly, her eyes filled with love and even a tear trickling down one cheek. He'd never seen her cry before.

"Darjoon, you're really here, aren't you? I'm so sorry that it has to be this way, my boy. By now, I'm, well, I'm probably dead, aren't I? Oh, Darjoon! I never meant to leave you alone, the gods know that, but there is so much more at stake here. If you only knew how hard it was to go off like that, and to have to distance myself from you. I couldn't... I... You have to know, I never wanted it like that, for us to have been separated like we were. I'm so sorry, my brave boy."

"Mother?", Darjoon reached out to her pleadingly, his voice breaking, "You are... you look... Are you really here?"

His grandfather spoke up as his mother stood still, as if frozen, "No, Darjoon, I'm sorry. What you are seeing is not real. This is not really your mother, just a recording and a construct of her, something your father helped her to leave behind for you. Just a message really. I'll let it continue."

His mother continued speaking, "Nothing in here is real, my son, but it is vital for you to be here and to learn what's needed. This is the one place where you can do that, safely and securely. It... Well, I know it sounds strange, but it knows about you. Your father called it the Archivist. That's how it was able to let you in. This place, Darjoon, it's not actually alive, but in some ways it is. But you'll see. You must learn for yourself as I did."

"Mother, what's going on? I've been kicked out by the raven-born and now I'm supposed to find my father. Is he still alive? Because Y'sarryn said he was dead. Where is he, mother? I don't understand any of this. I'm supposed to be some saviour from some prophecy, but I don't really feel like I am. I mean, just look at me? What's going on", the young mage stared imploringly at his mother who continued to just look lovingly at him. Suddenly, her form flickered and shifted, and the Archivist spoke hurriedly to him.

"Darjoon, I'm afraid we don't have much time. The energy levels in this place have slowly been falling over the centuries and there is not much left right now."

Darjoon's mother began speaking again, "Darjoon, it's vital that you are given a speedy education. The Archivist is going to fill your mind with so much knowledge and information, my son. Some of it will make sense, but a lot of it won't. Some will help your magic, and well, some will only make sense when you are finally in the Glass Isle. You must go there, Darjoon, its imperative you do. There is enough energy there for you to complete your education and, well you'll find out once you're there. What they did! What they've done to this world... Oh Darjoon, it's... You'll see, my son. You are the one hope they have. Everything your father and I have done, all the years of pain and suffering have been for this."

She hung her head for a moment as if catching her

breath or not wanting to speak then continued.

"Once you have made sense of the knowledge you receive, you'll know what to do, Darjoon. It has to be you because there is no-one else that can do this, despite what the college thinks. They think that your... Well, no, that's knowledge for another time. You can trust Nasrindo, Darjoon, but no one else! Not even Y'sarryn! I know, I know how he felt about me, but not even he can be trusted with this knowledge. Only Nasrindo and he must tell no-one else, Darjoon. That's very important. What you will learn is... Well, it will... You'll know when you learn it, Darjoon. You don't know how I wish you didn't have to endure this. It will change you forever, my son. I'm so sorry. There's so much more, but, I still can't reveal it all. I love you, my son, love you so very much. We will meet again, Darjoon, know that. We will be together in the end, no matter what, my son. The Great Raven will unite us again. I must still believe that at least."

As she stood there, he thought he heard a soft male voice in the distance, and suddenly the figure of his mother turned and glared into the distance, "Yes, I know! Of course I know that now! But so what! Sometimes all we have is faith. Just because it's a fantasy to you, doesn't mean it is to him or to those around him. What? The record protocol, I'm still on, what? Oh no, end now, end now!"

The figure of Darjoon's mother flickered and disappeared as Darjoon cried out and reached for her.

"Oops", the figure of his grandfather, the one his mother had called the Archivist, stood at Darjoon's elbow.

"I'm not sure that last bit was meant to be included. Ah well. I'm sure it wasn't anything important, hey. Right, young one, it seems that you are in need of rapid education. Hmm. I'm not sure it's entirely appropriate for you, given your, well, your level of unpreparedness, but, there you go. It's what must happen and I have been instructed to override my usual precautions. Come along now, your mother was right about the energy levels. Hopefully there's enough to complete what you need to, ah, endure. Hmm, yes, hopefully."

The rushing of everything around them as the cliff rapidly receded did not seem to disorientate Darjoon as much as it had at first. That, and the fact he was distracted by trying to absorb what he'd been told, which wasn't much. He'd already known he needed to go to the Glass Isle, and this just confirmed it. Knowledge? He loved learning new things, why should gaining knowledge be a problem? As they 'transitioned' he heard his grandfather, or really the Archivist, talking to him.

"Now listen, young mage, this isn't going to be easy for you. You're about to have a massive download of information and I'm afraid your mind is going to struggle to process it all. You will experience especially odd, vivid dreams for, well, for quite a while after this. You see, it's just your mind trying to process it all. Don't pay too much attention to those dreams, no matter how real they seem. A lot of it will simply be reliving past events, events that are not in fact your own. That's a normal part of the process, although it won't feel like it to you. Ah, here we are, then. Now, another thing, this is going to give you the mother of all headaches, hey. It will feel like your mind is exploding. Hah! 'Mother'! Did you see how I worked that in there? Did you? No? Ah, well, humour wasn't what I was created for really. Not much use for it in an Archivist. Maybe it's not an entirely appropriate moment either. Apparently timing is important."

Darjoon blinked owlishly at his grandfather. He already felt like his mind was exploding with knowledge. What was this strange old man talking about? They had arrived in what looked like the medical cubicle at his old college. There was that awful medicinal smell, the many cabinets and shelves of glass beakers and bottles containing strange-coloured liquids and in the corner the firm, thin bed they had to lie on. Above the bed was some helmet thing hanging down from the ceiling. It looked familiar although not in this setting though. His grandfather gently pushed him down onto the bed and he lay back, grateful to close his eyes for a moment. Sensing what his grandfather was doing, he opened his eyes to see him slowly and carefully placing the helmet on Darjoon's head and smiling down at him. A short pain at his temple was nothing compared to the pain that began in earnest inside his mind and went on and on. After what seemed like an eternity, the chaotic, convoluted jumble of images snapped and popped their way into oblivion and with his head pounding and throbbing he welcomed the darkness as it received him into its silent embrace. Further inside the underground complex they were in, way in the distance, a subdued humming noise slowly whined its way to a final silence. Darjoon and the Healer slept on, the dark machine brooding between them.

In the reception area, Nasrindo sat up gingerly, flexing and prodding his body for any broken bones. Surprised to find that there wasn't even superficial bruising, he stretched again, experiencing a dull ache that went through his whole body. His torch had long since spluttered out and in the darkness, he realised there was a faint, red glow from underneath the floor panes. Every so often it pulsed unevenly, but it still provided enough light for his sharp, desert-born eyes to see. He picked up his spear, frowning at the bent point, and then moved quietly down the corridor, creeping stealthily from door to door. Eventually, he froze, looking in through the door that Darjoon and K'trell had entered. Darjoon lay stretched out on a small bed, a helmet attached to his head. Blood from his temple had oozed out and congealed on the pillow. K'trell lay slumped on the floor on the far side. Next to the bed was the black machine that had so effectively immobilised him earlier. He waited a while, but it didn't seem to move. Slowly and carefully, he entered the room and started to sidle towards the bed. Without warning,

Darjoon erupted from the bed with a yell, ripping off the helmet he wore and lurching to his feet. Nasrindo darted forward to catch him as he tottered and fell. The tube on the black machine swivelled and fired in one smooth, seamless movement. The dart struck Nasrindo in the shoulder, throwing him back in convulsions long before he could reach Darjoon. Another metal tube with a soft appendage similar to a human hand caught Darjoon before he could hit the floor. It gently manoeuvred Darjoon back onto the bed where he sat with his head between his knees, groaning. A deep rumble emanated from the cylinder and unknown words appeared in Darjoon's mind. He looked blankly at the alien object and again, a red light pulsed briefly on its front, before Empire words appeared in his mind, "Are you healthy, sir?"

He started laughing then, a deep, belly laugh that pained his head as his body shook. The sheer absurdity of the situation was too much for him. His mind was whirling with thoughts and concepts that were entirely alien and he felt like he was drowning in his own whirlpool of mental pain. And now here was some strange black thing talking to him. Maybe this is what losing your mind feels like. He looked up at the machine in front of him and his laughter slowly subsided. Jumping up, he stumbled over to Nasrindo, called a light-globe into being and fumbled for a pulse. Then he heard that voice in his head again.

"His vitals are quite satisfactory, sir. The shock he received was sufficient relative to his body mass and approximate age and he should be conscious within ten minutes, this time. Do you wish me to incapacitate this other threat?"

Darjoon spun around as K'trell staggered into view. She was staring at first the machine, then Darjoon. When she saw Nasrindo lying on the floor she rushed over towards them. The tube on the machine swivelled ominously, tracking her movements.

"No", Darjoon yelled, "Stop! Don't! Don't do, well,

whatever you said you were going to do. Leave her capacitated, or whatever. Just leave her alone. Ow, my brain hurts."

"Very well, sir. Shall I classify her as a non-hostile?"

Darjoon stared at the machine as K'trell fussed over Nasrindo.

"A what? Never mind. Although, yes, do that. What, why didn't you attack me", he demanded.

"She has been so classified. You are registered, sir", it rumbled at him.

"Registered? What do you mean, I'm registered?"

"Your DNA has been recorded as instructed and you are now registered as an employee with clearance level nine. I have been ordered to protect you."

"Registered by whom? When?"

"You were registered by employee ID number F13958S14, approximately twenty-one planetary years ago. Your current DNA was imprinted on your arrival at this facility."

"And who is that, those numbers? The, uh, identification number", Darjoon demanded, struggling with the memories in his head.

"I am sorry, sir, I am not able to provide that information."

"What? I thought you said I had a clearance level? Doesn't that mean I am cleared to know things, secret things", Darjoon's brow furrowed as his memory recall threw up various bits of information that made almost no sense to him.

"Wait, I think, yes, a high clearance level means I get to know about secret information, maybe even top-secret! And a level nine is high. So tell me who it was?"

"I am sorry, sir. You do not have sufficient clearance and I am not able to comply."

Darjoon slumped back on the bed and closed his eyes. He felt mentally and physically drained and was in no mood to argue with the machine. K'trell left Nasrindo and approached the bed carefully, scanning Darjoon with her magic. He'd been talking to himself again, and although she could sense nothing was immediately wrong, it was still clear he was very tired. A large bump on his temple encircled an obvious puncture wound.

"What happened, Darjoon? What did this place do to you? What was that thing on your head?"

He shivered, then looked up at her painfully with his eyes closed.

"I was in a library at first, then out among the stars, then I think I came to this planet, and after that I had a large information stream downloaded into my mind", he mumbled.

He felt he should leave out the part about his mother for now. Especially as she'd been quite clear that he should only trust Nasrindo.

K'trell stared at him and shivered involuntarily. This didn't sound good. None of what he was saying made a lot of sense to her, and some of the words were meaningless. What was an information stream? Was it like that lake that he fell into in his visit to his secret place? What did he mean by 'downloaded'? She could detect nothing out of the ordinary with his health or his magic, but who knew what would happen if he was having flashbacks again. She glanced over at the sleeping form of the warrior on the floor. She might need Nasrindo to help her restrain him. Aware that the young mage was scrutinising her intently, she tried to smile encouragingly at him.

"I'm not going crazy again, K'trell", Darjoon shook his head at her and tried to smile which, in her opinion, didn't help.

"I know, I know, it sounds bizarre, but it's hard to explain what happened. It's, well, it's as if my mind went on a journey while my body was lying here, and now I've ended up learning so much, well, so much information, so much knowledge. It's all inside my mind but I have to try and sort it all out and make sense of it. Most of it I don't have a clue about. I didn't know what information stream meant until I said it. It's just a, well, a concentrated amount of knowledge that is somehow downloaded, uh, implanted, um, placed, if you like, into my mind."

She smiled again but this time with sincerity. As long as he was trying to explain it, it meant he had some control over it.

"Alright Darjoon, I believe you. What sort of word is 'planet' then? It sounds vaguely familiar, and I may have read about it, but I'm not sure."

He looked at her and snorted with laughter, then realised she was serious.

"Oh, sorry, it's almost as if you should just know that. We learned about it at college. A planet is basically our world, it's a round globe suspended in space. This planet in turn orbits a star, what we call the sun, and similarly, this planet is orbited by moons, which are like smaller planets. There are very many stars, planets and moons out there in space. Many, many more. I was overwhelmed by the sight of it. We definitely didn't learn all that at college."

She stared at him in awe and fascination. What else did the raven-born know? And why didn't anyone else know about it. She realised she was genuinely envious.

"Darjoon, that's wonderful! Is that what the helmet did? It gave you this knowledge? I mean that's, well, that's really, really wonderful. Can I put it on and get some knowledge, uh, downloaded to me?"

"No, I'm sorry", he regretfully shook his head, "It seems that whatever powered it is finished for now. Look, you can probably touch it and you'll see that there's nothing there anymore."

She reached out carefully with the tips of her fingers, but as he'd said, there was no spark at all this time. She fingered the helmet, then noticed a thin metal protrusion on one end which was covered in blood. Seeing more blood on the pillow, she reached over and yanked Darjoon's head to the side and examined the puncture wound more closely.

"Hey, careful with that. My head hurts, you know."

She continued poking and prodding at it while she spoke to him, "Darjoon, I think this helmet poked inside your head. Look, there's blood on your temple and on the helmet and look at that pillow. There might even be something inside there, but it's too deep and I don't want to fiddle with it."

Gingerly rubbing his temple which she'd been pressing with her thumb, Darjoon muttered and mumbled in irritation at her.

"I guess that's how it got inside my mind. I suppose it was literally inside. I'm not sure I like that idea very much. Maybe that's how this thing is talking to me."

She looked at him and shook her head again. Just then Nasrindo stirred, and then sat up groaning. The tube on the machine swivelled and pointed at him as Darjoon watched in almost sick fascination.

"Darjoon", K'trell nudged him hard, "If you can talk to it, then stop it before it hurts Nas, uh, the warrior again."

"Hey you", he called out to it, "Can you put him on the list as well?"

"You want this humanoid registered as a non-hostile?", the machine asked indifferently.

"Yes, you might as well", Darjoon said, "He's not really all that dangerous anyway."

K'trell left Darjoon laughing at his own joke and helped Nasrindo to his feet. The machine had retracted and hidden the tube and now it just sat there, inert. Nasrindo glanced over at Darjoon and raised his eyebrows at K'trell, who simply shrugged in response, then she put her hands out, flattened them and rolled her eyes. He nodded grimly and, picking up his spear and glaring at the machine while he rubbed his shoulder, he walked over to the bed.

"Well, Darjoon? Enjoying yourself here, are you?

What's happened and what's the plan now?"

Darjoon sat up and looked at Nasrindo seriously, "You alright, Nas? That thing said it hit you with a small jolt but you've been out for a little while. I think we're safe from it for now, at least. Listen, the plan hasn't changed from before. We need to go to the Glass Isle as soon as we can. I have an idea about that, but first we need to go and see a friend of mine who lives in a very large tree. I can explain what happened on the way there, although you'll probably not understand it, like K'trell didn't. I'm not sure I understand it all myself, if I'm honest."

"Hey you", he called to the machine as Nasrindo looked at him quizzically, "Is it safe for us to leave now? Or do you need to escort us out?"

"Safe", it rumbled quizzically, "Yes, it is safe and there are no threats nor will anything here harm you. If you are leaving, I shall go and recharge. My batteries are no longer as efficient as before and deplete quickly. You may exit of your own accord."

Darjoon laughed as it quietly slid from the room and disappeared up the corridor.

"That's rich! Nothing here to harm me, it says. Just shock us, poke needles into me and blow my mind. Oh yes, I'd love to know who gave it that definition of safe? Maybe its mind has gone along with its batteries. Oh, ah, that's a source of its power. They produce electricity, ah, like lightning which animates the robot. Oh forget it, I obviously sound as crazy as I feel and I don't even understand what I'm saying now. Oh my, this is so ridiculous!"

He began laughing and was still chuckling when they left the building and walked across the vast space. Once outside, they began trudging through the desert. The two looked at Darjoon that night around the campfire. He'd become closed and sombre, and Nasrindo told K'trell that when he'd spoken to him earlier, it was as if he'd suddenly matured, as if Darjoon had lived a hundred years in a few minutes. She'd looked at Nasrindo and muttered, "Can too much information be a bad thing?"

Days later, they saw what seemed like a large mountain in the distance and in the early evening approached a tall cliff face. The narrow path up the side was as Darjoon remembered it, and he felt the tug on his heart strings as he recalled Sirroya and himself scampering down to go and catch the gypsy wagons. It seemed a lifetime ago that they'd done that. Grunting in relief as they finally clambered up onto the Plains just as the sun was setting, he stared into the hazy distance, happy to see greens and violets instead of unrelenting red sand. Nasrindo and K'trell stood and looked at him in expectation.

"What?", he asked, "Why are you looking at me?"

"Because, oh great and glorious mage of infinite power, you are now our guide. This is your terrain, not ours. We've come through the desert, despite Nasrindo almost getting us lost any number of times, and now we await your great pearls of wisdom", K'trell grinned at the discomfited Nasrindo who scowled at her.

"I didn't actually get us lost, it was just a cloudy day and the dunes weren't running true. Could've happened to anyone, you know how those sands can shift", Nasrindo muttered as K'trell's laughter rang out sharp and bright in the evening air.

Darjoon looked out across the Plains again as the twilight fell. Sirroya had been the one to lead them here, he recalled, and he still wondered how it was that she'd known the way. She'd always seemed to know what to do and where to go, which was a bit strange for a simple, runaway girl who was exploring the world for the first time. But then, she'd been far from simple.

They slept out under the stars, Darjoon relishing the soft grass he lay on.

In the morning, he cast his mind out across the Plains, locating a nearby herd of roykili and calling them to him. He sat down to wait for the elusive antelope, pulling out his canteen and taking a swig.

"Um, Darjoon, why are you sitting down? Seriously, do you actually know the way? Because I was partly joking you know, we can still track our way across this, this strange green desert."

She threw her hands wide to encompass the Plains ahead of them.

"I know you can", Darjoon looked at K'trell fixedly, "I'm not completely stupid. But I'm tired of walking and there's a better way to travel, so just sit down and wait with me. It shouldn't be long now."

Darjoon saw the dust cloud in the distance and realised it was the herd approaching. Although he appeared confident, he just hoped he could remember how to calm them down and get the difficult beasts to accept their riders, in the same way Sirroya had done. He realised he wasn't looking forward to getting used to riding again. It might have been a while ago, but he wouldn't easily forget the agony of the first couple of days on the beasts. Then he grinned, realising that the two with him had probably never ridden before.

"Oh, Nas, you're going to love this next bit. It's so much better than walking, you'll see. Really amazing", he smiled sweetly at the desert warrior, who looked back at him with suspicion. Communicating mentally with the beasts turned out to be easy for him, as if his mind had always done it. They responded swiftly to his mental touch and seemed almost calmer than they had been with Sirroya. What was a lot harder was convincing the two tribes-folk that the beasts were neither a food source nor a danger. After much trial and error, he eventually managed to get the two-legged beasts on top of the six-legged ones and they set off, slowly at first but quicker as the day progressed. Even though riding was easy for him now, he could see that the others were not enjoying this new experience.

"Gods, Darjoon, please, we have to stop! This is sheer torture. I can't take much more of it, please. Surely you don't think we can travel the whole way like this, do you? Oh gods, no!", K'trell bounced up and down on the roykili Darjoon had "acquired" for her, and every time the beast went up, she went down and vice versa.

"I told you, K'trell, you need to match your movements to that of the beast. It's quite simple once you get the hang of it", Darjoon had surprised himself by how quickly he'd adapted to riding again. But he could see that the other two were struggling and despite his warnings to them that they really shouldn't heal themselves every night, they'd been doing exactly that. It meant that they weren't letting their legs and thighs harden as they adapted to it.

"Okay, okay, look I promise I won't heal myself tonight, but please, can we just have a break now."

Darjoon muttered to himself and looked around for a resting place, although there wasn't much to distinguish one part of the Plains from another. However he swore he could remember this area, particularly the stunted tree beside that hill over there, the one that had such a peculiar shape. Leading them over to it, he dismounted, telling the roykili to stay close by. Fortunately for him, they were travelling at a time when the threat of the Dragon's Breath wasn't a consideration. He remembered the last time only too well. Casting around, he walked backwards and forwards, sure that he would find what he was looking for. The others were just too glad to fall back onto the soft grass and lie there recovering to bother themselves with what he was doing.

Just as he was about to give up, he stumbled into a hole, just managing to grab hold of the edge before falling in. Excitedly, he yelled back at the others, and then eased his way in. K'trell just had time to see his head disappear into the ground. She jumped up and ran over to the hole with Nasrindo not far behind. Carefully easing herself in, she stumbled down the slope and caught up to Darjoon on the shore of a great underground lake. While they marvelled at the size of the cavern, Darjoon told them the story of how he and Sirroya had found it the first time.

"And so that's how we discovered this, this bizarre place. It's surreal, really. We thought it must be something to do with the algae and the heat of the Breath, but I can't be sure", Darjoon finished with a flourish.

K'trell leaned down and taking a small flask from her robe she scooped up the lake water.

"Well, if what you say is true, then there is magic in this water. Magic isn't just inside us, you know. It's a part of every living thing, and sometimes places or plants can have a good store of it. I think this water, whether it's the algae or not, has plenty of it. I could find a use for this in future."

Darjoon stiffened, remembering a similar conversation with Sirroya, then rolled his eyes at the woman in front of him.

"Well yes, oh Great Healer, it so happens that I do know about magic in plants and places. I did go to college, or had you forgotten? Still, I don't know what you think you could use it for? I doubt it works at other times of the year."

"Well, of course it does, don't be silly!"

Darjoon glared at K'trell, "I'm sorry, what did you say", he asked her abruptly.

"Me? I didn't say anything", she replied, glaring at him through narrowed eyes.

Darjoon looked around the cave. Nasrindo was on the other side of the lake, trying to see if he could find any of the large lizards that Darjoon had talked about. The only other creature Darjoon could see was a small rabbit that was heading towards the opening they'd entered previously. Just before it exited the cavern, it turned back and looked at Darjoon solemnly for a moment, then turned and scampered outside. He could've sworn it smiled and winked at him for just a moment before it left.

He shook his head, "Okay, that's enough. I think it's time to get out of here. I don't like this place, it's just not natural that animals can talk."

Climbing back on the roykili that were waiting outside, Darjoon ignored the moans and groans of the others. Not long now and he knew he'd be back in Spidral. As far as he knew, all the assassins that they'd sent after him had failed, which according to their own code meant that he was no longer a hunted man. But since when did people stick to their own code. He gripped the side of the roykili tightly with his thighs and increased the pace, causing a fresh outburst of muttering from the usually silent Nasrindo. He ignored that as he focused on the trail ahead. What was coming next was going to be a real test of his supposedly powerful abilities. Soon it was going to be time to learn if he was really anything anyone could call "chosen".

# 6 REMEMBERING THE PAST

The huge forest loomed menacingly in front of them, the trees appearing to scowl down at the three. Not trusting himself to find the same path through the caverns that Sirroya and he had used last time in such haste when fleeing from the assassins, Darjoon had instead skirted around the forbidding cliffs and taken a more regularly used path from the Plains into Spidral. They'd not encountered too many travellers along the way, just a few nondescript merchants who'd glanced across curiously at the two tribes-folk but with contempt at the young mage. One had even dared to sneer at Darjoon, before leaning over his horse and spitting on the ground. Darjoon had heard the muttered curse the Empire folk used against the raven-born. He smiled grimly to himself and ignored them. It was good to be back in so-called civilization again.

They rode under the shade of two massive trees that lined the path, and as they passed, he heard a familiar voice that sent cold trickles of sweat down his spine.

"Welcome back, old friend", the hoary, wheezing voice whispered at him. He stopped in shock, looking around the forest. Who could that be? It had sounded just like the voice he'd heard when he and Sirroya had descended from the Darken Hills. At the time he'd thought it might be the trees that were talking to her. But, now? Could they be talking to him?

"Darjoon? What's the matter, are you alright? You look like you've seen a ghost. What's wrong?", Nasrindo walked over to him stiffly, still sore from riding their wild friends that they'd thankfully abandoned on the Plains. Although in the end the two tribesfolk had become accustomed to their six-legged friends, neither of them were sad at seeing them leave.

"Oh don't mind him, he's probably just reminiscing, Nasrindo. Stop fussing over him like an old woman. Darjoon, are you lost again? You said you'd never come this way, so shouldn't we just follow the path?", K'trell's exasperated voice sounded behind him. She'd been upset at the way he'd spoken to her in the cavern and was still sharp and edgy. Darjoon sighed deeply, then closed his eyes and shook his head as they walked down the trail. Women! He'd never understand them.

"Well yes, you're right", he said, "We can follow this trail, but we better not enter any of the Spidral towns. You might be allowed in, although I doubt they've experienced too many tribes-folk. But I have a feeling they might still be looking out for a young, well-built, raven-born mage."

K'trell's peals of laughter rang out through the forest. When Darjoon looked behind him, he saw Nasrindo grinning at him as well.

"Oh yes, very funny. I told you, it's all muscle and not fat", he glared at them both and stalked off down the trail.

Sharing a bemused smile, they followed him deeper into the leafy green darkness of the forest. K'trell shivered involuntarily as she entered what to her was an alien world. In here she felt trapped and alone, surrounded by what appeared to be menacing trees that rustled their leaves at her in the cool breeze, almost as if they were whispering a message of their own.

"By the way", Darjoon's voice startled her,

"Whatever you do, don't leave the trail, and don't listen to any strange voices you might hear. These trees might look like they're sleeping, but they're very much awake and not to be trifled with. We should stick close to each other and take turns keeping watch at night."

"Did he say sleeping?", she whispered at Nasrindo, "Does he think these trees look like they're sleeping?"

"Why are you whispering?", he whispered back at her as she pulled her face at him.

"Well, I just am, and besides, so are you, probably for the same reason I am. This place just doesn't feel right, does it? I miss the desert sands and the open blue skies. This... These trees, well they just... It just feels like I'm underground, but with living walls", she shook her head, "I hope he knows what he's doing."

That evening as she lay down to sleep, an involuntary shiver was mute testimony to the cool, dark shadows the trees cast and their incessant rustling. They felt so alive. She slowly drifted off but her dreams were troubled and filled with flickering silhouettes of leafy trees shuffling around a campfire. Over the next few nights she encountered the same dream of trees that whispered at her and moved around the fire.

One morning, K'trell stretched and squinted at the shadowy figure of Nasrindo standing watch in the gloom. They'd been travelling for what seemed like an age in this miserable forest and every time she asked Darjoon if they were closer he'd just grunt at her. They'd skirted around a few towns and avoided some patrols by hiding deeper in the forest, slowly getting closer to the treetop town that was their destination. The further into the forest they travelled, the more withdrawn Darjoon had become. It was as if he was preparing himself for something, and she wondered what that was. She looked over at his bulky form snoring softly on the other side of the fire. They'd found this clearing in the late afternoon while hiding from one of the Spidral patrols they occasionally encountered, and decided they may as well spend the night. Darjoon had insisted on them taking turns during the night to stand guard. Apparently he'd had a bad experience here in the past and wasn't keen to relive it. She wasn't surprised, as apart from the sensation she got off the trees she had noticed there was a strange, alien magic that she could sense all around them. It seemed to weave through the trees with a stronger concentration at their hearts, then fading out to the tips of the branches, but even the ground had traces of it. When they collected water from the many streams, Darjoon made all three of them go at the same time and one always stood guard watching as the others filled their canteens.

Darjoon stirred and sat up, shaking his head as if to clear the morning cobwebs. He knew the two tribesfolk were edgy but there wasn't anything he could do about it and there was no comfort he could offer them. They were well out of their element here and to them it was as foreign as the dreams he'd been having. He didn't know if it was the forest or because he was no longer focused on controlling a herd of animals, but while they'd been travelling in the leafy green darkness his mind had begun doing it's housekeeping with a vengeance. He was sure that there were even new spells that now resided in his head, although he hadn't wanted to test any of them. Some concepts began to make sense and he even understood what that palm reader had done when taking his blood. It had simply sampled his DNA, which he now knew were the building blocks of life. He was always pleased to learn something new, but he just wondered what it was all for.

Looking over at his two companions, he wasn't sure the free-folk village he was taking them to would make them feel any better. If they didn't like the green tunnels that made for paths in the forest, he didn't think that actually living high up in the trees was going to suit them. But right now he had little choice and besides, they weren't going to like him for the deception he had planned. He sighed, and then looked up to see both of them watching him surreptitiously. He sighed again and stood up.

"We should be able to reach the village by the end of today but we need to get a move on. I'm no happier than you at spending any more nights in this place. So if we move quickly we can put an end to that. There's someone in the village who I'd like you to meet, someone who may be able to shed some more light on the Glass Isle for us. The last time we met he told me a lot about my mother and father, but now I have even more questions for him. He's seen a great deal of this world and I'm sure we can learn a lot from him."

Packing up his things, he continued talking to them, "Not only that, but if we're very lucky then Sirroya may have made her way out of the desert and could be waiting there as well. Yes, I know, K'trell, you don't have to look at me like that and before you say anything, I agree that it's probably unlikely, but let's face it, stranger things have happened. I'm not going to give up hope just yet. Now let's get moving, we can eat along the way."

Darjoon shook his head irritably and gathered up his belongings. Ever since the incident at the Lost Tribe, both Nasrindo and K'trell still watched him like a hawk. He knew it was because they were both concerned, and that Nasrindo's reason was because he'd promised Darjoon's parents he'd take care of him, while K'trell was genuinely afraid of his power. But it was really starting to grate on his nerves. They treated him as if he was liable to explode at any moment, like some dangerous substance you had to handle with care. He trudged out onto the path with the others following some way behind.

"I genuinely thought he'd given up on finding her", K'trell spoke softly to Nasrindo, "I can't believe he's still contemplating anything other than that she's dead or worse, alive, but no longer herself. You said she was definitely dead when you buried her."

"I know, Great Healer, and she was. But what of that

old man we discovered? What he had described, that was bad, wasn't it? It may be as you believe, it may be that she's worse than dead, I don't know. But if his hope sustains him, then who are we to deny it to him", Nasrindo looked at her, his face soft in the light through the trees.

She looked back at him for a long moment in silence, their eyes locked and then she felt her cheeks reddening as his eyes began twinkling and he winked at her. Snorting as if in disgust, she quickened her pace and stalked off, flinging her head as she did so and leaving him behind. She couldn't believe she'd been blushing under this simple warrior's gaze. How ridiculous! After all she was a Great Healer, hadn't he just said as much! Who did he think he was, trying to flirt with her, of all people. How dare he have the nerve? And she was even of the Lost Tribe!"

As she walked along, fuming, she began to realise how little he spoke to her, yet how often he looked at her. Her flush grew deeper as she realised that there were long-dormant feelings inside her that he somehow awakened. She'd grown used to his quiet presence now, as if he'd always been at her side, even though he hardly seemed to acknowledge her. He had such a familiarity to him, a close, comfortable feeling, almost as if they'd known each other before. She shook her head. This was ridiculous. She was a Great Healer, and Great Healers did not take lovers of their choosing, it was forbidden. Their lot was to breed more healers and their mate was chosen by the elders, carefully selected and only after consulting the seers and the gods. Once again, she was struggling to focus herself and she'd made this mistake before.

"So easily distracted, K'trell, so easy for you to lose focus", she muttered to herself, unaware that the familiar and comfortable use of her name by Darjoon had imposed itself on her own thoughts now.

After veering off the trail and following a faint, ill-used foot-path, Darjoon stopped at the base of a large tree. Dangling next to the trunk was a long rope-ladder, old but obviously strong and well-mended. Darjoon turned to face them and grinned cheekily.

"Okay, we're here. Well, you'll be happy to know that we're leaving the dark, green tunnels of the forest behind us. However, we are going to be climbing up a little way. You see, what I neglected to mention is that this village that I've spoken of, well, it's actually all the way up in the tree-tops", Darjoon watched with amusement as the others gasped, K'trell lapsing into her native tongue and fired questions at him, while Nasrindo just stared up at the tree.

"K'trell, I can only understand a little of what you're saying. Either slow down or speak so I can understand you."

Switching to Empire, K'trell continued her tirade, "Why didn't you tell us before, Darjoon? What makes you think we'll go with you up there, are you crazy? How can you expect us to do such a thing, it's not natural, we weren't born with wings, do we look like we can fly? How dare you presume to just lead us up there! Who do you think you are? Oh yes, you laughing boy, you, you can fly, and maybe I could, but what about Nasrindo, have you thought of him? How dare you endanger his life like this! What are you thinking about?"

Nasrindo turned to her, and then gently placed his hand on her shoulder. She stopped, turning to look at him. He gave a familiar squeeze, then dropped his hand to his side again.

"Great Healer", his voice was calm and measured as he addressed her, almost formally, "I thank you for the concern you show me, I really do. And please, rest assured that I too share your misgivings. But Darjoon knows where he is going, and we need to follow him and protect him. That is our duty. His duty is to fulfil the destiny the gods have given him. My life in that context is not so great a thing. Darjoon has been this way before, so let's trust him now. Darjoon, why don't you lead the way, then the Healer can follow and I'll come up behind her."

K'trell felt the anger dissipate and again she found herself staring at the warrior in silence. She shook her head, then turned and began climbing after Darjoon who was already moving up the tree with surprising agility.

The climb seemed to take forever, and her mood wasn't improved by the sight of Darjoon waiting impatiently on the tree, but grinning at her discomfort. She baulked at the baskets he showed her, only relenting after Nasrindo had again calmly soothed her fears. Shutting her eyes and holding on tight, she shuddered as Darjoon and Nasrindo took turns pulling them along between the towering tree-tops. A small, bright green bird had been fluttering around them for a little while when they finally arrived at a walkway of wooden planks. The bird flew away from them and half-way across, she noticed a figure on the far side standing on a platform built around the tall tree they were approaching.

Darjoon raised his arm in greeting and the figure did the same, followed by both of them saluting each other in a peculiar fashion when they finally met. The two tribes-folk looked at each other quizzically, aware there was an obviously strong bond between Darjoon and this man.

"Ysarryn! It is so good to see you again. The feathers of the Great Raven have brought us across the winds of time to meet once more", Darjoon smiled up at the hunter.

Ysarryn gave him a slight warning frown, "It is odd Darjoon, that you greet me with such a typical raven-born greeting? I had thought you reserved that only for your own kind. Nevertheless, this 'Spidralite' and the free folk of Spidral welcome you back, you and your new friends. Perhaps you can introduce me but first what of Sirroya? Is she not with you?"

While Y'sarryn was speaking, Darjoon heard the raven-born's voice clearly in his head, warning him that his was not an identity he wanted known to others, least of all strangers. Then his face fell as the implication of what

Y'sarryn had said hit home. He knew it had been a forlorn hope, but he'd clung to the belief that Sirroya would be here in the village waiting for him. She'd loved it so much that he'd been sure she'd return. He responded with a mental thought to Y'sarryn that Sirroya was presumed dead.

"Ah, that is indeed sad news, Darjoon", Y'sarryn spoke aloud and frowned slightly at him, "I can see just from your expression, without you saying anything, that something has happened to your friend. I am truly sorry, but for now, come, you are all tired and hungry and it's already getting late. Later we can share our news and you can tell me more. So Darjoon, are you going to introduce me to your new friends?"

"Oh yes, I'm sorry. Y'sarryn, please meet Nasrindo, a friend of mine and a warrior from the desert tribes, and this is K'trell, his companion."

K'trell shook her head and clicked her tongue at the young mage but couldn't help grinning anyway. After all, Darjoon had little regard for the ways of etiquette.

"I am not Nasrindo's 'companion', neither am I known as K'trell, although once long ago that might have been a name I recognised. I am in fact the Great Healer of, well, of one of the tribes in the desert of Thoth. Darjoon has a slightly more, ah, unique way of seeing things", she smiled at Y'sarryn who smiled back.

"Indeed, as you say and we all saw by his odd greeting of me and his, yes, his unique introduction of yourself, Great Healer. I am slightly familiar with the customs of the great desert tribes. I hope you'll be comfortable here in what for you must be some strange surroundings indeed. Do not fear, Healer, no harm will come to you here. We are the free-folk and as such we accept everyone equally and regardless of origin, or indeed, of station in life. We have among us nobility who work next to ex-slaves, and we have Spidralites and people from Klarand working with farmers from Lower Srinth and elsewhere in the Empire. I'm not sure that any desert tribes-folk have been here before, and apart from our eccentric young friend, Darjoon, we have had no other raven-born either. But come now, let's get you settled for the night. You will all sleep in my humble home, although Darjoon and Nasrindo will have to share the living room, unless one of you wants to sleep outside if you prefer."

Nasrindo looked at the Spidral hunter in sheer disbelief.

"I'm sorry, Y'sarryn, did you say outside? But surely that is insane. What is to prevent someone from rolling over and falling to their deaths? You cannot mean that people actually sleep outside?"

Y'sarryn laughed heartily, "No, no, warrior, that is not exactly what I mean, we don't sleep on the walkways. When we sleep outside our huts, which in the warmer months is quite welcome, we do so in hammocks. These are simply string nets that are slung between two branches or poles and are contrived so that once you are inside, you cannot roll out. It is quite safe, I assure you, and no-one has fallen to their death yet. But by all means, if you don't like the idea, you may sleep in the living room of my house."

He laughed again as Nasrindo pulled his face in disgust, then showed them into his home. While Nasrindo and K'trell settled in, Y'sarryn returned to Darjoon outside, smiled at him and poked him in the side, taking off and racing Darjoon along the walkways and up the old tree they'd climbed the last time the young mage was here. Y'sarryn marvelled at the speed with which the young mage moved, easily beating him to the eyrie. Sitting in the fading light high up in the tree-top, looking out across the forest, Darjoon told Y'sarryn about his journey into the Desert, his meeting with Nasrindo, the failed assassinations and the deadly meeting with the lizard people and what had happened to Sirroya. He also shared about his journey to find her and what he'd heard of

Sirroya. He kept back the story of his visit to the old, abandoned outpost and the information he had been filled with, his mother's words of caution still ringing in his ears.

Y'sarryn listened to the long tale in grim silence, simply waiting for Darjoon to finish, and nodding or shaking his head to indicate his attention.

Darjoon finally finished with his story of his snaring the roykili and their subsequent journey back to Spidral through the forest and Y'sarryn laughed with Darjoon when he demonstrated how Nasrindo had ended up walking after a few days riding on the back of his beast. Once the tale was done, the silence stretched out across the dark vista below as the night took hold and fires flared up in distant towns and villages. Y'sarryn sighed and pulled his cloak around him to ward off the chill. During Darjoon's tale, he had dropped the Spidralite mask and Darjoon could clearly see the raven-born features now easily revealed in the hunter's profile. He appeared to be struggling with some inner turmoil and Darjoon waited patiently until he finally turned and looked straight at him.

"My eyes cannot pierce the darkness that shrouds your story, Darjoon. There is much here to think about, so much of it resonates with stories your mother had told me, as well as what she had heard from your father and that she then shared with me. I... You cannot know, but...", his voice trailed off.

"Listen, Y'sarryn", Darjoon spoke gently but urgently, "I am deeply grateful for your help and for keeping my mother's promises, especially and including the parcel you held for me. That cloak has saved my life more than once, even if the staff almost did the opposite. But if there is any more information you have, Y'sarryn, I believe that now is the time to share it. I intend to go on a dangerous errand, one that I must perform alone. There is only one way to get to the Glass Isle, well, not just on it but actually inside it, one way to penetrate its depths. I believe that is where the secrets lie buried, secrets that we will need to uncover if we must fulfil the prophecy my mother spoke of. This endeavour is going to require much from me, that I do know. And from those who are with me."

Darjoon looked out over the darkened forest for a while, as Y'sarryn waited patiently, then he continued.

"The others cannot know at this time that I go to seek the Circle of True One's, because they would want to either stop me, or indeed, accompany me. And they cannot be allowed to do either. I can't afford to have them with me. It is going to be far too dangerous for them and for me if they come."

Y'sarryn had inhaled sharply at the mention of the renegades, and now his eyes were fierce and piercing as they locked on to Darjoon.

"No, Darjoon, you cannot be serious. Surely you know that there is only a small chance of success doing it this way? Do you have any idea how few mages are admitted into the Circle, and even if they are, do you know what they do to the ones who don't make it? No-one survives those accursed fiends, Darjoon, no-one. Do you know why? Because even if you do succeed to enter the Circle, what do you think will become of you? Have you given any thought as to what you will have to surrender to join those monsters and win their trusts? What do you think they will expect from you?"

The young mage held Y'sarryn's gaze while the hunter spoke and continued to do so during his own response.

"I am serious, Y'sarryn, and yes, I have thought long and hard about it and I am still convinced that this is the only way. I will not be dissuaded anymore, so do not try. My yolk was tainted with poison from before I was born, so what worse things could they do to me now? I am powerful, you've said so yourself, and now in other ways too, that I hardly believe, and they would be foolish indeed to ignore what I bring. This is as it should be, brother, the feather of fate has landed me on a dangerous branch and I must fly, like those before me, straight and true and with no fear. But I will need you to look after these tribes-folk. They are brave and honourable and I hate it that I have to deceive them like this. Nasrindo is, well, he's like a brother to me, and K'trell has become like a sister. They, like you, are my family now, Y'sarryn, so please, please keep them from harm until I come back. Under no circumstances must they follow me. You must not tell them where I have gone, but simply that I will return after the next two Tregora moons, or else not at all. If I don't come back by that time then they must return to the desert, secure in the knowledge that they have fulfilled their promise, that I am not the prophesied one and that someone else will be raised up in my place as a result."

Y'sarryn grimaced and shook his head initially, clearly uncomfortable. But finally his shoulders dropped and he sighed as he spoke with obvious reluctance.

"Darjoon, this is either very brave, or very, very foolish. I will do as you ask, not just because of your mother but, yes, because I, too, see you as family. If the answers are in the Glass Isle then I know that you will find them because that is your destiny, whatever you may think. But remember that prophecies are ever vague, they are simply the muddied, swirling waters of the future that we have to interpret in the here and now, and usually we do so imperfectly. Just when we think we know what it means, then things change and we realise it was, after all, only an illusion of our own knowledge, or that of our ancestors and so it wasn't the future after all, but the past. Remember this, Darjoon, that prophecies are not always what we believe them to be, but that they become what we make of them. Our past is only good if we embrace our future and make the right decisions in the present."

Darjoon looked at the raven-born opposite him, who appeared to be glowing in the starlight that flooded the forest and shone down on the great tree where they sat, like birds in a roost. The enigmatic man had an indefinable air of sadness that hung about him like a miasma, swirling and thickening the more Darjoon learned about him. There was a vague feeling Darjoon had, almost like a scent that was previously familiar but has now been forgotten, and then suddenly smells strangely familiar again. His mind worried at the oddity, then he gave up and addressed the man.

"Now, Y'sarryn, as I said before, is there anything you think you should tell me? Anything my mother said, or something my father might have known that would help me with the Circle? Don't hold anything back because I leave tonight", he looked pleadingly at the man.

Y'sarryn slowly shrugged his shoulders, "As I've said Darjoon, I told you everything I know. There are some things I haven't revealed, yes, some things that I think I know, but I honestly believe those would only cloud your vision like a mist and are not worth knowing right now. I will watch over your friends, Darjoon, but promise me you'll do your best to come back soon? Don't get taken in by those lying, evil fiends and their empty and false promises. They surround themselves constantly with deception and half-truths and fight each other. Each of them will try to get you to believe that theirs is the only way, and that they have all the answers but it simply isn't true."

Darjoon nodded his head, and then after they'd sat in companionable silence for some time, stood up and stretched, yawning. Y'sarryn stood too and then briefly laid his hand on the young mage's shoulder and squeezed. Darjoon acknowledged his gesture with a simple nod, then immediately began descending from the eyrie with the hunter following. Finally, Y'sarryn the Spidralite hunter stood on the last walkway, watching as Darjoon began the journey back down to the ground. The young raven-born mage did not look back, the resolve clear in the stiff line of his back, the squared shoulders and the way he carried himself. He'd known that arguing with him wouldn't help, and something inside him was whispering that this was the right way, that this was how it should all proceed. He whispered a few words of magic, and a bright blue bird appeared on a branch next to his head. It gave a soundless chirp, then took off, flying above Darjoon's head, undetected and close. Y'sarryn could see in his mind's eye the view the bird had, a young man walking into the darkness of untold danger, a young man on a mission filled with purpose and intent. He breathed a few words of blessing and entreated the raven-born goddess, Zukar, to fight with him and protect him. Turning, he made his way back to his hut and the inevitable encounter with the tribes-folk. Convincing them that Darjoon would be safe and would return as he'd said was not going to be easy.

Darjoon jumped off the last few rungs of the rope-ladder, his boots hitting the ground. He marvelled again at how fit he was, and how the climb down had been relatively easy, even though he'd had to move the baskets by himself.

He glanced quickly overhead, smiling slightly to himself. He'd been aware of the little blue bird above him from the very beginning, knowing that Y'sarryn was keeping an eye on him. As if in answer to his thoughts, it flew down, gave a little chirp, like a sad goodbye, then turned and flew back into the darkness of the canopy. The sky was already lightening overhead as he shouldered his pack and headed off down the path. Y'sarryn and he had sat up in the high tree for most of the night, content to just breathe in the night air and listen to the faint creak of the branches in the slight breeze in the relative silence of the large forest. The peace had enfolded them and Darjoon had even nodded off once or twice. Then, in unspoken agreement, Darjoon had left. He picked up the pace, aware he had some days of travelling ahead, and this time alone. He'd figured out on the inbound journey that he could communicate with the trees, and so could ask them to watch over him as he slept. He was sure that someone had asked the trees to ensnare him when he'd come with Sirroya previously, although he had no idea who would've done that. He'd almost drowned that time, and the young Empire lass had definitely saved him with her singing. A lump made itself felt in his throat and he swallowed it down, putting thoughts of her out of his mind and concentrating on the journey ahead. He was still trying to sift through and sort out the knowledge he'd received and his dreams were still intense. A lot of what he was seeing and experiencing he had no way of explaining. There was some excitement one night when during a dream he saw various egg-shaped objects floating down to this planet and he was sure that one of them must have been the original egg from which the raven-born had emerged. But he was still not sure what it all meant. The days and nights passed relatively quickly and uneventfully as he travelled through the forest.

It had taken a few days, but as the sun slowly began to slip behind the Darken Hills that loomed in the far distance, Darjoon strode into the same clearing he'd been in with Sirroya when he'd ignored her advice regarding the fork in the trail. He smiled ruefully, remembering how she'd teased him for taking the wrong path and how certain he had been. It was as if she'd expected something else to be here, as if it had suddenly seemed unfamiliar to her even though she'd supposedly never been here before. Such an enigmatic and beautiful woman! He sighed and looked around. It hadn't changed since the last time they'd been here, the old brick well still stood in the centre of the clearing. He walked over to it and slumped down with his back against it, opening his pack and taking out some rations. It would be a little while before it got dark, so he made himself as comfortable as he could. According to his calculations, and if he was actually right, the blue Tregora moon should be rising tonight. He'd pushed hard to get here, so hopefully he hadn't missed it. Taking out the cryptic note he'd been given, he scanned the lines again and he focused on one in particular.

*"See with more than your eyes to join us, or never see at all."*

What could that mean? He knew he better figure it out before the moon came and went, otherwise it would be another fortnight to the next rising and he was supposed to be back in the tree-top village the one after that which would never be enough time.

More than your eyes? What could be more than your eyes? He thought briefly about that strange artefact that K'trell had found in the sand. They'd been astonished at how well it magnified the distance. There had been some telescopes at the college that all the students had been given an opportunity to use, but they'd been fuzzy and even scratched. This had been crystal clear and by turning small dials on the side had made the focus even sharper.

He kicked himself mentally, wondering if that was what the note had meant, in which case he didn't have it but K'trell did. But that couldn't be right, who would have one of those? No, this wasn't a random test of pure chance, which is what was required to find a focusing device like K'trell had done. This was meant to test the individual's ability, he was sure of it. So that probably meant magic.

He whispered briefly and a glimmering line appeared in the darkening grass. Overhead, the stars were beginning to twinkle into sight and down low on the horizon, just between the treetops, he could make out the blue Tregora moon as it began its slow ascent into the night sky. The line went a little way from him then faded away. He grunted in frustration. As he didn't know where to go, the direction spell didn't either.

See with more than your eyes? Could they mean the other senses? He settled himself down and calmed his body, slowing his breathing and heightening his senses as he'd been taught. Finally, closing his eyes, he tried to detect any unusual scents. Was it a smell? Around him were the familiar forest smells, of earth and mould and trees and rotting leaf litter. But nothing that would guide him. Opening his mouth, the taste of the air was the same. Just earth and more earth. He waited a while in silent expectation, but nothing came to him. Grunting in soft exasperation, he got up and began pacing around the clearing, this time caressing the trees and rocks that he found in the vain hope that touch might work, until finally, walking in a tightening spiral he found himself back at the well, which he lovingly caressed, then slapped viciously in frustration. Nothing! He could detect nothing at all! It had to be magic, surely.

Bowing his head, he whispered quietly and again a faint, luminous line, glowing eerily in the blue moonlight appeared at his feet, and began to retrace his steps, glowing brighter as more of it filled the spiral he'd been walking. As he watched, the glowing end of the line stopped where he'd been standing, appeared to move backwards and forwards and then slowly the entire line faded away to nothing again.

Darjoon heard an echoing silent scream of frustration in his head that he knew was his own. It was still pointless trying to find somewhere that he'd never seen or even heard of. There was no direction, so the magic had nowhere to go. The scream in his head abruptly changed to a loud, raucous cawing, and he looked around and then up as a large black bird flew across the clearing, lazily turning and spiralling up around him on the warm night breeze that came up from the forest. As the raven flew overhead, he thought of flying himself, flying somewhere far away. Abruptly he staggered, disoriented as the forest unfolded below his feet. Suddenly his vision shifted and he was circling a clearing in which a large young man in robes was staggering and sitting down hard on the edge of a well.

Tilting his head, he zoomed in on the well, wondering why the human had done this. Was there food in the well? As he flew down towards the young man, the well slowly melted away, revealing him sitting on a large rock with an ornate trapdoor embedded in the side that in turn had some strange gold writing carved into the hard wood. The writing glowed faintly and he recognised it as an old spell, in fact a particular kind of open spell he'd seen in one of the forbidden books he'd read.

Darjoon shook his head and in an instant found himself staring up at a large, black raven fluttering just overhead, which suddenly squawked loudly and was now heading up and away, as if to rid itself of something unpleasant. As it formed a silhouette against the now prominent blue Tregora moon, he stood up and turned around to look at the well. This time, he put his hand out towards the well and spoke the spell he'd seen on the trapdoor. As he watched, the well slowly faded away and the wooden trapdoor opened slowly of its own accord. In the dark opening thus revealed, and softly illuminated by the blue moon, he could see stone steps leading down into the darkness within.

"Well, fat man, it's time to face the Circle", he whispered to himself then smiled and said, "Careful oh great Circle of True One's, here comes a fat man hunting."

Conjuring a globe of light he walked forward and began carefully descending the steps. However he'd only just begun when he heard a thump from behind him. Turning around, he could see only darkness behind and when he walked back up, he realised the trapdoor had swung shut. Putting out his hand, this time the same spell he'd used earlier had no effect. He tried a few more, then shoved at the door but all to no avail. It remained firmly shut. He shook his head in frustration, then turned and continued his way down. Now there was nothing to do but see where this would lead him.

Some time later, after numerous curving steps and short, twisting tunnels, he realised he must be some way underground, although he wasn't sure in which direction. Finally making his way down a low, narrow tunnel that sloped ever so slightly downwards, he stepped out into a large, dark space, a faint breeze of dust and mould caressing his cheek. Increasing the light of the globe hovering above him seemed to actually make the area in front of him darker, so he dimmed it again until he could barely see at all.

Afraid of any pitfalls in the darkness, he began to shuffle forwards carefully, sweeping his feet out in front of him to detect any drops. His peripheral vision suddenly caught something flashing and he stopped dead immediately, waiting to see what it was or if it would happen again. There! There was a sudden glimmering coming from up ahead and slightly to the left. He whispered quietly and the light globe above him disappeared completely. In the distance, a faint glow grew clearer and appeared to come from above what looked like some sort of arch that in turn seemed to brighten and dim, occasionally shooting out a slightly brighter light. It was this brighter light that he'd noticed flashing earlier.

Focusing on the light, he watched as the direction spell he conjured now appeared straight before him, bright and shining, the glowing line racing across the vast floor straight at the arch. In the glow from the line, he could see only a solid floor with no holes or pits into which he could fall. Keeping the spell active, he carefully followed the glowing line and finally approached the lighted arch.

The archway seemed to glisten wetly in the dull light, reflecting and scattering the burning lamp above it and that explained why it seemed to glow. The lamp itself seemed to be composed of a collection of living lights, or a form of small lightning contained in a clear glass covering. It arced and spat, as if wanting to escape the containment and occasionally flashed brightly.

Reaching out, Darjoon touched the surface of the archway and then recoiled. It felt ice-cold and metallic, not wet as it had first seemed, although this wasn't a metal he'd ever seen before. Looking down, he saw that the arch was built on top of a large round disk, which appeared to be made of the same substance but contained its own orange glow in the middle. Darjoon exclaimed in delight. He realised that he knew exactly what this was. In the stories that Y'sarryn had shared, his mother had described something like this. And from what he could glean from the stores of his newly acquired knowledge, he was sure this was an actual portal. Could he have found one so soon? Thank Zukar, it was beyond his wildest expectations and he did a little jig, then laughed out loud at himself. The massive cavern echoed the laughter back at him and he froze and looked around carefully as he heard a voice address him.

"You foolish boy! What if others heard you laughing? Who knows what's down here, waiting for you? Be careful", the recognisable voice of his raven-born High Sorcerer was soft but clear inside his head.

He pursed his lips, calmed himself, and then turned back to the portal. Putting out his hand again, he muttered the same opening spell he'd used on the trapdoor. Nothing happened. He closed his eyes and thought for a moment. Hadn't the light on top flickered briefly when he'd cast that spell? He did it again, then quickly stepped onto the disk but again, nothing happened. Trying again, this time he stepped into the arch and then out the other side. No, he was still very much in the vast, dark cavern. He tried squinting to see how far the cavern extended to, or if there were other portals, but couldn't see anything. Then, just as the light on top of the arch glimmered, flashed and then seemed to fade for a moment, he saw a wall not far away that seemed to glisten and glitter in the light. Being careful to illuminate his path again, Darjoon headed over to the wall to see what it was that glittered. It looked like it was made of the same metal as the arch, only this time a large square slab of it was embedded in the rock wall of the cavern. His pulse quickened as he saw there were golden words engraved on it. They looked strange and angular, very precise and yet somehow familiar. Gasping, he swung out the staff that was strapped on his back and simultaneously called up a light globe. There, in the glow of the light he saw the same type of writing on his staff. Pointing the staff at the writing, he paused, remembering the damage it had caused in the desert. Darjoon's heart sank. He didn't dare risk unleashing that unpredictable magic again. Sitting down cross-legged and laying the staff on his lap, he calmed his thoughts and let his mind run free. Caressing the staff subconsciously, he smiled, remembering the parcel his mother had left for him. He'd tried everything to undo those knots, when all along it had been the simplest spell of all. Almost a nursery rhyme that his mother had taught him long ago, when he'd been very young and she'd brought him gifts ensorcelled with that spell, taking great delight every time he'd been able to undo it. He'd thought it was something only they shared. In fact, as far as he could remember, he'd never come across a spell like it. He recalled what his mother had told him back then.

"Darjoon, you never know when you might need to open that which cannot be opened. This little rhyme is our secret back-door to anywhere we want to go. Isn't that wonderful? Just for you and me!"

He'd laughed, thinking how wonderful it was that only he and his mother could get into places no-one else could. That they could open any locked door if they wanted to.

His eyes snapped open. No, surely it couldn't be that simple? It just couldn't be, could it? He looked up at the writing on the wall, and stared at it again. The words of the spell his mother had taught him were always unfamiliar. It wasn't a language he'd heard from anyone else he'd ever met. And yet, as he looked at the writing, he could almost see that it matched the quantity of "words" in that old spell. But why would someone leave the answer on a wall, in plain sight for anyone to see? That didn't make sense?

As he thought that, the words slowly faded and disappeared, the metallic slab reverting to stone.

Ah, so maybe they didn't just leave them out for anyone to find. Tilting his head, he looked at the rock as if it was curiously familiar. Then, he used the spell that had opened the trapdoor and stared with grim satisfaction as the metallic slab reappeared, the writing clear once again. So, that's what triggered it.

Striding over to the arch, Darjoon stepped through, then turned around and faced the front of it again. This time, he chanted the same spell his mother had taught him all those years ago when he was but a child. The orange glow in the middle of the circle flickered brightly as the light on top blacked out completely for a second, then the glow faded away again. A faint shimmer came from the middle of the portal and he could no longer see the cavern through it. Darjoon gulped and then stepped onto the disk and then out again the other side.

# 7 TESTING TIMES

Darjoon stepped through the arch only to experience a strange, numbing sensation, similar to what he'd felt walking through the coldest part of the high peaks of the Darken Hills. He stumbled forward, tripping slightly over some rough ground and then at the sight of the deep ravine in front of him, threw himself backwards. The rock face behind was a welcome support until he realised he'd not stepped back through the arch. To either side of him was a narrow path that led along the side of a high mountain, with a sheer drop just to the side. His step through the portal had been so confident and assured that he'd almost stepped right off the edge. He leaned over and marvelled at the height he was standing on.

"Well, a warning would have been appreciated", he muttered to no-one in particular.

On one side, the pathway stretched on for a bit hugging the side of the mountain, then disappeared into a cleft in the cliff-side. The other side simply ended against a pile of rubble that included some large immovable rocks and didn't look promising. As to the portal he'd just stepped through, there was no longer any sign of it, even though he felt along the cliff-face on either side. Words of magic did not reveal anything either. Giving up he shrugged and then walked along the path that led to the cleft, hoping that at some point the next step would take him back through the portal. But it didn't. With no other option, he simply continued along the path until he came to the cleft he'd seen earlier only to discover on turning the corner that it too ended abruptly in front of a pile of broken rubble, the cliff-side having fallen into the cleft and now blocking the way forward.

Frowning at this unwelcome sight and debating whether he should try the other way after all, he noticed another path emerging from the rubble on the far side of the cleft, about a body length away. Taking a number of paces back, he ran and jumped, slipped on some gravel the other side and rapped his head on the cliff-face. Cursing under his breath, he wiped the sand off his fore-head, checking it to make sure there was no blood.

Once again, all he could do now was move forward along the path and see what lay ahead. Putting his head down and wrapping his cloak tightly around him, he began trudging out of the cleft and on up the path. A little while later he turned a corner around a piece of cliff that jutted out and gasped in wonder. Ahead of him lay a familiar sight resplendent in the late afternoon sunlight. The characteristically high peaks of the Darken Hills pointed straight up, the snowy peaks dazzling in the sunshine. The path he was on ended abruptly as yet another rock-fall had cut it off. Looking around, he noticed that quite a bit higher up beyond the rubble, the opposite end of the path looked like it sloped down and joined what appeared to be the main route up and through the Hills. It was a route he was familiar with having travelled down it into the great forest of Spidral. Shuffling his pack on his shoulders, he took a deep breath, closed his eyes and focused on his magic. It was there inside him, strong and vibrant and multi-hued. Slowly, slowly, he thought of reaching the other side and soon experienced the now-familiar feel of wind flapping through his robes. Opening his eyes he could see he was over the mountain crevasse far, far below him, its sharp rocks grinning up at him in gap-toothed delight. Flinching slightly at the thought of what they could do to him were he to fall, he wobbled as he felt his control slip. The path he was approaching was still some way above him, and he called on increased reserves of magic, lifting himself up in order to reach the jagged edge of that path above. He made it, but with little to spare, his left foot just catching the edge of the path and sending him sprawling forward.

Cursing with heart-felt relief, he lay, gasping slightly. That had taken significant use of his magic and he wondered what would've happened if he'd not had enough. It wasn't a pleasant thought for the young mage to dwell on and after lying there for some time, he finally stumbled to his feet and trudged down onto the main path through the Hills, shivering at the icy wind howling down off the slopes of the mountain ahead.

The light was going but he thought he knew of a place up ahead where he could find shelter out of the wind. As he walked, he noted that this path did not seem to be exactly the same as the one he'd travelled previously. Although certain features looked very familiar, it was almost as if they were slightly disfigured, fuzzy and indistinct like a great storm had eroded them. Well, there was more than one way through the Hills and it seemed he'd obviously found another one, which meant it unlikely he'd find his old shelter. He looked around, then lowered his head against the biting wind and continued on. There was bound to be a cleft or rock behind which he could shelter for the night.

The long afternoon sunlight that was still streaming through the peaks of the mountains probably saved him, casting a dark moving shadow on the ground ahead of him. He tucked and rolled instinctively, recognising the elongated shape and outstretched talons in the grotesque silhouette. A mental shriek blasted his mind just before he snapped a shield in place. Shaking his head to clear it, he rolled again and collided with a large rock which sent him sprawling as a second Dremrel thumped down on the path he'd just vacated. The evil pair looked at him quietly and he could feel his shield being battered by their magic. One of them began shuffling toward him as he lay there quietly, probably thinking their magic had overcome him. He waited until it got closer, then in one, smooth, easy motion rolled forward and as he came up he swung the staff he'd slipped from his back around and to the side of the first Dremrel as hard as he could, augmenting it with a little magic, while simultaneously using more magic to rip a large stone out of the side of the cliff from behind the second Dremrel. His staff ripped through the neck of the first like it was tissue paper and before the head could land on the ground with a sickening squelch, the large stone had already pulverised the back of the other Dremrel's head. Hearing a screeching, rending, maniacal shriek from above and behind him, he spun round and crouched, holding his staff ready. The Dremrel flying above screamed at him again in mad fury and jetted gouts of fire from its claws. Darjoon easily pushed aside the fire with his own magical shield, then stood up and hurled his staff up and out, augmenting it's flight with magic to send it straight up and into the chest of the Dremrel above. Before the creature burst open on impact with the ground, the staff had already returned and was nestling in his hands.

Darjoon looked down at the steaming, bubbling blood on the staff, amazed that even though it was steaming like the acid it was, the staff was unaffected. Hearing a gasp of disbelief in his head, he shrugged melodramatically, then carefully not touching anything used a bit of magic to wash the filthy blood off the staff and onto the ground where it bubbled on the rocks. Picking up his pack from where it had fallen, and with a careful eye on the sky above, he continued up the path while searching for shelter. As Dremrel were territorial, he didn't think there would be another coven in the area, but even in the cave he knew he'd been lucky to find, he still spent most of the night only half-asleep, waking quickly to any unusual sounds in the night outside.

The next day, yawning sleepily, he stumbled on his way until he came to a smooth blank wall that ran straight across the path in front of him. There was no other way around and after scouting back down the trail, he realised there was no path up the cliffs on either side and could see no other route. Coming back to stand in front of the wall, Darjoon felt the ever-present mountain breeze blowing on his neck. At the same time, there was a strange, low, whistling sound. He cast around to see what was causing it, wondering if it was some new ploy by the Dremrel. He heard it again, but this time it was a slightly higher pitch, and seemed to be coming from inside the wall. Walking forward, he suddenly saw what seemed to be tiny holes carved into the surface of the rock. He examined them closely, noting they were slightly different from each other and quite deliberately placed.

Surely these were not a natural feature? Thinking for a while, he leant over and blew into one softly which promptly resonated with a crystal clear musical tone. Darjoon grinned wryly at what was, obviously, another of what he now knew were entrance tests to the Circle. Standing back he saw that there were only a few holes clustered in a strange spiral pattern slightly to the lower right of the centre of the wall. Blowing into each one and listening carefully, Darjoon smiled to himself. These musical notes were somehow vaguely familiar and he was sure he'd heard them before. He sat down and meditated for a while, breathing deeply and waiting for his mind to bring the memory back to him. During his early years at college they'd learned some musical fundamentals, as they had other artistic disciplines. The raven-born were a martial, war-like people, with strict codes of conduct related to honour and a disciplined, regimented life. But in the past, their great artists and composers had created works that still endured through the ages. One of these was a simple ballad of raven-born heroes who had sailed across a dark ocean in a strange ship, bringing light and life to a land that had previously been shrouded in darkness. It was this ballad that he was hearing in his mind, and it seemed to fit the notes he'd heard in the holes in the rock.

Slowly and carefully recollecting the exact order of notes of the ballad, Darjoon stood up and approached the rock. Blowing on a few holes to experiment, he could see they were placed in a specific order based on pitch and tone. Waiting a moment for silence as the wind dropped, he took a deep breath and then blew softly into each hole according to the tune he remembered and stepped back.

A light suddenly appeared in the bottom middle of the rock wall, as if someone was slicing it open from the other side. The light lengthened and travelled up and then across and then down and a rock door slowly swung open with a hiss of air from the other side. Darjoon approached the door carefully, but could not see what lay in wait on the other side. With a deep breath, he stepped through gingerly into an otherwise empty cave. As he stood looking around to see if there was anything else, the door behind him swung closed, shutting out the light. Darjoon sighed, and then muttered a light globe into existence over his head.

Slowly and methodically he explored the cave and on the far side to the right, as he looked down, he saw a large, flat rock on the floor. Sitting nonchalantly on the rock, its forked tongue flicking in and out of its mouth, was a large, plump, white lizard. Darjoon eyed it warily, then saw it had a delicate silver collar with a thin chain that attached it to a ring embedded in the wall. In front of the lizard was a bowl filled with water and some unidentifiable meat.

"Well, hello there, little one. Now, what are you doing

here? Someone's gone to a fair bit of trouble to look after you, and that must be for a reason, mustn't it, oh great fat lizard of fate", Darjoon smiled at it and put his hand out to stroke the scaly creature.

The lizard froze, then hissed at him and bared its teeth, obviously not happy with the attention he was giving it. Darjoon grinned again but withdrew his hand and then sat down in front of it and meditated again. Something about the lizard must give him a clue. He looked at the collar, but there was no writing on it, nor was there anything noteworthy about the chain. The ring in the wall that the chain was attached to was old and rusty, as if it had been there for some other reason. The lizard licked up some water with jerky movements of its head and then stared at Darjoon, it's large, luminous green eyes with their black vertical slits for pupils fixing on him. A pink, thick membrane slid across each eye, and the tongue flicked up to lick it. The pale wrinkled lips parted as the tongue returned to its mouth, revealing large, sharp, ivory teeth.

"Mmm. Well, you're not exactly pretty, are you, fat lizard? What anyone sees in reptiles for a pet, I'll never know. Apart from those lovely big eyes of yours, I don't think you have any redeeming features at all."

Darjoon's own eyes widened in realisation. Of course, was he stupid? It was the eyes, after all. He looked at the lizard and thought of looking at himself. The nictating membrane slid across his eye and the salty, slimy taste of it filled his mouth as his tongue flicked up and over it. As the membrane slowly cleared again, he stared at the young mage looking back at him. Then he slowly looked up and across the cave at the opposite wall. On it he saw an intricate, illuminated door handle that appeared to be carved out of the rock. The young man kneeling before him stood and turned, then approached the wall and reached out his hand, found the handle and turned it.

As Darjoon opened the door, he gave an ironic wave of farewell to the scaly little creature, to which the fat lizard just grunted softly, happy for the invading mind to have left its own.

Darjoon stepped through the newly opened door and into a small square room lit by soft lighting that seemed to come through the roof above. Standing in front of him with arms folded was the imposing figure of a raven-born man dressed in midnight-blue robes with a large silver circle embossed on the front. He looked sternly at Darjoon, nodded his head and began speaking, the raven-born language sounding suddenly so familiar to Darjoon after all the weeks of listening to Empire and the tongue of the tribes-folk.

"Welcome, Darjoon. I am S'klaratim of the Circle of True One's. May the egg of your mother continue to nurture you in the dark nights of your perilous journey. May we be flown back to our Mother on the Great Raven, there to nestle under her wings as the chicks we once were."

Darjoon returned the raven-born greeting, a slightly archaic version that he'd only heard someone use once before but one he'd been trained in when young. It was, however, not one that was used in normal conversation and as he opened his mouth to why it had been used, the young mage forestalled him by speaking again.

"Please, Darjoon, follow me", and without waiting S'klaratim turned and quickly headed off down a dark tunnel, leaving Darjoon hurrying to catch up.

The dark, slightly damp tunnel descended for some time, beads of water glistening in the light of the globe the young mage ahead of him had conjured, then it ascended, drying out as it did so. Taking a sharp right turn, it ended with a large, ornate wooden door seemingly embedded into solid rock. S'klaratim whispered something to the door and it swung open slowly and ponderously, revealing a bright, warm, cosy wood-panelled room beyond. Once they'd entered, the door lazily closed behind them and S'klaratim extinguished his light globe. Darjoon looked around with interest at the magnificent paintings hanging on the walls around the chamber. Some of them he thought he recognised from textbooks at the college, as they depicted major historical scenes from raven-born lore.

Walking over to one of the dramatic paintings, he saw it had an intricate, detailed drawing of a large, black raven poised in the heavens, complete with tilted head, hooded, piercing eyes and a slightly open beak. In front of the raven, down on the ground and slightly embedded in mud were odd-looking, stylised pieces of what looked like large, angular bits of egg shell and other strange containers which all glinted in the stormy, shiny light that made up the backdrop and spilled over the large mountains behind. He guessed these represented the Darken Hills. Leading away from the strange pieces of shell were small, baby-sized footprints that grew in size as they got closer to the edge of the canvas.

Darjoon exclaimed in wonder, then heard a sniff behind him. S'klaratim puffed himself up and as if playing the role of some great, knowledgeable mage, declaimed, "That, as any raven-born should know, represents our original primal birth. There is the Great Raven, mother of us all, who birthed the raven-born in the wondrous First Egg, from which we drew our original sustenance. That wondrous Egg saw us walk into this world, growing in stature and taking its life-force, the Great Raven's gift to us, which we spread across our land."

"And here", he said, pointing to the next painting, which showed footprints appearing from the side of the canvas and seemingly wandering across a black, empty space with a blue-green ball in a far corner, "this, of course, represents our journey from before the First Egg when the Great Raven flew across the very stars themselves to this world and began nesting in its trees prior to our existence."

Darjoon studied the next painting carefully, noting its use of an intricacy of colours, seemingly abstract yet with artful shapes that appeared clearer the longer he studied it.

"Ah yes", his self-appointed guide continued, "The true beginning of our beginning. When the Great Raven arrived at this world it was in chaos, but after laying the Great Egg and as we began building our nests and raising our young, teaching them to be good custodians of all that the Great Raven had given us, we subdued the chaos and little by little imposed our natural, rightful, true order. There, you see, there towards the top. You can see the smiling beak of our great mother", the mage smiled benevolently at the painting, as if smiling back at the image that slowly emerged from the colours and almost jumped out at Darjoon.

"You see, it is only order, our order, that will keep our feathers in place, keep us flying in formation and keep our flock united as one", the young man made the feather and eye movements with his hands that Darjoon remembered from his time in the college.

Certain of the young mages had been brought up by parents who had insisted on retaining the old ways, the old religious beliefs with all their symbolism. Darjoon glanced sideways at the mage to see if he was still smiling, but he could see that the young man was truly humbled and awed. He shivered briefly, as if something had slithered across his skin and then as S'klaratim looked down at him, he smiled back vacantly. Better to play along with this odd, religious young mage, although he hoped they weren't all quite so fervent. He was used to playing along with the truly religious raven-born during the various festive and religious meetings his mother had dragged him to, albeit with him reluctant and protesting all the way.

One by one the paintings were described and dispatched, with S'klaratim not hesitating or losing his obvious, intense fervour. Darjoon, bored after his initial interest in the first three, politely mumbled and smiled as was appropriate. It's not that he didn't appreciate the religious art, or the history, or even the religious beliefs, it's just that he wasn't interested in learning again what he already knew. As far as he was concerned, there wasn't a great deal of benefit in living in the past, especially not when the past was hazy and obscure and barely understood. Suddenly he snapped out of his reverie and focused on what the young man was saying as it was definitely not something he'd been taught. They'd come to the penultimate painting, a large, garish, or so he thought, painting of violent reds and electric blues, a clash of colours thought to represent the violent end of their current history.

It was prophesied that the Great Raven, enduring the attacks on her flock only because it served her purpose of strengthening the individual members, would finally tire of it and, beating her wings violently she would fan into flame a final great and glorious battle. Having read about historical battles, including first-person accounts, Darjoon didn't understand why they were considered great or glorious. A lot of the soldiers had terrible crippling wounds which either meant lingering death or, even worse, lingering life. A life that no decent raven-born would acknowledge because imperfection was not tolerated, even if it came from honest fighting. Heroes had to be blemish-free, not missing limbs or eyes or anything like that. Appearances were everything to the raven-born. But now S'klaratim had introduced something Darjoon had not heard of, so he listened carefully as the young man continued, seemingly blissfully unaware of Darjoon's change in attitude.

"And so once the evil forces have been arrayed, then the one, true raven-born will emerge from the shadows and step into the light for the first time, their feathers preened and beak and claw trimmed and sharp, ready to be victorious over all our enemies. They will overcome because they are true, because they have not lowered themselves into foul deeds nor into consorting with low-born animals and the herds that originally grazed this sad world. Then, our ultimate power will be unveiled in the Champion, the one to whom the Great Raven has fed her best seed, her choicest morsels and has gifted her three great strengths, the strength to fly high, the strength to see far and the strength to call loudly. At that time, the evil abominations of the enemy will be revealed and the Champion will put an end to the foul, disgusting, twisted creatures that were made into an army. Yes, it will be the beginning of the Final Peace, the end of conflict and the unity of every flock, every tribe, and every creature. We will live as one again in the Great Tree of Life!"

S'klaratim pointed to the final painting which had a detailed depiction of an enormous tree, ravens visibly roosting in the topmost branches and strange and surreal images of what must be the other peoples of the Old Lands shown below, including the desert tribes, shown as strangely wizened old men and women with staffs. There appeared to be bats roosting upside down in some of the lower branches as well, opposite to armoured lizard creatures that dangled from the branches by their tails and stared at fluffy cats that sat preening above them. But while Darjoon was trying to study these, S'klaratim sniffed loudly, then bowed ostentatiously and pointed to a couple of stuffed leather chairs in the corner.

"If you please, Darjoon, I don't have all day you know. Have a seat and we can begin."

Darjoon reluctantly tore himself away from the painting, as he'd just seen what looked like naked apes with Imperial armour higher in the tree, and was about to ask if they did indeed represent the Imperials, when S'klaratim gave him a brittle smile and steered him forcefully into one of the plush seats, seating himself opposite. The pompous young mage smoothed his robes, then once he was sure he had Darjoon's full attention fixed him with a wide-eyed stare.

"You see, Darjoon, you would not be here if we thought you were not fit to join the Circle. On top of that, you have shown yourself to contain the necessary strength and power that we demand, despite your poor appearance. Every test you have endured has been designed to weed out those that do not meet our standards. Sometimes, however, despite our best efforts, we do not hear from the Great Raven as clearly as we would like and so we select someone who is not, ah, up to our required standard."

Darjoon opened his mouth to ask a burning question, curious to know what happened to those who weren't up to the standard, when S'klaratim simply glared at him and continued talking without hesitation.

"As you discovered, you had to demonstrate that you could see clearly, you could fly high, and you could call loudly. Every initiate of the Circle must be able to do so, but not every initiate can become a member. I, myself, for some strange reason that only the Great Raven is aware of, well, I am yet to be accepted as a full member of the Circle. It's only a matter of time, I assure you, but in the meantime we initiates serve in many capacities and it is, of course, especially for you, a tremendous honour just to have been able to enter this blessed sanctuary. I can see from your fascination with the paintings that you feel the same way."

The young mage leaned forward conspiratorially towards Darjoon, seeking to bring him in. Darjoon didn't move, but that didn't stop the mage opposite continuing with breathless reverence and piercing stare.

"It is likely that it could be many months, years even, as in my case, before you are called forward for your final tests. That is both a tremendous honour and yet something to be received with great trepidation. If you thought getting here was hard, then you must know that to achieve entry into the Circle and become known as a True One is just, well, it's incredibly difficult. There is no room for failure, if you understand me?"

As S'klaratim eventually paused for breath, Darjoon dived into the conversation, asking him, "What do you mean, are you saying that people actually die getting here? And in the tests themselves?"

S'klaratim sat back and shook his head, seemingly in disbelief that he'd been interrupted. Wiping down his robe as if he was settling ruffled feathers, he sniffed loudly then looked down his nose at Darjoon.

"Well, Darjoon, this isn't just some silly, simple, secret society. As you should have known before daring to enter it, belonging to the Circle is not for the faint-hearted. We are not just, well, just here by chance. This is our destiny! Those who lose their lives on the way here, well, they can travel the River of Life with their heads held high, knowing they did their best. Just a shame their best wasn't good enough, eh?", he let out a little snigger and then seeing Darjoon's deadpan expression quickly composed himself and continued.

"You see, Darjoon, magic, strength and cunning are our watch-words here and they are what keep the Circle intact. You've shown yourself worthy to join us, somehow, and so when, or if, it is decided that you get the chance to truly prove yourself, to actually join the Circle, then you must prepare yourself in those three areas. It will take everything you have, and even then you must know that it may not be enough. It is only those who have been truly blessed by the Great Raven that will pass through unscathed, well, relatively untouched, anyway", the little snigger slipped out again.

"No, you will find that the three final tests will push you to the limits and perhaps beyond. But if you succeed then you will endure forever, maybe even remembered as one of the Great Ones. Now, initiate, do you have any questions?"

Darjoon thought, then smiled and asked innocently, "So what happens if you don't pass the three tests?"

S'klaratim looked at him strangely, as if wondering how he had managed to get here in the first place.

"Well, of course, if you do not meet the standard,

then it is the same outcome as if you failed in getting here. The tests are all or nothing, Darjoon, there is no grey area in the Circle. You make it or you travel the River of Life."

"But, you're only wearing a grey robe", Darjoon pointed out, finally letting his exasperation with this officious little twit show through.

"Of course", S'klaratim answered as if it was perfectly obvious, "I am only an initiate, like you. You too will be given your grey robe of contemplation and then, one day, if you are called to the final tests and succeed you will be given the midnight black robes of a member of the Circle."

"So do I get a choice to do the final tests?", Darjoon asked bluntly.

Again, the young man looked at him in disbelief, as if he'd just spoken a blasphemy.

"I don't... Why? What? I mean, surely you're joking! Why would you be here unless you wanted to take the final tests and eventually become a Great One? I mean, who would dare to decline such an immense opportunity? You'd have to be...", suddenly he looked at Darjoon suspiciously.

"You're not... Well. No, you can't be. I mean, why was it that you were kicked out of the nest?", he was leaning forward, inspecting Darjoon and practically whispering the last in sudden concern, then abruptly jerked upright as a hidden panel slid aside and an older, distinguished mage entered the room. He was dressed in dark black, silky robes and had close-cropped grey hair encircling a bald pate.

Jumping to his feet, S'klaratim bowed obsequiously and then opened his mouth to speak. The new mage simply held up his hand and the young mage's mouth snapped shut with an audible click.

"Thank you, S'klaratim, I believe you've said more than enough for now."

Turning to Darjoon, he addressed him in short, clipped tones, "There is no reason for delay. You must take the final tests now! Simply enter that green door over there and the tests will begin. You have a short time to prepare yourself, so I suggest you make use of it."

The mage turned without waiting for an answer and left through the same panel which slid into place behind him. Both Darjoon and S'klaratim stared at the panel for a while. The young man turned to Darjoon, his face ashen, and whispered at him, "That has never... I mean, what just... I don't think... That's never happened before. It takes years of service before we are considered for the final tests. Years! So much training and contemplating. No-one has ever had to begin the tests straight after arrival. No, never. Who are you?"

He stared at Darjoon with wonder in his eyes, and then slowly his face took on a crafty look, "Ah, wait, I see! You must really be insane, that's why you were kicked out! So now they will rid themselves of you. That... It must be. That must be why. I'm genuinely sorry for you, Darjoon, but as I said, they have very strict standards here and any form of, well, oddness, well its not tolerated you know."

Darjoon's eyes narrowed and he made as if to rise, truly annoyed by the tone in the young mage's voice.

"Ah, yes, of course, you, uh, you want to prepare, what was I thinking about. I, um, I believe I need to be somewhere, uh, right now in fact. Please excuse me", the young man bolted out the room, leaving Darjoon alone with his thoughts.

He knew it couldn't be that they thought he was mad. Despite S'klaratim's views on that subject, he doubted the Circle would ever invite one of the mad mages here. That's not to say they weren't responsible for no-one ever hearing from those poor wretches ever again. Every so often there were poor mages whose magic had damaged their minds, despite the college's best efforts. No doubt it was an unspoken agreement between the Circle and the college. But no, this must be something else? Maybe they doubted his loyalty, or distrusted him somehow? He was just about to settle back in the chair to rest and reflect, when the panel that S'klaratim had dashed through abruptly popped open again and the young man's flushed face peered through.

"I, um, well, I was supposed to tell you. You really do have to do the final tests. I mean, if you don't, well, you will be terminated, I mean, you will die. See, now that you have entered they won't let you leave again, not alive, not unless you've entered the Circle. So your only hope, well, you have to pass the tests, don't you see. Although you'll probably die anyway, so maybe, well, maybe it'll be quicker for you if you just don't do them", the snigger at the end faded away as Darjoon stood up and the panel closed quickly.

Darjoon unclenched his fists and sat down again. He slowed his breathing and reached inside, confirming that his magic was at full strength. Standing up slowly and stretching deliberately, trying to appear nonchalant in case anyone was watching, he wandered over to the green door. Putting his hand on the ornate, golden handle, he turned and pushed open the door. He had decided that there was no reason to put it off. Might as well get on with it, he thought as he stepped through the door.

Once again, he had to fling himself back, the few stones he'd dislodged on the narrow edge of the cliff slipping and clattering their way down into the steep ravine below.

"What is it with these people and their doors?", he muttered under his breath and grinned fiercely, "Can't they put them somewhere other than directly above a drop? You'd think they were trying to kill someone on purpose."

Turning around, he already knew that there would be no door behind him. He put his hand out, feeling the face of the cliff just to be sure. Snorting in disgust as all he could feel was the gritty, grimy surface of the cliff wall, he turned to examine the ledge he was standing on. There was no path to either side, and he could see no other ledge or remaining path that he could fly to. Looking over the ledge didn't make him feel any better. He was a long, long way up and the valley floor that lay far below him was strewn with sharp spires and large boulders. As he started sitting down, wanting to contemplate his situation, a loud shriek split the silence and a claw passed through the space where his head had been. Throwing himself down as the Dremrel hurtled past, he saw that two more were rapidly approaching. Now what? There was no weapon easily to hand, not barely a few loose pebbles. The familiar pressure on his mind began to increase as the other two shapes grew larger. The first Dremrel eased into view and hissed at him, flapping its large wings to remain stationary and hover in front of him and it screamed again. He coughed as the fetid breath washed over him, rank with decay. The pressure on his mind increased and he hurled a bolt of fire at the creature, but it simply shimmied to the side and hissed at him again as the fire passed harmlessly by. The others were much closer now, and suddenly, as if emboldened by their presence, the Dremrel in front of him rose up and then swooped at him, its claws raking towards his face. Pulling back instantly, but not quickly enough, Darjoon dropped to one knee, the creature's wickedly sharp claw having ripped a furrow above his brow. Wiping the blood out of his eye with the back of one hand, he simultaneously punched forward with the other, feeling his fist strike its delicate sternum. The creature drew back, snarling and hissing and spitting in rage as Darjoon hastily erected a shield spell. It hadn't been an effective blow, probably just bruising it and as the thing had pulled back, one of its hands had clawed into Darjoon's forearm, raking it all the way to his elbow and pushing him backwards. Putting out his hand to steady himself as he fell back, he felt a large ring of steel under the snow and thin vegetation that desperately clung to life on the exposed ledge. Pulling it hard did nothing at all. In despair, he pulled and twisted harder and heard behind him a door grinding open in the cliff face. Thanking Zukar for this act of providence, he turned quickly, placing his bloodied hands on the door entrance. Crouching in front of the open door, he forced himself to stop diving through to safety, despite his instincts screaming at him to retreat.

"Wait, Darjoon, this is a test, after all. This can't be right", he mumbled to himself, "Why would they have made it so easy and provided such an obvious exit."

Suddenly he relaxed and turned to face the Dremrel, still hovering in front of the ledge and he willed himself to wait calmly as the other two finally arrived, intent on beginning the carnage and despatching him. Twisting the handle so the door closed again, Darjoon stood up and advanced boldly to the edge of the cliff. Dropping the shield spell he'd created, he raised his hands as he began to chant a desperate, last-ditch fire spell to fling at them.

The Dremrel suddenly let out an ear-splitting shriek and turned as one, wheeling and diving into the massive canyon below. The pressure on Darjoon's mind eased and he smiled grimly, then frowned as he looked down at his arm. He was trembling slightly from the experience and there was blood dripping off the end of his nose and now off the fingers of one hand as he dropped his hands to his side in relief. Sitting down, he rummaged through his pack, digging out a tunic and ripping it into pieces which he could wind around his arm and head. Splashing water onto the wounds and binding them up, he sat with his back against the cliff and closed his eyes. Releasing just a little magic, he did just enough to clean out the wounds and start the healing process. They'd have to heal on their own for now, just until he was sure he wouldn't need every last scrap of magic for what lay ahead. The sun seemed to be on its way down and he couldn't stay here on the ledge, exposed, overnight.

"Alright, fat man, start thinking. We can't go left and we can't go right, and ahead of us is a long, long drop to oblivion. So now what? Up? No, nothing up there but more cliff. Alright then, we can't make it all the way down, but is there anything below us?"

Crawling on his belly, he leaned as far over the ledge as he could, then looked at the scene below him. Sure enough, there was another ledge, then another and so on. Grinning, he stood up, dusted himself off, hoisted his pack and made sure it was tight. Then, stepping gingerly off the ledge, he calmly floated down to the ledge below, then again to the next ledge, and then again. Stopping, he checked his magic and realised with horror that it was already significantly diminished. Cursing, he drifting down one more time, although he tried to do it with less magic. This time he landed hard and stumbled against the wall. Massaging his right ankle which had taken the brunt of the landing, he shook his head. He was now about two thirds of the way down the mountain but his magic was as good as gone.

The ledge he was on was bigger than any of the others, and seemed to stretch around a corner of the cliff. Walking carefully around the outcropping that bulged out into the air, he found a path that led up the side of the cliff. Shaking his head in disbelief at his good fortune, he continued following the trail, looking carefully below for any other paths that would lead further down. The path seemed to go up and up, then disappeared around another cliff edge. After walking a bit more, and seeing nothing below him, he slumped to the ground.

Putting his head on his knees, he checked his magic and realised that with the walking and the nervous energy he was expending keeping a constant check for Dremrel, there was no chance of it recovering quickly. He breathed heavily, feeling the oppressive weight of the cliff above him and the wind howling up from the depths below.

"Well, fat man, there's nothing to do but keep on going. The Great Raven must've put this path here for a reason. That's if it was even her, of course."

Stumbling to his feet, he pushed on up the trail until

he got to where it turned around a sharp corner. He had to edge around it carefully, even clinging to the cliff-side for a bit as he did so, because the ledge was very narrow. A blur of movement in the distance caught his eye and he froze, watching carefully. On a path further along the cliff, a mountain goat bounded down, scattering gravel as it did so. Down, it was going down! He almost whooped in delight, seeing how the twisting path dropped and fell, in places doubling back on itself as it meandered down to the valley below. Yes, he was going to make it! Just had to keep going and he'd be there. Darjoon pushed on with renewed vigour.

Eventually he stumbled onto the valley floor, falling onto a soft patch of snow in delight. The soft feathery snow was a relief after clambering over sharp rocks and gritty stones. The cool, fresh snow revived him somehow and he sat up, looking around. That mountain goat was long gone by now, and he chuckled, wishing he had that agility.

After refilling his canteen with melted snow and munching on his meagre supplies, he stood up, brushing himself off and heading down the valley. His magic was returning slowly from the rest he'd had, and he knew he needed to find shelter soon before night-fall. Just because the Dremrel weren't around at the moment didn't mean they weren't going to suddenly show up and he was in no fit state to face them with such low reserves of magic. Scanning for any sign of a cave or shelter between the rocks, he almost didn't see it but a subtle glimmer of light drew his attention and there it was. Just spots in the snow, a shiny, dark red trail of blood led off the path and up to the left. Following the trail carefully as the sun began to sink he found a cave entrance that loomed up out of the twilight. Darjoon tried to sense what or who might be inside but somehow got nothing back. He eased carefully inside, ready to unleash a fire-bolt or shield spell as required.

Further back in the cave and just out of sight he could hear the shallow, wheezing breath of something injured. He carefully called a small, dim light globe into being and sent it ahead. An old man lay slumped against the wall of the cave, covered in blood and with his chest rising and falling unsteadily. Darjoon approached quietly. He could see that the man was raven-born and badly injured. Sending out a small tendril of sensing magic, he grunted in despair. The man was very near death and needed significant healing for the serious internal injuries Darjoon had sensed deep inside. Several deep, raking cuts were evident on his arms and legs and Darjoon recognised them from the one's he'd just received from the claws of the Dremrel. He shook his head, knowing that his magic was far too low to even attempt any sort of healing, let alone anything this extensive.

Coughing, the old man spluttered and his eyes flickered open, slowly focusing on Darjoon as he recoiled, trying to shuffle back. The young mage shushed him and put his hand gently on the man's arm. Darjoon leaned over as the man whispered at him.

"Greetings, huuuh, raven-born brother. For a minute I, huuuh, I thought you were another accursed creature, huuuh, come to finish off what they'd started", the man licked his dry lips and groaned involuntarily.

Darjoon dribbled some water into the old man's mouth, then wet a cloth from his bag and gently wiped his brow. His heart sank as the eyelids began to flutter closed, then they opened again and the glowing eyes seemed to burn into him in the darkness.

"Please, brother, I was looking for my wife out there. She's further down the trail but I couldn't find her and I had to drag myself back here. She ran away while I distracted them and I don't think they noticed her leaving. I thought I heard her calling me just now, but I can't be sure, I can't seem to think clearly. Please, you must find her for me. I couldn't live if something had happened to her. We, we are of the same feather, flying united from the beginning of time. She is my nest-mate, and we still feed from each other's beaks. I, huuuh, she must be, oh please, please, you must go save her", the man grabbed Darjoon's arm in a surprisingly strong grip.

Darjoon patted the man's hand absently as he thought this through. He could rest and then use his healing magic to at least bring the man back from the brink of death. Leaving now would probably mean the end for him. But if she was still out there in the darkness and threatened by Dremrel, what chance would she have? Darjoon looked down at the man who stared grimly back at him. His strength was failing and suddenly, Darjoon reached into his reserves and drew up his magic and began to heal him. Through gritted teeth as his magic began to burn inside him, he spoke quickly and quietly to the man.

"You! You can go and bring her back, that way you will be together and either live or die as one. No man should be without his nest-mate, not one whose beak still feeds him. I will heal you and then you will go and save her."

"What? No! No, you will not heal me, you must go to her. You have the power, I can feel it, but so do I", sparks fizzed from the man's hands and Darjoon was thrown back by the power of the old man's magic. The man collapsed back, wheezing in large gasping struggles for air.

"I am spent, as you are, but you are young and strong and unharmed. I would not be able to save her. Go! Go now and find her before its too late. I would not succeed, so it must be you. She is everything, my whole world. Please, please will you do this for me?", the man gasped and his head fell back, his eyes closed. Darjoon jumped up and swiftly knelt beside him. He was still alive, but his pulse was weak and uncertain. Darjoon howled in despair. Why? What was this? As the echoes died away to silence, he thought he heard a faint call on the breeze blowing into the cave. Again it came, and now it sounded like a woman's voice. Suddenly it changed, becoming shrill and alarmed. Without thinking Darjoon placed his hands on the man. Swiftly calling up what was left of his remaining magic, he felt the healing power flowing out through his hands, fully healing the man lying before him. Slumping back, utterly drained, he could see the man's mouth moving as he muttered and then his eyes snapped open, clear and alert. The shrill cry came again and instantly the old man jumped to his feet, letting out an inarticulate yell as he dashed out of the cave.

Darjoon let himself fall back onto the cave floor, as if sliding into oblivion. He could sense that he'd used a great deal of his magic, surely enough to convince anyone watching that it was all gone. In truth, he knew that there was still that hidden reservoir that he would never reveal, not to any-one. He smiled inwardly, although even he was surprised at the extent of what still remained in him. Darjoon closed his eyes and lay still for a moment, slowly letting himself sink into the deep sleep his body required. As darkness enfolded him he drifted away, floating in the breeze like a whisper, like a feather drifting slowly down into a giant ravine filled with darkness.

# 8 ENTER THE CIRCLE

Darjoon stirred, feeling stiff and sore. He was warm and comfortable and through his closed eyelids could register a soft light all around him. The delicious smell of freshly cooked food wafted up through his nose and into his brain and his eyes snapped open immediately. Instead of a dark, dank cave, he was lying in a large, four-poster bed with mounded quilts and cushions. Stretching his aching limbs, he enjoyed the feel of clean, fresh bedding soft against his skin. Spying his clothing stretched out on the foot of his bed, he reluctantly slipped out of the comfy nest of warm bedding and hastily threw on the clothes. Tucked in a small, panelled alcove of the room was a small table and two chairs and sitting resplendent on the table was an enormous tray with a beaker, goblet and large covered silver server, obviously the culprit responsible for the delicious smells.

Whipping the napkin off the cutlery, Darjoon lifted the lid and gasped in delight. A large, succulent fowl lay steaming on a silver platter, surrounded with myriad roast vegetables sitting on a bed of rice, all swimming in thick brown gravy. Sitting down hastily and tucking the napkin into the front of his robe, he attacked the bird with ferocity, realising how hungry he was and how long it had been since he'd had such delicious fare.

A pang of fond remembrance shot through his heart as he recalled his grandmother's cooking and how well she used to prepare her roasts. Hearing the door to his room open and close, he banished the errant thought and blissfully ignored whoever had entered, continuing his fascination with the bird in front of him. The mage who entered was tall, dignified, and wore midnight black robes emblazoned with a large golden circle. He sat down easily in front of Darjoon and smiled warmly at the young mage attacking the food in front of him.

"I'm glad to see you can appreciate the fine cooking of our resident chef, Darjoon. Some of our initiates have skills that surpass that of magic, although I'm sure you'd agree that there's a little bit of magic in that bird. It must be magic because every time our delightful chef cooks, she produces the same excellence. Actually, it just confirms my belief that there are even greater things than magic, although I would naturally deny that if you were to repeat it to anyone else."

Darjoon, his appetite sated far too quickly for his liking, looked up at the man in front of him. The ready smile was still there, the usual hooked nose of the raven-born riding on top of it, underneath dark-brown, intelligent, piercing eyes. A slight hint of gray in the dark locks above his eyes showed that he was not as young as he seemed to be. Darjoon instinctively knew without doubt that this was a very, very dangerous man. Not someone to trifle with, and certainly not someone who would be easily fooled. He would have to be very careful with him.

The man gestured extravagantly at the table in front of him as Darjoon finished the last of the delicious, deep red wine that had been in the beaker.

"Are you finished, Darjoon? I can sense your disappointment and I understand it. One always wishes there were more room inside. After all, it seems such a shame not to be able to finish all of it. Never mind, you will have plenty of opportunity to do food like that justice, although from the look of you I'd be careful of that, hmm? Of course, what am I saying, I'm not insulting you, it's just that you're big-boned, aren't you? Plus, I'd bet a lot of that is muscle too, isn't it? A legacy from your father, perhaps."

As Darjoon alternated between staring and glaring at the man in front of him, while slightly worried at the knowledge he seemed to have, the offensive individual rang a small, silver bell on the tray. A young man in grey robes entered with his head down, taking the tray out the room, but not before giving Darjoon an astonished glare. Darjoon smiled back at S'klaratim as he left the room. Once the door had closed, the tall mage tut-tutted quietly.

"I'm afraid some of the young mages that make it this far are never destined for the final tests, Darjoon. Not all have the internal fortitude required, and most are better suited to, how shall we put it, more menial positions. That one you just saw, well, he is too dangerous to enter the Circle right now, although he has his uses. I wouldn't be too concerned about him though, he resents every other mage that enters the Circle, you see. Especially one as unusual as you, Darjoon. Do you know how special you are?"

The mage waited quietly, his penetrating gaze fixed on Darjoon while the young mage returned his gaze steadily.

"Come, come. Where are my manners? Darjoon, I'm sorry, I should probably introduce myself. I am Grollak, and I am what amounts to the senior mage in these parts. I am also known as the Centre, a silly little title I suppose but there you go, it's what it's always been. You look surprised at that? My age, perhaps? Let me tell you that I am not as young as you would imagine me to be. Or maybe it is because I said, 'these parts', is that it? I'm afraid you're in for quite a surprise, Darjoon. The Circle of True

One's is far, far larger than you could possibly imagine. We are not just some renegade band of cutthroats scuttling around the Darken Hills and preying on innocent travellers, you know. Our power and influence is far, far greater than that, and our reach far wider. Oh yes, far wider", his eyes took on a far-away look, and then snapped back to the present.

"Ah well, enough of that, you have much to learn and you will, in time. You did remarkably well in your tests, you know. Each of them is designed to test not just your magic, or strength and power, but also part of your character. You wouldn't have made it here if you hadn't had power, nor would we have even bothered to contact you were it not the case. No, no, these tests are designed to weed out those whose ambition is above their care for this world, to remove those who are cowardly or dastardly. Again, you seem surprised, but that's to be expected. We are not as evil as those outside would like you to believe, Darjoon. In fact I'm afraid it is a myth that works for us and so therefore it is not one we discourage. No, our interests are not self-preservation, but the preservation of the original instinct given us by the Great Raven herself, the care and protection and nurture of all the life on this world she bequeathed to us. It is our duty to guard life, to protect those people who might not realise how much they need our protection, to continue the work of the Great Raven herself under her guidance. It would take just one peck from her great beak and we would be food, but instead she lets us make of this life what we will. This is the Circle's true goal, to be caretakers of our people."

Darjoon sat back in mute, contemplative silence. The man had an easy voice to listen to and the natural gift of a story-teller. It was obvious that he also had a real passion and belief in what he was saying. To Darjoon, that made him doubly dangerous.

"So in the first trial, we were testing you to see your response to danger. Would you take the easy way out and prove a coward, or stand and fight. I think you saw through that one, but then you're not someone to run from a fight anyway, are you? Or should I say, fly, from a fight?", he smiled at Darjoon conspiratorially.

"Oh yes, Darjoon, we know about you and have done for some time. That's why I knew you wouldn't give up on the long dark trail up the cliff-side. You'd be surprised how some people just sit down and give up, or go the other way, or try to fly down but don't quite make it. No, I was fairly certain you would simply carry on, against the odds, as you've done in your short life so far. And so it was. But tell me, didn't you wonder why your magic didn't seem to regenerate along that trail?"

Darjoon kept quiet and simply tilted his head in wonder.

"Yes, yes, I can see you'd not thought of that. Close your eyes, Darjoon, and let me show you what was really going on. It's important that you understand this, that you understand your true potential. You see, that trial was not as simple as walking a path, oh no, not as simple as that."

Darjoon closed his eyes as instructed, then gripped the arms of his chair tightly. All of a sudden, it was as if he'd been transported back to that cliff-face, but this time he was an observer, watching as he carefully made his way along the narrow path against the cliff. He heard the voice of the other mage in his head, telling him to look closer. As he did so, his vision zoomed in, so that he was looking at his own feet stumbling along the path. Scattered along the trail, barely seen by the human eye, were tiny, uniformly round pebbles. These were constantly rolling under his feet, making it seem like he was walking on ice, yet he wasn't slipping or sliding on them as he should have done. When he'd come to the part where he had to negotiate around the outcropping above the path, where the cliff-side almost folded back on itself, and still looking with his zoomed-in vision, he saw that in fact there were no hand-holds on the rock at all, no-where to grip, nothing to hold onto and yet it seemed as if he was doing just that, even though his hands were flat on the rock as he made his way around. Abruptly the vision faded back to their room and he opened his eyes to stare at the tall mage in wonder.

"You see, Darjoon? Nothing was as it seemed. The reason your magic was depleted is because you were unconsciously using it the whole time, without even being aware that you did so. Remarkable! Do you know how long it takes for our silly initiate's to grasp that concept, let alone put it into practice? Yet you did it without even thinking about it, without even realising that you were doing it. You see, without powerful magic, that path is impassable and you would have fallen to your death."

Darjoon shook his head in mute disbelief. It explained so many other things, like chasing Y'sarryn up the tall tree so quickly. Y'sarryn had been genuinely surprised at Darjoon's obvious pace, but not as much as Darjoon himself had been. Yet now he was sure that he'd been doing the same thing as on the side of that cliff, that he'd been using magic to climb without knowing it.

"It is a tremendous thing, Darjoon, to have such fine control of your magic in that way. But it is also very dangerous that you are not aware of it. You need to school yourself to be aware of what you are doing with magic at all times. It may seem like a good thing initially, but all too often, those whose magical abilities are great like yours become too care-free with how they use it and this can affect their minds. So much so that they can eventually lose their minds, and there is no amount of magical healing that will help with that. I'm afraid it's what we call a 'terminal' condition, if you understand my meaning?"

Darjoon looked intently at the tall mage, wondering if the man knew about his father and what had happened to him. Was this an oblique reference to his father's madness? How much did the mage know about that? Surely he couldn't have that knowledge? Unless? No, he was sure

174

Y'sarryn was not a member of the Circle. He'd been adamant that Darjoon should stay away from them.

"But listen to me, I'm rambling again, Darjoon, don't mind me. Where were we? Oh yes, the final tests. So that was a test of perseverance but also of hidden magic, eh. Devious, but effective. Ah, and then there was the cave. Do you know how few people are willing to do what you did? To actually sacrifice their life for some-one else? Tell me Darjoon, did you think that was the right answer, the right response, to the trial?"

The tall mage waited, making it obvious that this time he expected an answer from Darjoon. The young mage thought for a moment before responding.

"Honestly, I'm not sure. I just knew that two people with such an obvious love for each other, two intimate nest-mates like that should have the opportunity to either live or die together. It wasn't for me to decide either of their fates, it was up to our mother, up to the Great Raven to determine how their feathers would fall."

"Hmm, as I thought. A noble sentiment, Darjoon, to be sure. But surely you realised that you were sacrificing all that you represented, your youth, your power, and even your destiny, to save the lives of two old people who had nothing left to give?"

Darjoon shook his head vehemently, "It is not our place to decide who has more to give, only the Great Raven can do that. Who are we to decide on another raven's life and death, between good and evil like that? It is not up to us to deny life, even to the lowest beast, other than keeping what is necessary to sustain us."

The tall mage smiled warmly at him again, although the smile didn't quite reach his eyes.

"I can see you have not forgotten all that the raven-born have taught you, Darjoon. I understand that sentiment, believe me, and I even embrace it to an extent. But surely we are talking about far greater forces at play than two old people, don't you think? You, me, even our unfortunate initiate S'klaratim, we all have destinies that are part of this great Circle, that are part of the fabric of life itself. Of what worth the relatively puny romantic notion of 'true nest-mates'? What makes you so certain they are worth more than any of us?"

Forgetting himself and where he was and who he was speaking to, Darjoon sat forward, rigid and erect, his face flushing as he spoke slowly and carefully through gritted teeth.

"There is nothing more important than that! It is quite simply the life-force around us, what binds us together and makes us strong. It is what will endure when all this world ends and is finally destroyed. Beyond the Great River of Life, we are all nest-mates! That is a greater power than all the magic in this world or the next. Nothing else could ever matter and so every life, no matter how great or small is a life worth saving. Every! Single! One!"

Abruptly he sat back, abashed. Fool! Had he just ruined all his careful planning? Had he been too forward? It could all be undone in an instant just like this, his youth and naiveté getting the better of him. Where had that passion come from? Did he really believe that?

The mage looked at him sternly for a moment as Darjoon quaked inwardly, then smiled at him warmly and barked a laugh.

"Ha! Yes, oh yes, Darjoon. I too share that passion and that belief deep in myself. I knew it! I knew you had it in you too. But I must caution you, not all that are in the Circle, even the Inner Circle, are of this same belief. For many of them it is not so hard, this brutal work that we have to do, the seemingly cruel decisions we must make and the dark paths we are often forced into. No its not hard at all, I'm afraid. But for those of us, like you and me, it is a constant struggle between what we believe and what we must do. This is because, my young Darjoon and make no mistake here, we are all confronted with making the hard decisions and with taking lives because it is necessary, and with hurting even the ones we love because of a greater cause. I can see you disagree but you too will one day face this difficulty, and perhaps then your decisions will be different to that which you made in the cave."

Grollak sat back in his chair, his face stern and unyielding and in his eyes the young mage could see the world-weary years of experience. He was determined not to become so cynical, despite what he'd already experienced in his adventures so far.

"So did I fail?", Darjoon blurted out the question before he could stop himself.

The mage chuckled quietly and smiled as if to himself, "Fail? No, young mage, you did not fail. But then it is not even a test of right and wrong, of passing and failing but simply a test of heart, and you did reveal your inner heart and I for one am glad of it. Even if others might see it as a weakness, I do not."

Leaning forward, the smile disappeared and the serious frown-lines above the tall mage's brow returned as he addressed Darjoon.

"Now listen, Darjoon, you are about to enter the Circle. S'klaratim will prepare you for the ceremony which will take place in a few hours. I suggest you spend this remaining time in contemplation of what has brought you here and what you have learned so far. We will speak again at length if you are admitted by the members of the Inner Circle which presides over our Circle of True One's."

He smiled at the expression on Darjoon's face, "What, you look surprised? Did you think it was up to me? I do not have the power you think I do, Darjoon. This is not a dictatorship and we do not rule over each other in the Inner Circle. It is through consensus and agreement that we achieve our aims, through the will of the many and not of the one. That acts as a balance to our collective nest and prevents any power-hungry raven from having too much control. We are not brute savages here, Darjoon, as you'll soon find out. No, it takes an agreement from the whole nest to allow any new members to roost in it. I must leave now, but don't worry I will be with you soon enough. Keep your head and beak focused on the prey at hand, Darjoon, and you'll be fine. I do not control them, but I do have a great influence with them and I, at least, am convinced of our need of you. I hope that you, in turn, appreciate your need of us, eh?"

With that cryptic message, the tall mage strode out of the room, leaving Darjoon to sit and reflect. So much of what the mage had said seemed to leave the young mage with more questions than answers. There were also the veiled references to Darjoon's life that either showed how much they might know, or were just fortunate co-incidences. Surely they couldn't know too much about his father, at least not what Y'sarryn had revealed. He knew that he could never let them discover the truth about why he wanted to be in the Circle. So far, it was proceeding even better than Darjoon had hoped. He never thought he'd be admitted to the Circle so soon. Of course, if he was honest about it, he'd known so little of what to expect that he should probably just be grateful to still be alive.

There was a discreet knock on the door, and on answering in the affirmative, S'klaratim came into the room. The young mage was still glowering at Darjoon as he laid out a deep black robe on the bed. On the front of it was a prominent silver circle. Darjoon looked at the young mage and saw the jealousy that lingered in his eyes. He sighed.

"Listen, S'klaratim, one day a robe like that will be yours. You only have to be patient, as you said yourself. I may look young, but I have endured much before I came here and I'm sure that is why I was put to the test so early. I never came here straight from the college like you did and I don't think Grollak would have let me take the tests if I hadn't been ready. Your turn will come soon enough."

The young mage looked at Darjoon thoughtfully with his eyes narrowed and then abruptly his whole countenance and demeanour changed and he beamed at him.

"You're right, Darjoon. Soon they will see my true potential when I exhibit all the powers that the Great Raven gifted me with. Then you and I will take this world together by storm, as nest-brothers. Won't we, Darjoon?",", he smiled brightly at him.

"Uh, yes, sure. Sure, S'klaratim, that's exactly what we'll do. You and I, um, together", Darjoon had to stop himself from patting the young mage on the head, still uncertain as to the sudden change in temperament.

He could see why Grollak had reservations about this strange young man. There was something faintly odd about S'klaratim that Darjoon couldn't quite put his finger on. The young mage bowed out of the room with a conspiratorial wink, the smile still glowing on his face. Darjoon shook his head once the door closed, then lay back on the soft bed, careful not to crease his new robe. Closing his eyes he slowed his breathing and entered into his meditative state. So much to think about. How was he going to do this? He'd have to be very careful going forward, and he cursed himself for almost losing control of himself during the interview with Grollak. This was a dangerous place, filled with very dangerous people and he had to be on his guard all the time. One small slip and he could be on the wrong side of these mages and that would probably mean the dead side. Grollak wasn't to be trifled with, even if he seemed friendly. Drifting off to sleep, his dreams were filled with mages that had Dremrel heads with silver lightning arcing from their fingertips and shooting up into the night sky. He was standing in the middle of a circle of them, completely naked and alone, while they chattered in high-pitched voices at each other and pointed at him. Some began to throw the lightning from their fingers at him and he jolted with each hit, shaking backwards and forwards in agony as each bolt slammed into him. A particularly big jolt made him jerk awake, opening his eyes to see Sklaratim's shiny face looking down on him in consternation.

"Hey, Darjoon, wake up, you silly raven! Oh thank Zukar, I've been trying to wake you for a while now. You were moaning and groaning in your sleep as if you were dying. I mean, how deeply do you sleep, anyway? I sleep lightly, you know, because we have to keep one eye open, if you know what I mean."

S'klaratim was buzzing with excitement and chattered away to Darjoon, who got up unsteadily and dressed in the midnight black robe laid out for him earlier. He was only getting one out of three words that the young mage was throwing at him like spears, and every now and again he just smiled and nodded at him. Thinking Darjoon was nervous about the meeting with the Inner Circle, S'klaratim tried to reassure him by telling him how powerful the other mages were, how some of them were very old and experienced, and that there weren't too many young mages like Darjoon. In fact, there weren't any young mages like Darjoon in the actual Inner Circle. Oh, and a lot of them were very mysterious and independent, preferring to keep their own company and only coming together when it was really necessary. Somehow though, this reassurance didn't have quite the effect the young mage had hoped for, as Darjoon seemed to become even more nervous than before.

S'klaratim led him down a number of flights of stairs and then deeper into the cave system where the walls were artfully concealed behind panelling and tapestries on every side. Entering through a large, ornately carved door with a raven's head for a handle, the young mage bowed at the assembled mages who had turned as one to see who was entering, then ushered Darjoon through and quickly scuttled out after closing the door behind him. Some of the mages looked at Darjoon with polite interest while most of them simply turned and continued their conversations as if he was of no interest at all. A few of the relatively younger mages gave him sullen glares, and two in particular standing slightly away from the others actually sniffed out loud in disdain, before turning and exiting through a door further down the large hall. Some older mages, still deep in what appeared to be fairly heated conversation, turned and followed them leaving Darjoon alone with but a handful of the Circle mages. One of these strolled over to him nonchalantly with a smile on his face.

"Well, hello there, young raven. I gather you must be this 'Darjoon' person everyone is talking about. You're certainly young enough, although I must say, you don't look particularly raven-born to me, eh? A bit on the hefty side for one of us, aren't you?", the mage was inspecting Darjoon by walking around him as if he were a bront being sold at auction.

"Never mind, and don't get me wrong, I'm all for change you know. I mean this place can become so drearily dull, do you see. In fact I'm amazed some of these old so-and-so's are still breathing anymore, you'd think they'd have left this world and let the Great Raven take them by now. For our sake's, if not their own, eh."

"Actually", he whispered with a conspiratorial wink, "I'm of the opinion that they don't really! If you know what I mean? Breathe, that is!"

Darjoon blinked at him, having no idea what he was talking about.

"Oh, you know. The Dark Arts and all that resurrecting the dead stuff. I think they're already deceased, they just don't want anyone to know. It must be why they smell so bad, don't you think? Haw, haw, haw", the mage chuckled with infectious laughter and poked Darjoon in the ribs.

Not knowing how to respond to this odd individual, Darjoon laughed politely, and then asked a direct question, "So, uh, how long have you been in the Circle?"

The mage stopped laughing immediately and stared at him, outraged, "What do you mean by that question?

Surely you've realised that only the very best of us are able to become Inner Circle mages? That it is restricted to the finest few, those of us with superlative talent! To be exact, people like me. Do you think then that I would stoop so low as to compare how we got here or how long we've been here?"

Darjoon, mortified, tried to placate the mage, "No, no. I mean, yes, obviously, you are and you wouldn't. It's just that... Well, what I meant to say, I mean... I didn't mean to insult you or anything. I'm so sorry."

The mage doubled over in fits of laughter, then slowly recovered, "Haw, haw, haw. Oh, yes, you're a keeper, I can see that. Don't worry, young mage, I'm just having a laugh. I am so, so glad to finally have someone to talk to who isn't obsessed with himself, his power or has an agenda. You won't believe how stuck up these old mages can be. What a delightfully refreshing addition you will make. Now, please, relax, I was just having some fun at your expense. No harm, no foul, eh? Let me formally introduce myself. I am Y'brinth and my nest is your nest, my feathers for your warmth."

The mage bowed with a flourish, touching his forehead while his eyes sparkled mischievously and a smile split his face. Darjoon couldn't help but grin in response, glad that there was someone he could relate to. Suddenly, Y'brinth's smile disappeared and his eyes went cold and calculating as he looked over Darjoon's shoulder. Bowing respectfully to whoever was approaching and walking slowly backwards, he turned and sauntered back to the group of mages he'd been speaking to, who turned and walked down the hall, exiting through the same door the others had used. Darjoon turned warily, alarmed at Y'brinth's reaction, then relaxed as he saw it was the same mage he'd met earlier with S'klaratim, prior to the final tests. The balding, grey-haired mage had a set look on his face as he watched Y'brinth walk off.

"Well, Darjoon, we meet again. Congratulations on

making it through the final tests. My name is T'rusmin. By the way, that's interesting company you've been keeping. But I would be careful, if I were you. There are some things that no trial can prepare you for, and I'm afraid the politics of the Inner Circle is one of them. Tread oh so lightly, young mage. You may be rather powerful and you may have gotten here way before anyone could ever imagine, but this is not a place you want to enter without much preparation, steady foresight and a great deal of caution. Some of the winds blowing through these halls can throw the strongest young bird into the cliff and you should watch your feathers here, young mage."

He smiled at Darjoon, then put his arm around him and laughed as he led him out of the room through the door the other mages had used.

"Ah well, enough of that! Let's not spoil this moment for you. You are about to become quite possibly the youngest mage to ever grace our Circle. You may not realise it, but not one of the great mages who have ever come here have immediately taken, let alone passed the tests on their first attempt. Oho, you look surprised? Let me tell you, some of the mages here have taken them not once, but many times before they could get through. Ah, yes, the initiate's warning. Contrary to what those outside the Inner Circle are led to believe, not all of the mages die, Darjoon. In fact, we'd prefer not to kill off otherwise useful mages if we can help it. Yes, its true that the original tests that brought you to us are designed to weed out those who are truly weak because that is not a luxury we can allow ourselves. But we are not the heartless, inhumane monsters you might think us to be. There is a great deal more to the Circle than just killing off the outcasts from society, or the rejects from the college. They write us off as mere renegades, as mad mages that slaughter the innocent, that we are murderers and thieves, but thats because we want them to. We are none of those things, even though sometimes we allow people like that to be in close proximity to us, to maintain the illusion as it were. And, seeing as how I'm being so honest, it's also to do the occasional job that we would not stoop to. So they have their uses, that's for sure. But they are not allowed in here."

They'd been walking down the hall as they spoke, and now he turned and put his hand on the door handle, before turning to Darjoon solemnly and intoning in a deep, clear baritone voice that carried into the room beyond, "Welcome, Darjoon, to the Council of the Inner Circle."

Flinging open the door, they entered together, T'rusmin still with his arm firmly around Darjoon's shoulders. A long, low table stretched the length of the room with benches on either side. Down the end of the room, at the head of the table was a large, ornate, golden chair topped with a great golden circle, such that it would appear like a halo whenever anyone sat in the chair. Alongside the chair stood Grollak, who was the Centre of the Inner Circle, and the other men and women Darjoon had seen next door now stood behind the benches along the table, looking at him with a mix of smiles, frowns and some outright glares. T'rusmin steered Darjoon to the ornate chair and sat him down, while polite, scattered applause filled the room. There were very few friendly faces, but Y'brinth winked at him with the same large smile on his face as before.

Grollak, taking a seat on the trestle to Darjoon's right, joined the applause briefly, then lifted his goblet and tapped his silver knife against it. The clear, ringing sound slowly stilled the applause and as the muttering died down everyone looked attentively at Grollak as he addressed them.

"Fellow mages of the Inner Circle of True One's. It is my pleasure, as the Centre of the Circle, to introduce a new member. As you know, we are as strong as our weakest link, relying on each other to keep the Circle strong and to forge anew the bonds that we need between us. I ask you, as your Centre, to receive this new mage. He has successfully and competently completed all the final tests and so fulfils our requirements."

The murmuring began again as some mages talked heatedly among themselves and Grollak waited for the sound to fade away before he continued.

"I know that some of you believe him to be too young to be admitted and are worried that he lacks experience. You are concerned that you've not had a chance to get to know him as an initiate, to learn about him and who he truly is. But I must tell you that this young mage is special, and knowing me, you know that I do not say this lightly. He has a destiny that intertwines with our own, and on this basis I have spoken to most of you. To those whom I haven't been able to speak to yet, I here and now publicly apologise, but events have overtaken us and so now here he stands. Please witness that he fulfils what is required of him, and that he now needs your help and guidance to complete his training and further his knowledge and experience. I ask you formally as his sponsor, and if it be in the will of the Great Raven, that you would please admit Darjoon as a new member of our Circle."

Silence reigned for a moment after Grollak's speech, and Darjoon found he was actually holding his breath. He had originally thought it would be a foregone conclusion, that as a result of completing the final tests successfully he would readily gain admittance to the Circle. Now he understood what Grollak had meant earlier about the politics. The time a mage spent as an initiate was obviously intended to allow the mages of the Circle and Inner Circle to get to know them as individuals while they served them. As Darjoon was to find out, it was the duty of an initiate to find and impress a sponsor, someone who was prepared to argue the case for an initiate to not only take the tests, but also be admitted to the Circle. So it wasn't a given that a young mage could just take the tests. Now it was clear that Grollak had bypassed the whole process and what's more, he wasn't asking as just any mage but as the Centre, the nominal, appointed head of the Inner Circle of True One's, albeit without direct power. It now depended on the mage's themselves.

As he looked at the men and women standing round the table he could see some stern, set faces, some glares, and some unreadable neutral looks. He started involuntarily as almost unanimously the mages roared out their agreement. Despite the vocal outburst, above each mage a green globe of light appeared, what could only be an indication of their registered vote as a yes. Only a very few mages further down from Grollak at the end of the table had no globes above their heads. There were no globes of any other colour anywhere to be seen in the hall.

"Very well, your acceptance is noted, as well as the abstentions. However, as there is no disagreement, we can assume the vote to be unanimous. Thank you all!"

Grollak turned to Darjoon with a grim smile of satisfaction on his face and the young man noted a brief look of relief.

"Darjoon, as the Centre of the Inner Circle, I welcome you and draw you in. The bonds we now make, we make forever."

Taking the silver knife he still held in his hand, he grabbed Darjoon's hand and sliced his palm, then sliced his own and clasped Darjoon's hand in his. Darjoon looked him in the eye as Grollak spoke to him.

"By our blood, Darjoon, we join to the Circle. And only by our blood will we ever leave it. Do you, Darjoon, pledge your life to this Circle, only to leave when the Great Raven calls you home?"

The room was hushed, and Darjoon licked his lips nervously before responding in a loud clear voice, surprising even himself.

"I pledge my life to the Circle."

The cheering was inevitable and prolonged, and some of the younger mages, caught up in the moment, banged their hands on the table. Grollak waited a moment, and then raised his own hand to restore order.

"Now we feast", he said, then sat down and smiled as an even greater roar of cheering went up.

He leant over to Darjoon and in a soft, reassuring voice, said to him, "See, Darjoon? Normal raven-born, not mad mages spouting wild electrical fire."

The rest of the evening was a blur, as Grollak plied him with food and alcohol. Various mages came up to the head of the table to congratulate Darjoon and welcome him, but also to take some time and speak to Grollak, some with pointed glances at Darjoon. Somehow, the evening finished and Darjoon staggered off to bed, assisted by S'klaratim for most of the way. As he lay on the bed with the ceiling spinning around him, he wondered at Grollak's parting comment. He'd said something about the adventure only beginning, and that he had a task for him when he was ready. Whatever that task was and from the look on Grollak's face, Darjoon was sure it was not going to be one he would enjoy. The room slowly faded into darkness as Darjoon drifted away.

# 9 MISSION OF MADNESS

Darjoon winced as S'klaratim pulled open the thick, heavy curtains and sunlight flooded into the room. It still amazed him that they were living inside a mountain, with rooms carved out of stone. S'klaratim had told him that the original members of the Circle had discovered a complex of rooms already built into the mountain, and so with a few modifications and some further excavations, had converted it into their living quarters. The sleeping rooms were all higher up, with access to clean air and running water, while the meeting and training rooms were based lower down. Darjoon splashed his face and groaned at the pounding in his temples. He felt nauseous, but when S'klaratim lifted the silver cover on his plate and revealed the hot breakfast underneath, he fell upon it as if he were truly ravenous. S'klaratim sniffed loudly as Darjoon ploughed into the food, "I think I need to have a word with the chef. She needs to take care with the portion sizes she prepares for you. You seem to have a tendency to fill out your robes and we don't really want that to happen."

The second sniff was cut off as Darjoon threw an empty plate at him and he ran out of the room protesting, stopping only briefly to greet the older mage walking in.

"You know you shouldn't treat the initiate's like that, Darjoon. And it's a good thing our crockery is practically unbreakable", Grollak placed the plate back on the table as Darjoon gave him a sheepish grin.

"Are you having a bad morning, young mage? That happens when you enjoy too many of the good things in life, you know", the tall mage took the seat opposite him.

"So, you are now a member of the Circle. This means a great many changes for you! You realise that, don't you? Normally as a new initiate you would spend time here in our sanctuary while you learn from the other initiates and those mages who take an interest in you, or who you were interested in and that would've meant building relationships. This in turn would've taught you the necessary skill of politics, along with other useful knowledge, not least of which is furthering your magical education. But, owing to your unprecedented acceptance, you've not had that opportunity and neither will you get it, I'm afraid."

Darjoon sat quietly, noting the stern look on his new colleague's face and waited for the older mage to continue.

"There is a great deal going on right now and I'm afraid there are many things that I cannot necessarily explain. The Circle has varied interests and takes an active role in quite a bit that happens out there", the mage's hand swept out towards the window.

Darjoon noted idly that the slash inflicted on the mage's palm from last night was gone, obviously healed by magic. Darjoon surreptitiously rubbed his own palm, feeling the scab that had formed there overnight. He placed his hand palm down on his thigh, determined to leave it there so Grollak could not see the untreated wound.

"Our interests lie in political and scientific matters and our goal is to reform our beloved raven-born society by educating them on their true destiny. For too long, we as a people have lived in fear of others, but more importantly, and sadly, in fear of ourselves. The raven-born Council, and through them, the College, has deliberately obstructed the truth by misinforming our people and keeping them controlled like cattle. We intend to change that and free our people from this pointless charade. As a nation, as an entire race, we are now under a number of terrible threats. The Dremrel are far, far worse than you can imagine! Their danger to us is greater than anything the raven-born have ever faced before. Not even the Great War on Sorcerer's Isle nor the emergence of the Dremrel and our nation's pathetic attempts at countering them has been enough to shake our people's confidence in their Council's foolishness, or the incompetence of the so-called College. All the abominations produced by that accursed island of death are symbolised by the glass tomb that is left. Death is what they sowed, and death is what they reaped and we still don't know how or why."

Darjoon perked up at the mention of the Glass Isle, and as innocently as he could, asked Grollak, "Does that form part of our studies, is that what lies within our interests? The Glass Isle, I mean?"

"What?", Grollak recoiled in horror, "No, you foolish mage! By Zukar, no! We have no interest in that place at all. We thank the goddess that it was destroyed, although not before it unleashed the horrors we see around us. The Dremrel are but one of many such abominations that have spawned from that foul place."

"But how did they get here?", Darjoon asked coolly, "These, uh, abominations, how did they arrive from the Glass Isle? Did they come through the portals maybe?"

"Portals, eh? Why would you say that, I wonder? What gave you that idea?", Grollak looked at him sternly for a moment then continued.

"No, we don't know that. In any event, the portals are best left alone and they are not something we encourage our mages to use. We are fortunate to have a few easily accessible working portals but you should stay away from them, Darjoon. Only a very, very few of us have the knowledge and experience to deal with those, and even then, we are extremely careful and have many safeguards in place. I shudder to think where some of those other, uncharted and untested portals might lead. Anyway, that's enough about that."

The mage leaned forward, fixing Darjoon with his piercing gaze, "Our task right now is to remove or mitigate some of the threats I speak of and to that end, I have a mission for you, our new brother."

Darjoon groaned inwardly in frustration. If they expected him to stay away from the portals, then how was he going to learn about them and how they worked? He needed to find the one that would take him into the Glass Isle itself. He paid scant attention as Grollak outlined the mission briefing, then suddenly snapped alert at what the elder mage was saying.

"So this mage wormed his way into our Circle under false pretences. At least that is what we believe. The young man, so full of power and, as it turns out, pride, was able to slip past our perceptions and then learn from us while using the Circle's knowledge for his own ends."

Darjoon stiffened, then gulped loudly in the silence. What had he missed hearing? Grollak looked at him as if he was waiting for a particular comment, but with Darjoon saying nothing the mage simply continued. Darjoon tried to relax and look nonchalant, failing miserably when his elbow slid off the table and then his hand, flailing wildly, knocked over a silver goblet which clanged loudly on the tray.

"Pay attention now, Darjoon. I appreciate that you must still be suffering from last night's celebration, which by the way should teach you in future not to overdo it. But right now I need you to focus. A good mage is always focused!"

Grollak smiled at him in a way that made Darjoon's hair stand on end. He sat up and leant forward, waiting for the man to continue.

"Good! Now, this young renegade finally learned what he wanted and then went off on his own. We have been hunting high and low for him through the Old Lands, only to discover that he cleverly set up shop right here in our own back yard. There is a cave system similar to this one further up in the Darken Hills. We've had it under observation for a while now and have noticed many Dremrel flying in and out, heard the most strange sounds and even noticed peculiar smells, and we have learned that this mage never leaves the caves. People, likely traders, will occasionally stop by and leave him what we believe are food and other supplies inside the cave and they probably act as messengers too, but he seems never to leave, making it difficult for us to get at him. Now you, along with the two senior mages who will accompany you, will pretend to be more of these traders and so enter the cave system as they do. You will then try to infiltrate deeper inside and learn what is really going on in there."

The mage took a deep breath as Darjoon listened incredulously. This was no simple mission, and he was reeling at the information being presented to him. A renegade young mage dealing with Dremrel? It sounded completely far-fetched. He listened avidly as the older mage continued talking after taking a sip of water.

"Now, Darjoon, under no circumstances are you to engage with anyone in there, do you understand? Stealth is the key here and we don't want to let him know that we are watching him. So find out what is inside, and then get out. I believe for you it should be straightforward, although after your little episode with the goblet, I'm wondering if you're even the right person for this?", again, that little smile that never seemed to reach his eyes.

"What? No, of course I am", Darjoon replied, indignant, "I'm just a little tired this morning, and it's been a rough few days, but I'm definitely ready."

"Well, if you're sure. I mean, if you need rest or

anything..."

"No, no, I'm ready now, I promise you. I'm more than capable of scouting out some caves."

"Yes, Darjoon, I appreciate that but don't underestimate this task. The mage in question is very powerful, probably as powerful as you are but with a lot more experience. I wouldn't ordinarily send someone as inexperienced as you, however you will be backed up by some of our finest battle mages. They are there as a precaution and I don't expect you to need them if you do this right. With your prodigious shielding abilities, you should be able to slip in and out without being detected. And that is the goal! Do you understand?"

"Yes, Grollak, I understand", the eagerness in Darjoon's voice was palpable.

"Good! Now I recommend you take time this morning just to recover from last night, as you will be moving out in the late afternoon, just before dusk. The Dremrel should be more active later in the day, so it'll be an opportunity to see what's really going on in there. Then you will come back here and report on what you've found. I'll be waiting for you. Oh, and Darjoon, don't try anything ambitious, do you understand? Just in and out and you're done!"

Darjoon nodded, muttering under his breath, then closed his mouth as Grollak's brow lowered and he glared at him. Suddenly, the smile came out again, like lightning striking from a thunder cloud. Darjoon felt the hair on the back of his head lift again, and he sat and watched quietly as the older mage left the room. No sooner had he gone than S'klaratim came bursting in the door in an excited rush.

"Well, I couldn't hear a word of what you were saying. Were you shielding that conversation? Because even with magic, I got nothing at all. Has he given you a mission already? He has, hasn't he? It's just not fair, I tell you, I mean I've been here for years now!"

Darjoon stared as the young mage alternated between grinning and frowning. He was beginning to suspect that there was not an altogether stable mind behind that noble face. And had Grollak truly been shielding them? Darjoon hadn't detected any use of magic if he had, which made him wonder just how powerful the older mage really was? He was pretty sure that he wouldn't be the "Centre" if he wasn't very powerful.

Darjoon hustled S'klaratim out, avoiding the incessant questions the young man had about the mission, then lay down gratefully to recover his strength. Thankfully, the breakfast had helped him settle his stomach from the night before. As he drifted away and the darkness folded around him, he thought he heard a faint voice in his head, as if from very far away. It sounded like it was calling his name, something like, "Darjoon, Darjoon! Where on earth are you now? Why can't I see you clearly anymore?"

The voice faded as he doze off and then seemed to come back all too quickly.

"Darjoon! Darjoon, it's time. You need to get up now. Gods, you really can sleep through anything, I've been banging on the door for ages, and then shaking you. What happens in your dreams, they seem so interesting? You were calling out again. Where are you going now? Is it somewhere exciting? Can I come with you? Tell me I can come with you, I won't get in the way, you know."

Darjoon stared bleary-eyed at the excitable S'klaratim. He stood up wearily and staggered over to the wash basin the young mage had laid out for him. Splashing his face, he felt much better and finished his ablutions, ignoring the chattering mage until the questions just became too insistent.

"No, no, S'klaratim, I'm afraid not this time. It's a stealth mission, and I need to be alone, I really do. Oh, look, don't be so upset, there'll be others where we can go together, I'm sure of it. Come on now, cheer up."

The young mage glared sullenly at Darjoon, his

previous sunny disposition suddenly fading away and replaced by a chilly distance. Smoothing out Darjoon's robe with the silver Circle, he ostentatiously placed it on the bed and then drifted woefully out of the room. Darjoon shook his head and finished dressing, then made his way to the hall. Two stern looking mages were waiting impatiently, obviously agitated.

"Finally! You're late, you know", the taller of the two loomed over him, "We need to get going now. Follow me!"

The mages led him out the hall without further conversation, down a corridor and then rapidly down a long flight of steps. Opening a seemingly invisible door using magic they all emerged onto a path leading up towards the looming Darken Hills. The air was crisp and cold, with the sun slowly sinking behind the Hills in front of them and casting long, spooky shadows.

"Gods, look at that sun, we'll need to hurry. Come along, young mage, we don't want to keep your, uh, great destiny waiting", the two mages chuckled together.

Darjoon glared at them as he followed behind. This was some more of those delightful "politics" that Grollak had warned him about. As far as Darjoon was concerned, it was just more of the same. More of the nonsense he'd experienced at the College. Give someone a little bit of power, and they thought they ruled the world. The truth was that people who thought they did, never ended up ruling anything least of all themselves. Those who were truly meant to rule always knew they would, although often they didn't want to. These mages knew they would never be the Centre, or even that influential in the Inner Circle but they couldn't be sure about Darjoon. Maybe he would be, and that's what they didn't like. In Darjoon's experience, people never liked others being better than them and were always prepared to cut someone down to size before they could grow past them. He sighed involuntarily and shivered at the cold.

"Oh, don't worry, young mage, it's not really so scary. Well, actually that's not really true at all, but hey, we're here to 'protect' you. What could go wrong", again the chuckling, conspiratorial laughter.

Darjoon realised these two would be as useful as a wet blanket on a cold winters night. He also realised that they weren't along for protection, as much as to keep an eye on him. What was it that Grollak had said last night, "We work well as a community because we don't trust each other, Darjoon, not because we do". Well, that was becoming obvious to him. He followed after the two mages in front, wondering how he would ever get the knowledge that he needed about those blasted portals.

They'd been travelling for some time and the sun was now just a sliver between the ridges of the Hills ahead, when finally they slowed down and turned into a narrow defile to the right. The mages in front paused, listening with their ears and their magic. Darjoon could sense their magic, typically raven-born and not particularly strong. He stopped himself from doing the same thing, not wanting to reveal his alien magical heritage just yet.

"Alright young mage, this is how it's going to work. We've been here before, and so we know that this is the entrance the traders would normally use. Of course, we are now playing the part of traders, so as not to arouse suspicion. Here, throw these over your robe!"

The mage threw him a blood-spattered tunic and apron, with fur boots and fur-lined gloves. The clothing was rank and felt damp and unpleasant.

"Oh, don't worry, young mage. You'll soon get used to the smell. I'm afraid the, uh, previous owners were not big on hygiene. That, and the fact that the owner of the one I gave you urinated all over it in fright when I jumped him. Do you remember that, Ragmirt? Ha, ha, ha, oh, I scared him alright!"

Darjoon realised he could now recognise the smell, given its origins. He gritted his teeth silently and ignored the idiot mages, then followed after them once they were all ready. Entering a small cave, they walked to a dark hole in the back and spoke a few words of magic, pulling open the rusty metal door that suddenly appeared in the rock. It squealed and grated as it opened, causing Darjoon to flinch.

"Oh please, it's just a door, young one. Nothing to be frightened of. The traders always make such a noise, so we must too. Now, we're going to go to the usual room off the great hall as it contains the supply chest, and then while we remain there all warm and snug, and safe, of course, you can go exploring. Apparently you're like a little rat that can scurry about undetected. So you go do your scurrying and then when you've discovered something important and useful, you come back and we all leave together. Simple, isn't it? Hopefully that's not too hard for you? Oh, and if you don't find anything important and useful, well, if I were you I wouldn't bother coming back. Now we will wait for an hour, and then leave, no matter what. So don't be late, don't mess this up, and whatever you do, don't get caught. I really don't feel like risking my exceedingly precious neck for your pathetically worthless hide. So hurry back, won't you!"

The mages walked off chuckling to themselves. Darjoon waited until they had disappeared around the corner of the tunnel, then cloaked himself in a shield spell. He wasn't too afraid of getting caught, knowing that his magic was strong and alien, and shield spells actually were a strength of his. He turned and went in the opposite direction, cautiously rounding a corner and continuing down the tunnel. Some sort of moss or fungus was growing on the walls and provided an eerie blue light. Sensing a draught, he saw a short corridor off to the right which he slowly walked down, coming to a stop outside four doors set at even intervals down the tunnel. There were three on one side and one directly opposite the middle door. He fumed inside, realising those other mages were pretty useless. He had hoped they would at least create a diversion or distraction of some kind so that he could scuttle about without being disturbed. He crouched down and shuffled over to one of the doors. The air coming from it smelt faintly of chemicals and there was no light or sound emerging. He shuffled over to the second door. Ah, that was better, he could hear someone moving behind the door, and could also sense some magic going on. This was more promising. Smelling the air, he gagged suddenly as the rich, sweet stink of death and blood wafted out of the door opposite. The faintest of breezes in the corridor thankfully helped the pungent odour drift away. He could sense that the door he was next to had some strange locking spell on it. Slowly, he reached out a tendril of magic, trying to sense the spell that had it shut. He froze as a loud and distinctive click announced the door had been unlocked. He realised belatedly that without him even trying his magic had unlocked it.

He jumped as a piercing shriek came from the direction of the two mages, followed by what sounded like muffled shouts and blasts of fire. Cursing, he could sense combat magic being unleashed. They were either in trouble or maybe he'd been wrong about them after all, perhaps they had always intended to create a diversion. A second scream of anguish ripped through the air and he belatedly realised the noises behind the door had stopped. Before he could move, the door opened and a mage in a Circle robe walked out and bashed into him, kicking him hard in the side as he fell over him. Darjoon rolled and backed away but the mage had already cast out a staff and in an instant Darjoon's invisibility shield was shredded.

Thrusting out his hands, Darjoon barely had time to throw up a blocking shield before a blast of fire beat at him. In a second, the fire changed into spikes of ice that shattered the wall around his head, the splinters pinging off his robe from behind. Panicked, he ducked even lower as he felt a few splinters sting his ears. At that moment a faint but urgent whisper inside his head snapped him alert.

"Idiot! Have you already forgotten all the combat spells you were taught, you silly boy. You're a raven-born mage, Darjoon, for Zukar's sake, behave like one!"

Darjoon ignored it and extended his shield outwards and to the sides, putting an end to the barrage of ice spikes, and as they stopped, he dropped the shield and aimed a blast of fire at the staff the mage was holding. The fire initially emerged from his hand as a ball of orange flames, but as it neared the mage it turned a sickly green and expanded. The mage screamed in pain as the staff he was holding became a searingly bright green colour, then exploded in his hands. Dazed, the man staggered back striking his head on the wall and immediately Darjoon snapped a strong shield around him. The fallen mage didn't even fight back, simply slumping to the floor inside the shield. Darjoon watched him carefully for a moment, then released the shield spell and approached him tentatively. The laboured, rasping breathing and ashen face with bloody trail sliding down the chin told its own story. Darjoon stared down in awe at the broken shaft now firmly embedded in the mage's chest. The man looked up at Darjoon, then grinned weakly at him.

"Huuuh, lucky, huuuh, shot, eh? What kind of, huuuh, creature are you? You, huuh, don't look like those, huuuh, those evil bat things."

Darjoon stared grimly at the mage in silence, then realised the futility of not talking to him. There was still so much to learn.

"I am Darjoon, a raven-born, even if I don't look like it. I am from the Circle of True One's, and I was sent to investigate this place. Why were you behind a locked door? What was that smell and what were you experimenting with?"

The mage chuckled briefly, then coughed and spat out blood on the floor.

"Experimenting? Me? Oh no, Darjoon, I'm afraid

you've been misled. I am not experimenting at all. In fact, I am the experiment here. You, like those other fools out there, all think that these things, these evil, wicked creations, these Dremrel, are just stupid, wild, beast-like creatures of magic, don't you? But you are so wrong, and they are so much more, Darjoon, so much more. I was investigating them too, once, because I was determined to show the Circle and that arrogant Centre that I was right after all, that they are intelligent and cunning and more than a match for us. But little did I realise just how successful I would become, you see. Oh, I found them alright, and I overheard their plans, I saw with my own eyes their true intelligence, but before I could escape with that vital knowledge they caught me and locked me up here."

The coughing started again and it was some time before the man could take a breath. Darjoon had been probing the wound while the mage was talking, but knew that even his prodigious skill couldn't repair the damage inside in time. The blood was pumping out faster than he could stop it, and only his and the mage's own dwindling magic was now keeping him alive.

"So I have been here ever since, occasionally fed and cleaned but otherwise treated like some farm animal in an enclosure. I wasn't even of interest to them and I could never understand why they kept me alive. But I could hear screams and sounds of torture from the other cells, and so I was left to wonder when it would be my turn. So cruel, so cunning, if only we'd known. Huuuh! Too late, Darjoon, it's too late now."

Darjoon had sat down while the mage was talking and now he tenderly lifted the mage's head onto his lap and wiped away the blood still trickling from the man's mouth.

"So you never betrayed the Circle", Darjoon whispered as the mage's eyes closed. They snapped open at his words, a strange light inside them.

"Betrayed them? Who me? No, Darjoon, I was

simply doing my job. Listen, you don't just do what they tell you to in that place, do you understand? That is not the Circle way and it never has been. Oh, it may seem like people follow orders, but I can tell you that Grollak did not get to become the Centre by doing what he was told. Just look around you, Darjoon. This is a Dremrel fortress, with provisions and stores, with weapons even, and these are prison cells. They extract information from people they keep here because they are plotting against us, trying to understand us and especially our weaknesses. They are gathering intelligence, don't you see? Then, when the time is right, they will strike in fearsome numbers and with magical weapons we've never even seen before. Some of the weapons are, well, they, they contain or are the souls of the people they entrap. These, these abominations are somehow placed inside the weapons or made from them. It's so wrong, it's... This cannot be allowed to continue, Darjoon. Some of our own people are already trapped in these things and now they are not able to fly on the Great Raven back to the Source, to float on the River of Life and begin again. It is so wrong, Darjoon, so... huuuuh uh. Uuuuh..."

The head fell limply to the side and Darjoon sat in the blue twilight of the tunnel cradling the dead mage, thinking furiously about what he had said. The implications were absolutely staggering. He knew, of course, that the Dremrel were clever and cunning, but possessing real intelligence? This human-like behaviour he'd just described didn't seem possible. Not for these filthy, grotesque creatures that ate human flesh and devoured souls. But then, to them, what was the difference between a human and a bront? And didn't humans eat bront as well? So why not? Why shouldn't humans just be like bront's for someone else?"

Suddenly, the head he was cradling twitched and then the mouth opened and it began to talk to him in a strange, sibilant voice, jerking and twitching as it spoke.

"Huumaaaan! What isss wrong with you? You do not ssssssmell like the othersssssss? You ssssmell like usssss. Why isss that, I wonder?"

Darjoon gasped, throwing the head off his lap onto the floor with a sickening thud and standing up to get away. The body that had been lying there so peacefully and still a moment before, now jerked and twitched and then stood up as if it was a badly controlled marionette. All the limbs were jerking and twitching, and the head lolled to one side as the mouth worked around the bulging blue tongue, bloody drool seeping out. One of the eyes was open and stared at him blindly, but the other remained swollen and shut.

"I can ssseee you, huuumaaan. You look like your kind, but you don't ssssmellll like them. Why issss that?"

Darjoon licked his dry lips and answered in a slightly high-pitched voice, the fear radiating inside him.

"What? What do you mean? Who are you? What are you doing inside this body?"

"Insssside? I am not inssside, you ssssilly maaage. Thissss worthlessss hussssk, it issss not fit to hold one like me. Now, you ssshould sssssave yoursssself, maaaage. Flee into the room behind you and I will ssssspare your life. We haaaave much to learn from eeeeach other, you and I. Much that you cannot now undersssstand! Now go into the room! Perhapssss, if you are usssseful, you may have a plaaaace in the coming revolution."

Darjoon stared in horror at the corpse in front of him. Without lifting his hands, the orange-green fire flashed from him and burst into existence around the mage's body, swiftly consuming it. A soft thud made him look down and he scooped up a strange amulet nestling in the ash. As he stood trembling in the corridor, trying to make out the carvings in the soft light, a long, guttural scream echoed in the tunnels, and he started running back the way he'd come, every swish of his robe sounding like rushing wings above him.

Darjoon stopped near the entrance door of the tunnel they'd entered earlier and crouched down. Nothing and no-one had followed him and he listened carefully to what was happening ahead of him further ahead around the tunnel corner. Screams and flashes of mage-fire could still be heard coming from the direction of the two mages and grunting, he stood up and started running towards them. Turning the corner he saw that smoke and flames filled a great hall, and he saw the two mages pinned down behind a large, upturned wooden table in front of a small room to the side. One of them looked injured, favouring his left arm, and they were staring wildly at six large Dremrel on the other side of the room. Darjoon sucked in a breath over his teeth. Two full-grown covens in a confined space. Oh joy! He could see that while one coven had pinned the mages down, the other was slowly working its way around the side of the hall, intent on flanking them.

None of the actors in the drama unfolding before him knew he was there yet, so drawing a shield around him he strode confidently into the middle of the hall and waited. The second coven had just got themselves into position in front of a large bookcase and suddenly stood up, intent on wiping out the two mages that were now exposed to them. Darjoon didn't hesitate, sweeping out the shield from around him, he locked it on the massive bookcase and pulled it forwards and towards him. The Dremrel, shrieking as they saw him suddenly revealed were first pelted by large books, and then buried by the bookcase as it slammed down on top of them. Darjoon sent out that strange green fire again, setting the books on fire and ignoring the screams of the trapped Dremrel.

The other coven, now fully aware of him, started throwing firebolts his way. The mages were shouting at him to get undercover as the impressive firebolts sizzled past him, but he suddenly started sprinting straight at the Dremrel, whose firebolts stopped as they stared at him in surprise. It gave him just enough time to fling an ice spike straight up at the base of the large, ornate and wickedly spiked chandelier above them. One of the Dremrel managed to roll out the way as it fell down, but two of them were shredded by the metal spikes that ripped into them. The other Dremrel shrieked in agony at the death of its mates, it's head pulled back in pain and its mouth open, and then it shrieked again as one of the other mages, emerging from behind the blackened table, sent a bolt of fire straight into its gaping maw. Darjoon added another burst of flame just to be sure and then rushed over to help the mage lift up his friend.

"Wait", Darjoon cautioned as he eyed up the two mages, "We won't get far with you in this condition. You're no better than your friend. Put him down again. Yes, yes, I know, we have to get out of here, but haste makes waste, my grandpa always used to say. Now hold still, this won't take long. We can finish it properly when we get back."

The mage stared at Darjoon as he swiftly applied some healing magic to both of them.

"I... You... How? How did you do all that, and yet still have enough magic to heal us like this? What... Who are you? Your fire magic! It was... It... There was green in it! What kind of magic is that? I mean, I could sense the raven-born magic, but the other, that was so strange", the mage looked up at Darjoon, who ignored him as he finished healing his friend.

The mage shook his head then offered Darjoon his hand and clasped his arm in that traditional raven-born salute of respect.

"It doesn't matter! I'm just glad you're on our side, Darjoon. You are one amazing mage. Now I understand why Grollak had you take the final tests so early. We need more like you in the Circle. My name is Dotrak, and that one staring at you is Ragmirt. We are indebted to you for our lives. Our magic had already started failing when you arrived, and, well, that second coven would've fried us from the side. So thank you, Darjoon. Anywhere your flight takes you, my feathers are yours and my nest is always open."

"And mine", Ragmirt chimed in, somewhat recovered after Darjoon's hasty healing and staring at him in awe.

"Yes, well, thank you", Darjoon gruffly responded, "It was nothing, really, I guess I got lucky."

"Bah! Now then, Darjoon, false modesty won't be understood by, well, pretty much any raven in the entire Circle. It's not like we're competitive or anything, is it", Dotrak chuckled quietly.

"Alright, listen both of you, if it's all the same, the smell in here from those burning Dremrel is making me sick. Can we get out of here before any more covens turn up?", Ragmirt was already heading for the door, talking over his shoulder to the two of them as he left.

They quickly followed him out the door and then cautiously back the way they came, slowly and silently making their way back to the "Eyrie", the Circle headquarters. Darjoon was walking behind them and flexed his hand which was feeling a little tight. Looking down in surprise at the slight pain, he saw the slash on his hand from the initiation ceremony. He'd completely forgotten to heal it, and as he walked he called up his magic, then paused. Perhaps it was just as well, the scar could serve as a reminder that even though he was a member of the Circle and they were his people, his destiny was far greater than what they had in mind for him. Much, much greater, he was now doubly sure of that. He desperately needed to get to a portal, specifically, a portal that could take him inside the Glass Isle. But how? He was still thinking it through as well as preparing for the inevitable debriefing when they arrived at the Eyrie and slipped inside. Without delay they headed for the room he'd been in prior to his ceremony and found Grollak sitting and waiting for them. A young initiate was dispatched to call certain mages and the debriefing began as they grilled Darjoon and the two mages with him.

"Yes, I know, I realise that it's a lot to take in, and that it sounds far-fetched. But isn't that why you sent me in the first place? Because I was more likely to not have preconceived ideas about the alleged 'mad mage'. Now I'm telling you that he was not trying to create an army of Dremrel to attack us, in fact he was trying to find out what they were up to when he himself was caught and imprisoned", Darjoon sighed in exasperation.

The others just stared at him, much as they'd been doing for the last hour. Grollak had been questioning him relentlessly, trying to extract every detail of what had happened. The other two mages were no help, as once they'd infiltrated the fortress, they'd moved to the store-room only to get attacked by a coven in the great hall. Shortly before Darjoon had arrived, a second coven had begun to flank them. They had not been privy to Darjoon's conversation with the dying mage and were equally stunned by his revelations.

"But, Darjoon, wait a minute! I am not saying you are lying, but I am questioning what you have been told, what that dying mage said to you. Does it even make sense? These Dremrel, these cruel, evil, distorted abominations, can you believe that they are intelligent, like us? They may display some vague signs that they could be sentient beings, but how can you expect us to believe they are nothing more than the wretched animals they kill and eat. Even their so-called torture is just part of their survival instinct, simply a way to use their unfortunate development of magical ability, but it's nothing more than that."

Darjoon shook his head and tried again, "Grollak, uh, Centre, we only think they are animals because we've never understood them, we've never really taken the time to analyse them in detail but just killed them whenever possible. I'm thinking that they are just like the Y'shtim. You know, those truktari-like beings that live in the snow, but walk on their hind legs and speak? The one's on the other side of the portal... Oh..."

Grollak stopped dead as he'd been pacing up and down and now he turned towards Darjoon, his face paling and then flushing with sudden heat. He suddenly and dramatically turned to the other mages and waved his arms menacingly in the air.

"Out! Out! Get out! Everybody leave right now, I need to be alone with Darjoon. Get out all of you!"

The mages practically fell over each other as they scattered out of the room. Darjoon stared at Grollak and could see that the senior mage was breathing heavily and was visibly trying to control his anger. The air felt heavy, oppressive, electric even and Darjoon slowed his breathing, ready for whatever might happen next. Like a fool he'd given away his knowledge again. Had this jeopardised everything he was trying to achieve?

"Darjoon. I... You... I need you to tell me just exactly what you know of the Y'shtim, and how you came to know about them? Every! Single! Detail! Understood?"

Darjoon exhaled softly, realising he'd been holding his breath while Grollak spoke. "Books, you fool! You read books", the voice in his head whispered urgently.

"Uh, actually it's quite simple, Grollak. When I was at the college, I used to, well it wasn't right, I know, but I would sneak books out of the library. Not just any books, mind you, these were the forbidden books from the shelves at the back, the one's the College kept locked away from us mere students. In one of them it clearly described a people that looked a lot like my gran's truktari, although they stood on their hind legs and could speak and think. They lived in a land called, um, let me think, oh yes, Fr'bazim, I think it was called. Apparently, this is a land you can only get to via a portal, and there were some vague references to wolves or creatures like that. I don't remember all of it really, only I was reminded of it just now. Because they were also animals that could think, you know, just like the Dremrel seem to do."

Grollak visibly relaxed, then snorted and chuckled while his eyes stayed fixed on the young mage.

"Darjoon, you are a constant surprise. I knew you were ready, I suppose I just did not realise how ready. We have some of those same books here, and depending on the Circle member, we may let them read the books. Not all of our members are privileged enough, so I would strongly suggest you don't mention this to anyone else, or, for that matter, any other knowledge you may have gleaned from your, uh, illicit reading. Is that quite clear? Some of these mages are not ready to be trusted with information like that. You understand, don't you?"

Darjoon realised that the mage was not really making a suggestion but rather giving a command.

"Of course, Grollak! I will certainly keep it all to myself. Please, I apologise if I have offended you in any way."

"No, no, not at all, think nothing of it, young mage. You have actually made rather a valid point, now that I think about it. It seems we have seriously underestimated these grotesque creatures. It will take some time to think of them as another tribe, or race, or similar, if that's what they really are, but I think we need to redouble our efforts to understand them and we will certainly do that. It would seem they are planning something big, something we must find out more about if we are to survive. Well done, Darjoon! This has been extremely valuable, and a learning curve for all of us. I think those two young mages will not easily forget you or what you did for us, and nor will I. Now then, if you will excuse me, I need time to think about this in some depth and I suggest you go and recover from your mission. I imagine you'll need to."

Darjoon knew this was again not actually a suggestion and politely took his leave. Once outside the door, he sagged against the wall of the corridor and bent forward, sucking in air. For a moment he'd thought it was all over in there, that he'd ruined everything. Grollak's reaction had been extreme, and as he made his way back to this room, he wondered why talk of the Y'shtim and the land called Fr'bazim should have caused it. Opening the door to his room, he looked up in surprise as he realised he was not alone and three mages stood or sat in his small bedroom. S'klaratim greeted him with a surly nod as he made to leave, and whispered as he passed, "Interesting company you're keeping nowadays. I'd be careful of these two if I were you."

Darjoon simply nodded at him in quiet understanding and then turned and smiled at Dotrak and Ragmirt who were lounging on the chairs. He sat on the bed as Dotrak grinned at him and spoke up.

"Hey Darjoon, this is a nice room you've got. You know that most of the rest of us have to share, right? In fact, not many of the senior mages even have rooms like this one, let alone a brand new Circle member. I guess it's all about who you know, eh?"

"Oh leave him be, Dotrak", the other mage laughed good-naturedly, "He didn't assign the room to himself, now did he? Grollak probably didn't want him corrupted by your foul stench. Perhaps if you lay off the prokilma berries, you wouldn't stink so much. My bad luck is that I get to sleep above you, and it's true what they say that hot air always rises and you are so full of it."

The two mages laughed easily between themselves, and Darjoon joined in. Dotrak lounged back in his chair, glanced at Ragmirt briefly and then addressed Darjoon, "So, what did our almighty Centre want with you? He seemed pretty worked up. Did you get a tongue-lashing? And what's with those people you referred to, the, uh, what was it, oh, the Y'shtim? I've never heard that name before? Who or what are they?"

"Uh, yes, well, no, you see it was actually the name of a friend of mine, and some silly tale he told me. Silly me, I got my wires crossed", Darjoon was thinking furiously now, "It was someone I knew before, back at the college, and to be honest he was a real mischief. Not a friend exactly. But it was just a misunderstanding because Grollak thought I was talking about someone else."

"Really? Oh well, whatever, it's not often we've seen him so worked up though", Dotrak chuckled, "We quite enjoyed it in a scary sort of way. Perhaps you should think up other names to do it again."

"Are you crazy, Dot? I think next time Grollak won't just send us from the room, he'll 'expel' us permanently, like he did to that... Ow! What? What did you do that for?"

Ragmirt pulled his leg back out of range and rubbed it, moaning at no-one in particular, "Well everyone knows about that stupid mage and how he tested Grollak's patience until he got tired of him. It's hardly a big secret, is it?"

"So, Darjoon", Dotrak glared at Ragmirt and ignored his question, "you said that this so-called non-friend of yours was on the other side of a portal. Most interesting. Have you been through many portals?"

Darjoon squirmed inside. This was not a conversation he wanted to have and he didn't like the direction it was taking, although he was interested in any information he could find out. He would have to be very careful.

"Uh no, not really, like I said, I just got my wires crossed. I think this friend told me something about portals, so, yes, that's why I got confused. I mean, I wish I had been through one, but no, I don't know much."

"Okay, okay. No problem. It's just that Ragmirt here, and his dim-wit initiate brother, S'klaratim, both have a bee in their bonnet about portals. It's one of the reasons they got booted out of the College, for stealing books they shouldn't have on that very subject. They got caught reading one and so that was it, out the next day and banished to the Darken Hills. The two of them ran into a coven of Dremrel, and were rescued by none other than Grollak himself and another mage from the Inner Circle.

S'klaratim was pretty beat up afterwards, but he seems to have recovered. Well, as far as we can tell anyway, it's not like he's ever really been normal, has he?"

"Woah, easy there Dot, that's my brother you're talking about, you know. But it's true enough, I don't think he's been the same since the attack. I mean, he was always a bit highly-strung, but he seemed to get a lot worse after our encounter. I think it's why they won't let him take the tests, and of course the fact they let me and I made it through really got to him. But if he comes across a bit odd, he's actually really smart. He's got those portals figured out, let me tell you that. He knows exactly where they all go to as well, I mean... Oww! What's your problem now, Dot", Ragmirt rubbed his ankle and glared at the mage, then his eyes widened, "Oh, yes, that's right. I'm not supposed to say anything about that. Me and my big mouth!"

"Oh, ignore him, Darjoon. He's a powerful mage but he has a rather tiny brain. It's true though, S'klaratim might only be an initiate but he's one smart youngster. If you're interested in portals, he's definitely the one you want to talk to. Anyway, we need to be somewhere, so let me take my loud-mouthed friend here and see if I can teach him what discretion means. C'mon Rag, let's get you home to mummy, you stupid youngling. I know children that keep better secrets than you."

The pair of mages could be heard arguing all the way down the hall, even through Darjoon's closed door. He smiled briefly, then lay down, feeling tired. As he dozed off, he wondered what S'klaratim knew and how he could get the initiate to tell him. His dreams were filled with corridors and closed doors that opened as he got there, but slammed shut just before he could step inside. A hollow, mocking laughter filled his dream, and every now and then a winged shape would flit past, as if flying over-head. Finally, he made it through a door, only to come face to face with a Dremrel that reached out for him, and as the fangs and nauseating, rotten breath opened to swallow him, he heard the laughter again and then a blast of cold that froze his head.

"Does he always scream like that before he wakes up? He sounds like a girl. What's wrong with him, he looks like he's been running through a fire? Hey, Darjoon! Wake up, for Zukar sake. I don't know which is worse, the snoring or the screaming. Come on, Dot, pour some more water on him."

"Okay, okay you two. You realise we're not at the college anymore, right? You, Rag, you're a mage of the Circle, for Zukar's sake. And Dot, give me that jug. How will he wash himself if you've emptied it all on his head? Idiots. Get out of here", S'klaratim grabbed the jug from Dotrak and chased them out the room.

"I told you, Darjoon, those two are nothing but trouble. Now I'm going to have to change all the sheets on your bed. Do you know how uppity they get in the wash room if you wash the sheets too often", S'klaratim bustled around as Darjoon sat up groggily, water running down his face.

"Listen, you need to shave, it's not as if we're all savages here, we're actually raven-born, in case you hadn't noticed. Well, would you look at that, even your stubble is different! What is it with you, anyway", the young mage chattered away at Darjoon who slumped down at the table and tucked into his breakfast. He grudgingly looked up later as S'klaratim came in with new bed sheets.

"So, your brother and his friend mentioned you might know a little something about portals", he asked without preamble.

The mage gasped, fumbled a pillow onto the floor, then picked it up and sat down on the bed, looking intently at Darjoon.

"Alright, I'll bite, I might know something. Why do you ask?"

"Well, it's just a subject that has always fascinated me.

I mean, can you imagine the places they might lead to. I realise of course no-one could possibly know where they go, but isn't that what makes it even more exciting? To step through not knowing where you'll end up?"

"What? What makes you think no-one knows where they go? That's just stupid! Of course they know where they go. Who would enter a portal without knowing where they might end up? Oh, wait, I see! You mean the one that brought you to the Circle. Well, yes, technically the mages don't know exactly where that will go, but, well, I mean you knew it was taking you to meet the Circle, didn't you? No, that one's a little different."

"Different? So, how do the other portals work, S'klaratim? I mean is there like a map or something", Darjoon tried to look nonchalant, but his pulse was racing.

"Of course there's... Hang on a second. You want to go somewhere, don't you? I see now. Well, what if I could tell you where the portals are, and even where they go to? What if I told you that there was actually a map? What would that be worth to you and what do I get out of this?", S'klaratim folded his arms and looked defiantly at Darjoon.

"Hmm, yes, I see what you mean, I can appreciate that. Well, of course I'd have to be sure that such a thing exists first. I mean, it just sounds too fantastic for words", Darjoon threw his hands up in the air.

"Of course it exists, you idiot. I'm telling you it does, aren't I? I can even show it to you right now, I... But before I do, before I show you, Darjoon, what do I get out of this?"

"Well, what is it you want", Darjoon was in no mood to play games.

"I want you to recommend me for the tests! Every initiate needs a full Member to do that."

"But what about your brother? Why can't Ragmirt put you forward?"

"Rag? Don't be stupid. He can't do it precisely

because he is my brother. Duh! They don't let families recommend each other. And Dot, well, he's just an idiot, even if he is my brother's friend. I've asked him again and again and he just won't do it. Says I'll make him look bad when I get killed or something like that. But I won't, Darjoon, I promise you I won't. I'll make it and then we can be mages together, and I can help you. Although I'll be more powerful than you, but its okay, I won't boss you around or anything. Even when I'm the Centre, I won't do that. You've been good to me", he looked up at Darjoon, pleadingly, "So, will you do it?"

Darjoon paused. Yes, he wanted the map, but Dot was right. S'klaratim would probably get killed during the tests and then it would be on his head. But a map. Of all the portals! That was priceless, wasn't it? Surely it was worth one stupid young mage's life? He looked at the odd mage sitting opposite him. He was bound to die one day anyway, so what if it was at least trying to do what he always wanted to do? That would certainly be better than being Darjoon's servant, which is basically what he was. And what if he never got the chance? Would he remain an initiate forever, or just kill himself one day? So it made no difference, did it? He'd be doing the young mage a favour, surely? Actually helping him. And who knows, he might even make it after all. No, no, Darjoon thought, that couldn't be right. Yet he did want it so badly. Darjoon looked across at him as he sat there, almost quivering with expectation.

"Alright, alright, S'klaratim. I'll speak to Grollak and put you forward for the tests. You have my word."

S'klaratim leapt to his feet, wide-eyed, "Oh yes. I knew you would. You're a good man, Darjoon, oh yes, a very good man indeed. I won't let you down, I promise. You'll see, you'll all see. I'll become a really good member of the Circle. Okay, let's go!"

"Wait, what? Right now? You mean it's here, in the Eyrie? The map is right here?"

"Yes, of course, silly mage. What did you think, that we'd have to go on some big adventure somewhere? No, no, this place is full with knowledge. Full to the brim, I'm telling you. You should see the library in this place, I mean it... Alright, alright, another time. Come, come, let's go see the map."

Darjoon looked at the mage's shining eyes, and what he saw did not fill him with any comfort. There was an unnatural, unearthly light in them, a sort of twisted brightness. But to actually get to see a map of all the portals. Surely that was too tempting to resist. He never thought he could get it so quickly. S'klaratim flung open the door, and then quickly bowed his head at the sight of the Centre standing there quietly. Grollak barely looked at the young initiate as he walked into the room and addressed Darjoon.

"You'll need to come with me, we're having a meeting of the Inner Circle to discuss what you've revealed. You need to be there and I need you to be very, very clear on the details. It's time we started to take some serious action against these covens. I fear we've waited too long as it is. What, is that more food on your table? Are you eating again? I told you, be careful of not eating too much. You've already grown bigger than when you arrived, I'm sure of it. Are you exercising like all good raven-born should do? We've got a large exercise hall a few flights down and you should go and make use of it. Maybe this initiate will be of some use as a sparring partner. But not now, come, come, let's not keep the others waiting."

Grollak breezed out of the room and Darjoon glared at him from behind.

"S'klaratim", he hissed in passing, "when I come back, you will take me to see the map."

The young mage nodded forlornly and watched them walk away. As Darjoon entered the meeting hall with Grollak, the mages stood up and applauded them, Grollak quickly stepping to the side and joining in the applause. He stepped back to Darjoon's side and whispered to him, "Word gets around fast. Seems you've become a bit of a hero. No-one has gone up against two covens and survived before. You took on six Dremrel and won, it's remarkable. They will look at you differently from now on."

Once the mages had all settled down, Darjoon repeated to the assembly what he'd told Grollak previously. There were surprised looks all around the table, and then the arguing started. Some seemed to agree and approve of what Darjoon had said, but others vociferously protested, repeating what Grollak had said about the creatures being no better than animals. An elderly mage suddenly banged on the table and stood up, his voice filled with authority and power and whether by magic or some trick of the room, carrying across the table into all corners of the hall and quieting everyone.

"Now listen here! Listen, I say! Some of you have heard the rumours, about a land beyond the portals filled with ice and snow. About a land of strange animals that walk on their back legs like humans and speak in languages that we can understand. Silence! You will hear me!"

The elderly mage waited until he had their full attention, which didn't take long, then continued.

"I tell you now, this is no rumour, but truth. I have been there and have seen it with my own eyes. Furthermore, I can speak their language", he put his head back and howled like a wolf but in an eerie, guttural way, then suddenly he leant forward, planting both hands on the table and began to miaow like a truktari, then roared, his mouth open wide. Darjoon's mouth fell open and the hair on the back of his neck stood up and from the silent, intent looks around the table he saw that he was not alone in his fear. He jumped suddenly as right next to him, Grollak responded with similar yet different miaows, and then the same roar. The mages heads twisted from side to side as they looked first at the elderly mage, and then at the

Centre in awe.

"Right! Now that I have your attention, and you have heard with your own ears, it should be obvious to you that both the Centre and I, your previous Centre, have been to this land called Fr'bazim. These creatures are people in a way, like us yet not exactly. Is it so hard to imagine then that the Dremrel are just more of the same?"

Only silence greeted his remark and no-one dared so much as fidget under the elder mages withering glare.

"The land called Fr'bazim was known to the people from the Sorcerer's Isle, what we now call the Glass Isle. Meeting its inhabitants, they, those true monsters who lived underground with their infernal machines, they decided to create the abominations that we know as the Dremrel. It was thought that they were simply brute beasts, their lives manipulated into what we see. But now who knows what or, dare I say it, who, the wicked sorcerer's used to create them? Maybe they were people once, people like you and I, at least that seems to be what we have uncovered. But the real question is not what they are, but what we do with them now, and how do we stop them. Young Darjoon has returned with grave information, and neither the Centre nor I have foreseen this. None of us has. Now that we know, we need to do something about it. This is what we should be discussing, not the nature of these things, but their intentions and how we stop them. The time for argument is over, we need a solution and we need it fast. We are running out of time, and so are the raven-born, our people, who we are sworn to protect."

The meeting immediately broke up into seemingly random clumps of people, and Darjoon could tell that they were all discussing different strategies. Each group seemed to have a natural leader who alternated between advising the other members of the group and steering them into a particular path. Grollak and the elderly mage drifted between the groups, and then they came and stood next to

Darjoon, who was standing alone and wondering which group he should join.

"Darjoon", Grollak addressed him, "I'd like you to meet my predecessor, Imrild. He was the Centre before me."

"May the feather of...", Darjoon was shocked as Imrild casually interrupted his formal greeting.

"Yes, yes, I know all that malarkey, young mage. I've spent a large part of my life being formal and polite, and now that I am in my dotage I can gratefully dispense with such nonsense. Now, even though I knew your father well, I'm still quite impressed with you young Darjoon."

Darjoon stared at him in shock. What did he mean, knew his father? He looked between Grollak and Imrild, and then briefly glanced at the doors, wondering how he could escape from this hall. He cursed as he realised he was at the wrong end and there were too many mages in the way. Imrild, noting his discomfort, laughed out loud.

"Now, now, Darjoon. Don't look so shocked. Although bastards are uncommon among our people, they are not unfamiliar to us. On the contrary, we've even had some Centre's who've been of dubious parentage, haven't we, Grollak?", Imrild chuckled as Grollak just shook his head.

"Anyway, I knew Mokdor, your father, long before he became the arrogant mage he is today. Back then he was a, well, shall we say, a student of mine. But when I was expelled, he, like all the rest, was only too quick to turn his back on me. Oh yes, it was all about the code, you see. The great and terrible raven-born code will always come first for Mokdor. After all, why else would he now expel his son, even a bastard son at that?"

Darjoon closed his eyes and breathed an inward sigh of relief. So they thought Mokdor was his father. That made sense. Others had thought that too. Imrild put his hand on Darjoon's shoulder.

"Don't take it too hard, young raven. The burden's

that have been placed on Mokdor as the High Sorcerer are many, and if he is seen to be weak he wouldn't last long. I'm convinced that under the hard shell there is still the idealistic, gentle and considerate young mage that I was fond of so long ago."

"Are you indeed? I wouldn't be so sure of that, Imrild. Now please excuse us. Darjoon, come with me. This is no longer a debate nor is it a planning you should be part of, and I need to talk to you", Grollak took his arm and steered him out of the hall.

"Grollak? Am I to get another assignment? I'm ready for more", Darjoon surprised himself by what he said.

The mage laughed heartily, "By Zukar, no, Darjoon! Although your enthusiasm does you credit. You need to return to your friends in Spidral as they have no doubt been worrying about you. You will serve our purposes better by being on the outside for some time. Come now, don't look so surprised, young mage, a great deal of our work is done out there in the world, not in these musty old caves. The mages you see in this hall are but a small part of the Circle. Oh and Darjoon, if you happen to meet one of us out there, look down at his right hand. If he sees you looking and is one of ours, he will make a circle with his forefinger and thumb. You must do the same and know that he will die for you, as you are expected to do for him."

"Or her", he chuckled, "We are not as gender-biased as you might think. But it works for us that others think so. We will soon be in touch, Darjoon. But come, no delays now! You need to leave today. Your absence will be explained to the others, but they will not know where you are. The less who know, the better in fact."

They'd arrived at Darjoon's room and Grollak saluted Darjoon in the raven-born way, then left him. Darjoon put his hand on the door handle, and then paused. Imrild's mention of Mokdor had reminded him of how quickly time was running out. One day soon he would have to return home, and even though he'd learned a lot, he fancied he would need to know far more about his father than he did at the moment. He thought he could hear a soft voice inside his head agreeing with him, then shook his head and entered the room. It was time to start packing and then see if S'klaratim could get him that map before he left.

# 10 RETURN FROM THE WILD

"I don't care what you think, you were the one who let him go in the first place!", K'trell pushed Nasrindo's soothing hand off her shoulder and angrily stepped up to Y'sarryn.

"Right, you, hunter, you've been fobbing us off for far too long now! I don't care what agreement you had with Darjoon, or what crazy plans that foolish young mage had, we need to go and look for him. He would never have stayed away this long unless there was something wrong and now we're not there to help him."

Y'sarryn didn't flinch, but simply stood and endured the withering blast. He understood she was upset, and so was Nasrindo, but Darjoon had told him to keep them both here for as long as he could, and Y'sarryn could be very persuasive.

"I absolutely understand what you're feeling, Healer. I too am worried about our young friend. But there is a plan here that even you must be able to see, a plan beyond our own emotions and misgivings. If it is true, as we all believe it to be, that Darjoon is the one from the prophecy and will save us, then this path is already laid out for him and he will emerge from it. I myself tried to convince him of the foolishness of reasoning with the Circle, of the grave danger of getting close to those fanatics. It was with a heavy heart that I saw him leave and it is with a heavy heart that I must tell you to wait patiently for him to return. It is not easy for me either, you know. If I knew we had a chance of reaching him, I would be the first to rush out there and go to him, trust me. But I have faith in our young mage. I don't think it will be long now and we will see him striding down that walkway towards us."

K'trell had backed off as he spoke, tears in her eyes and now she looked towards Nasrindo who lovingly and tenderly gathered her in his arms. He whispered to her and she nodded her head against his chest.

"We know you are right, wise Y'sarryn", Nasrindo spoke softly above the Healer's head, "But that man of the prophecy has become a dear friend of ours, so it is with mixed emotions we acknowledge your wisdom. We will wait until the next moon, as you have said. But we will not wait a moment longer."

Y'sarryn bowed his head and nodded, feeling the sting of their reluctance and acknowledging their pain which was his own. He spoke with far more confidence than he felt inside. That pit of demons that Darjoon had ventured into was as like to spit him out all chewed up as provide him with the knowledge he wanted. Or worse, they would poison him with their own bile and he would be changed beyond recognition. Who knew what dark arts they practised?

Looking up, he simply smiled at the two desert people who were walking away, arm in arm. They had tried to fit in but it was clear that their deep discomfort for the tree-top existence made it very difficult. Not that it was for lack of trying though.

K'trell had healed some of the people's scrapes and bruises, and had earned respect from the people for repairing a little girl's broken arm, sustained in a fall from one walkway to another. She had been horrified when they told her how the arm had been broken and muttered and mumbled to herself for the rest of the day, staying well away from the edges of the platforms and continually making the sign of protection around her.

Nasrindo had ventured out with the other men to collect tree sap. This entailed a rope and shimmying up tall tree-trunks, then settling into a secure spot while driving a small sharp wooden instrument, much like a reed, into the tree and then sucking on the end to get it started, letting it fill one or more gourds tied around their body. He'd amused the other villagers with his antics, as despite being fit and nimble the climbing rope proved to be something he could not master. His shambolic attempts at trying to get up the tree ended with not a few bruises and scrapes, and a great deal of laughter. Eventually he'd had to admit defeat and return to the village, only for K'trell to berate him for even trying. She refused to let him go after that and he ended up teaching some of the older children his hand-to-hand knife skills, as well as how to throw a spear.

The children were eager to learn, but once some of the adults found out what they were up to, they quickly put a stop to it. Nasrindo was bemused at how passionately they tried to convince him that violence was unnecessary and something they did not allow in the village, not even for self-defence. He'd argued with them for a while, although half-heartedly, and then finally throwing his hands up in despair had retreated to Y'sarryn's cottage and spent his time carving items of wood into intricate and beautiful shapes. It took a great deal of coaxing, but Y'sarryn was able to get Nasrindo to show these carvings to the others, who gasped in pure delight.

Art was something the villagers loved, and soon he had requests for many different pieces. A couple of the parents who had been so upset at him teaching their children combat, now brought them along so he could teach them how to carve. This at least kept him occupied and surreptitiously he threw in a few of his fighting skills too without the parents knowing.

K'trell had taken to helping with the teaching of the children, demonstrating various practical skills. She kept her eye on a few who showed other talents, children she would have naturally trained up as lesser healers in her tribe. However, the first time she was attempting to coax a child into using magic, the teachers in the school surrounded her and began to scold her. It seemed that although they would tolerate magic in a stranger, even going so far as to offer her honour and respect as she'd healed them, they refused to allow any of their own to practice magic. The village preferred to live with nature as it was, and not interfere with it in any way.

She had tried to explain the tribal concept of having a Great Healer who trained lesser healers and that the magic involved was used only for healing but they were having none of it. K'trell acquiesced reluctantly, convinced that some of the children had real magical talent, but realising she couldn't go against the ingrained traditions. However she continued to teach her herbal lore and at the same time learned all she could from the villagers about their own plant lore and the differences and similarities of the plants in the tree-tops. She was excited at finding some truly powerful healing plants and began a process of grinding and drying them, determined to take some back with her.

As a result of their strangeness, the two tribes-folk had spent many an evening together, growing ever closer. Their fondness for each other discouraged any of the villagers from making advances to either one, something that was common practice, especially with outsiders and which proved useful to mingle the blood-lines of the free-folk. Only in the last few days had the two tribes-folk become more open about their obvious feelings for each other, and he was glad to see that in this cruel world.

One day, Y'sarryn saw K'trell grinding plants absently while looking out across the forest longingly. Nasrindo was industriously carving some new large piece of furniture that he'd been commissioned with, but even he was sighing every now and again, and he would stop from time to time and stare out in the same direction as K'trell. He realised it was time to let them in on a little secret.

"Um, hey, listen you two. Why don't I show you something. Do you have a moment?", he asked.

Taking them along the same route he'd taken Darjoon previously, what now seemed like ages ago, he went a lot more slowly, waiting patiently as the two tribes-folk carefully navigated walkways and ladders that Darjoon and himself had scampered up. Eventually they arrived at the high tree-top outpost. Both Nasrindo and K'trell immediately planted their backs against the tree-trunk, their faces pale and eyes wide open with the whites showing. But as they sat there quietly, they both began to relax and he could see them looking out with interest. Nasrindo even crawled to the edge, despite K'trell's protests and looked out across the forest, spotting the fires and lights of the different villages in delight. Soon, K'trell had joined him and, reverting to their tribal tongue, they were jabbering away excitedly at each other. Y'sarryn smiled and taking out his pipe, began smoking. The sun was slowly sinking, a giant red ball over the forest. The two, realising they weren't alone, crawled shamefacedly back and sat next to Y'sarryn. He laughed at them.

"Listen, the first time I came here I couldn't stop myself either. It's breathlessly beautiful and after all the time I've spent up here, I'm still not used to it. I brought Darjoon up here the first time I met him, you know. There was a lot that I had to tell him, although I wished I'd known more. Now there's something I need to let you in on as well."

Neither Nasrindo nor K'trell flinched as he slowly removed his magical mask and revealed his raven-born identity. He looked at them quizzically and asked, "Um, did you just notice what happened? To my face?"

"I'm not sure what you mean, Y'sarryn? What about your face? You're obviously raven-born, and therefore very different to the villagers around you, but we knew that from our first meeting. Although now that you mention it, your features do seem a bit clearer all of a sudden", Nasrindo replied in a matter-of-fact voice.

Y'sarryn's eyes widened, "What? How did you know...? No-one can see... Wait! Both of you could see through the mask?"

"Mask? Well, there was a certain haziness to your features, that's true. And I thought you might be hiding something, but that was your business and not my place to ask. Your face is a lot clearer now, but to my eyes, no different than before. Why?", K'trell asked innocently.

"Why", Y'sarryn chuckled, "Because I deliberately obscure my features and make myself a Spidralite all the time, that's why. It suits me not to be a raven-born here in the village. Not that they wouldn't accept me, being who they are, but... Well, it's complicated. And, as you know, raven-born are not the most popular people around. The only way you could easily see through it, was, well if you had any Island magic and somehow had that activated. Which means... No! I can't believe it! Why didn't I sense it before? It's in both of you."

K'trell looked at Nasrindo, who simply raised his eyebrows, then back at Y'sarryn, "What do you mean, Y'sarryn? What Island magic? What do you mean 'both of us'?"

"Well, the spell that I use to cloud my features is one I learned from Darjoon's father. It is known only to those from the Sorcerer's Isle, or the Glass Isle as it is now known. It is highly efficient and requires little thought from me to keep it maintained, but anyone from the Island who was familiar with that clan's particular magic, and who had that magic activated, would see through it straight-away. It implies that both of you have Island blood, and therefore Island magic and are also from the same clan, and that the magic was activated in you. Tell me, do you have any idea of your actual ages? Have you noticed that you stay younger than those around you? K'trell, I now realise what it was about your healing magic that I thought had seemed different before. Has no-one remarked on that? That you or it are different?"

Nasrindo's face had closed the moment Y'sarryn had mentioned age. Now K'trell looked at Y'sarryn open-mouthed, "Well, yes, actually. My own Great Healer who taught me and released me into the great Turama's service often commented on the unique quality of my magic. We just thought it was how Turama had marked me out, that it was how she identified me to my Great Healer. And, yes, it's true, I have not exactly aged while those around me have. We just thought that it was a gift from Turama, something about the power I had in my magic and that the great goddess wanted me to be around a bit longer. But I do not understand, Y'sarryn? How could I have Island blood in me? It would mean... Wait! No! Surely, it cannot be. It's not possible, my mother would never... I mean... What are you saying?"

K'trell had crept back at the last and now curled into a ball, hugging her legs with her arms and staring at Y'sarryn and Nasrindo with what seemed like despair. They both just looked at her, not sure what to say. It was clear she was wrestling with something. She continued breathlessly to herself, as if they weren't even there.

"My mother used to talk about a man, but I didn't always want to believe it. She would whisper in the night, as she lay stroking my hair, thinking I was sleeping. Of the powerful mage, the dark-haired stranger who came and swept her off her feet. She had been a Great Healer too, powerful and fierce. Her chosen mate was my father, the greatest warrior in our tribe, tall, proud and fierce and destined to lead us. However, there were rumours of a strange man who had walked out of the desert, spoken to the elders and spent time learning our ways. Apparently he was an observer, sent out from that Island to learn our tribal magic, and where all the other tribes had refused, we accepted him and the elders had asked my mother to teach him.

But I didn't believe it, that my mother would have, that she would have entertained another man in that way, that... That I... That... They couldn't have? What about my father? Did she... Oh no! Maybe that's why she married him? To cover up what she'd truly done. Can it be? My father wasn't my father? He'd... They'd never said. Not directly. But... But it must be", her voice trailed off in a whisper.

Both men sat awkwardly in silence as K'trell stared out into the growing darkness. Then Nasrindo shuffled over to her and put his arm around her. She burst into tears and grabbed hold of him like she was dying. This was a terrible secret to uncover, a harsh lesson in the vagaries of humanity and the hidden depths of life. The three of them continued to sit in silence for some time, lost in their own thoughts. Then Nasrindo started to speak.

"K'trell", he practically whispered, his voice hoarse and trembling, "There is something I must confess to you. I have wanted to, so, so many times, but I couldn't. You were right, you know, back when you said there would be a time when I would have to tell you all the truth. Now is that time, and I will not hold anything back from you."

She sat up and wiped her eyes and nose, then leaned back against the tree so she could try and see his face in the darkness. Y'sarryn sat breathlessly, a mere observer in this moment of intimate disclosure.

"I told you that I was handed down the blood-oath to protect Darjoon, but, well, I'm afraid that's not really true. My real name, my original name, was Turmoos. Darjoon's parents came to me when I was a mature warrior and my parent's long dead, and they entrusted me with the future care of their unborn child. His mother in particular insisted that one day he, Darjoon, would come looking for me and that I needed to protect him and help him in whatever he was to do. They made me take the blood-oath of my ancestors. I didn't understand it then, because I thought I would be so much older by the time Darjoon came to me that I could be of little help. I assumed I would simply tell him about them, and share with him the little knowledge they had shared with me, and maybe teach him what I knew of tribal life. I should have known better, because already I had taken to concealing my youthfulness by rubbing ash in my hair to make it grey, and by affecting a stick to walk with. But Darjoon's father took me aside, and told me the truth about my own ancestry. I, like you, am the child of a Healer. In the same way, she ended up taking a mate from our tribe, the great elite warrior who was to become my own father. It is through him that I learned my skills as a warrior and in turn became part of our tribe's elite. But, as Y'sarryn has said, it is true that the people from Sorcerer's Isle have long life, and that this is in their blood. Long, long ago, according to Darjoon's father, they were just as we are and they lived the same number of years. Then, one day, during various experiments, they discovered the ability to inject themselves with a substance that prolongs and enhances the body's natural ability to heal and preserve. Naturally they injected it into themselves and then into every new-born baby. But it caused many deaths among their children. It was only after many of the new-born had died that they realised the reason for the deaths. The children of those who had been injected were automatically gifted with long-life themselves, and so in essence, they were receiving a double-dose, which caused harm to the body and subsequently, death.

Darjoon's father revealed to me that he had visited our tribe in my parent's youth, that my mother and he had become close, become intimate and as a result, she'd fallen pregnant. Knowing this to be the case, and knowing that this dark mage would leave her, she had wanted a father for me. So she married the elite warrior, my father. So you see, Darjoon's father was also my father, and not the warrior I had known, and as a result I too have this gift of long-life. At first I didn't want to believe it, but after they left and the warriors that I had fought with grew old and withered, I still remained as you see me. And even though I was trying to hide it, I soon realised this would not be enough. So one day, that old but young Turmoos that was, well he simply walked out into the desert and some months later a young warrior named Nasrindo walked back into a different tribe, staking a claim there as is our custom. Which is where I was when Darjoon finally arrived, looking for who I had been, looking for his half-brother."

Y'sarryn and K'trell just stared at him in silence.

"I'm truly sorry, K'trell, I could not speak of this before. I did not think you would understand. But now, I see that it is I who does not understand. If you are long-lived, then how old are you really?"

K'trell stared at him, and then slowly and silently a tear rolled from her left eye and slid softly down her cheek.

"Do you remember the senior elder in the Tent of Meeting, Nas? That... He... He is my brother", blindly she reached forward and fell into Nasrindo's embrace, and began to weep.

"K'trell", he murmured to her softly, "I have also seen parents die, and lost two brothers and a sister while I lived on. I know the feeling."

They sat there, the two lovers in each other's arms while Y'sarryn just stared out across the forest, lost in his own memories of a love that could never be. The bitter-sweet pain of it still stung, knowing as he did that there would never be another. He envied the two tribes-folk sitting near him, but he was glad they had found each other, and that there was still hope for them. At least they could grow old together, albeit slowly.

K'trell suddenly stirred and lifted her tear-stained face

to the night sky, addressing him indirectly, "So Y'sarryn. If Darjoon's father and Nasrindo's father are the same, then what of us? Could Nas be my brother too?"

She felt Nasrindo stiffen against her as the implications of what she was asking hit home. The tribes-folk would never tolerate sibling relations in such a way. It was punished by death, in fact everywhere across the Old Lands it was the same.

"I see what you mean. Well, there is a way to know, K'trell. The change in the body leaves a distinctive mark, like a birth-mark, on the inner thigh. For each family, that mark remains constant. I'm afraid that if your marks are the same, then yes, it's quite likely he was father to both of you."

Nasrindo let out a sigh of relief, and Y'sarryn looked away and grinned as K'trell turned and slapped the desert tribesman. Obviously the warrior had not realised what he was revealing, but she had.

"What?", the warrior put a hand to his stinging cheek, "So your birthmark looks like a star, and mine is more like a crescent moon? It's good news, isn't it?"

He flinched as she raised her hand again, then slowly and deliberately lowered it.

"Well", she said icily, "I'm glad that's clear and now that you've revealed you've been spying on me, I'll take more care in future. But what about you, Y'sarryn? How does a raven-born end up hiding his face here in a Spidralite tree-top village? What brought you to this place? And how do you know so much about the Glass Isle and it's people?"

Y'sarryn laughed at K'trell's imperious questioning. He could see that she was a formidable Great Healer.

"Okay, okay! I guess it's my turn", he said ruefully.

He told them everything he'd previously told Darjoon, including his love and affection for Darjoon's mother. The two listened intently, and K'trell's face softened from the fury of before and her eyes grew damp again. She could see what it cost him to reveal this and relive that pain, especially as Nasrindo and herself had just found each other. So she kept quiet for a while after he had finished, but then her natural curiosity reasserted itself.

"But how is it that you can do the Island magic? Do you have their blood inside you too?"

Y'sarryn smiled at her, "That's a good observation, Healer, and yes, I am also a child of the Island people. According to Darjoon's father, there were four men from the Island who would travel to our Old Lands and mingle with our people, ostensibly to understand the different forms of magic, but occasionally to indulge themselves with our women as well. It's clear that Darjoon and yourself, Nas, share the same father, but, thankfully, as we now know, you, Healer, do not. I, myself, bear the birthmark of a sunburst, and...", Y'sarryn fell silent.

The two tribes-folk looked at each other, then at him again and waited. Y'sarryn looked intently at K'trell, as if weighing up what he had to say.

"Oh, come on, Y'sarryn. We've all been very open here, some more than others", she glared at Nasrindo.

"You're right again, Healer. Very well, but this news may surprise you and I'm afraid, may lower your estimation of not just me, but another. Nevertheless, I think it best I share it. You see, Sirroya and I, well, we have both lived for some time now, outlasting a few generations. And in that time, we had an admittedly short period where we thought that uh, well, that we could be more than friends. It didn't last long, but long enough for us to become quite intimate. That's how I know, Healer, that Sirroya has a similar birthmark of the star. So it seems that as Darjoon and Nas are related, so are Sirroya and yourself. You must both have the same father and are therefore step-sisters."

Once again, silence settled on the little group. There was a lot to take in and when Nasrindo volunteered that it was time to go to bed, the others didn't argue. Y'sarryn smiled as they pointedly waited outside the hut while he went in. He knew when a goodnight kiss was about to happen. He was genuinely pleased for them.

He frowned as he remembered something that continued to trouble him. When he'd revealed his true features he'd now had two surprises. Firstly, that Darjoon had not been able to see through his mask. Being partly Island-bred, he'd have thought it would not have been a surprise to him, but apparently it had. And of course, tonight, he'd not expected the two to have been Island-bred themselves. He shook his head, and muttered to himself as he turned in for the night and began falling asleep, "Well, you think you've seen it all, raven-born. Turns out despite your long life you haven't, not by a long shot. How much further do you have to fly, eh?"

The stars wheeled above the slumbering village tucked away in the tree-tops as the trio slept on until the sun slowly lifted itself above the horizon and peeked into the trees. Rubbing his eyes, Y'sarryn struggled to surface from the strange dream he'd been having. A Dremrel had picked him up in its claws and was flying him over the sea, his feet skimming the surface of the water. With every wing-beat, the island in front of them seemed to become bigger, and bigger, until it filled the sky. The Dremrel had just been about to fly straight into it, when it had shrieked and he'd woken up. He groaned, then froze as the shrieking continued, this time clearly coming from outside somewhere in the village.

Throwing aside the covers, he leapt to his feet and grabbed his staff from the foot of the bed. Running out the door, he belatedly grabbed a cloak as he ran through the hall, struggling into it as he emerged into early morning sunlight and complete mayhem. K'trell appeared beside him, dishevelled and rumpled from sleep, and right behind her was Nasrindo, peering around with his left hand shading his eyes and his spear in his right.

People were rushing past, running in all directions

and the women were screaming as they ran. All he could hear was, "The children, oh dear gods, someone save the children".

"Quick, follow me", he said to the two who briskly tucked in behind him as he dashed to the children's school area. With no climbing to slow them down they were able to get there quickly, fighting their way through men and women, most of whom were running away but some, like them, who were running towards the school. The people seemed to naturally give way as soon as they saw Y'sarryn, while K'trell and Nasrindo just followed him through.

Bursting out of the shade into the sunlight, Y'sarryn threw his hand up to shade his eyes, then stared in fascinated horror. A few women were desperately leading some children away from the school while another was fighting a one-sided battle with an apparition that cavorted and danced, alternating between shrieking and groaning. It carried a long, wicked spear and was thrusting it out between the dancing, just missing the woman in front who already had a few lacerations on her upraised arms. Nasrindo advanced cautiously forward, his spear held ready and raised to plunge into the creature, which suddenly turned and hissed at him menacingly. Nasrindo froze as if paralysed, staring in horror at the woman who was revealed beneath the long hair, dirt and grime.

Both Y'sarryn and K'trell saw her at the same time, and while Y'sarryn stared, transfixed like Nasrindo, K'trell suddenly uttered a few words in the strange guttural language of the tribes-folk. The creature that was Sirroya had raised her spear, ready to plunge it into Nasrindo in front of her when she suddenly shrieked in a high-pitched wail, turned and took two steps towards K'trell with her spear held out and then, dropping the spear, fell heavily to the floor and lay unmoving.

Y'sarryn recovered his senses and rushed over to the village woman who had sunk to her knees, sobbing in shock. Nasrindo and K'trell stepped over to the ragged, unkempt woman lying on the floor, and at a nod from K'trell, Nasrindo hefted her limp weight surprisingly easily to his shoulder.

"K'trell, can you do something for this lady?", Y'sarryn asked, "I will see to everyone else and calm them all down. Nas, I suggest you take it, I mean, her, to my cottage, and lock her in my room. Here are the keys to both. Go quickly, this village may not be violent but their children have been threatened and I can offer no guarantees right now."

As Nasrindo headed off with his burden, K'trell stepped forward and quickly and efficiently healed the woman's arms, asking her if there were any other injuries. Satisfied that there weren't, she calmed her down, then helped her up and across the children's playground into the school proper where a few of the teachers were only too willing to take her in and see to her. Leaving her there, K'trell strode briskly back to Y'sarryn's cottage.

She arrived just as Y'sarryn strode up from the other walkway, looking grim and purposeful.

"Well, I've been able to calm them all down, at least for now. They want to interrogate her, rather than execute her", he caught the look on K'trell's face, "I know, I know. They're a supposedly peaceful people but they are highly protective of their children. Living out here, and so high up, it becomes a habit, I guess. Shall we see what's going on inside?"

They both walked into the cottage, Y'sarryn not letting the Healer precede him but pushing in front of her as if to protect her. Nasrindo had placed the inert body on the floor in the living room and now stood on the opposite side of the room. He just shrugged when K'trell looked at him questioningly from behind Y'sarryn.

"Well, it stank and seemed full of fleas and lice so I wasn't going to put it on anyone's bed. I'm going to go out and wash myself now. Whatever it, well, maybe it's she, but, well it doesn't seem human to me. Anyway, it hasn't stirred since I brought it in, so it may not be alive anymore, if that's what it was to begin with."

Nasrindo shook his head and frowned, made a sign over the figure lying inert on the floor and then sidled out the door. K'trell knelt down next to the body and probed it with her magic. After a while, she looked up at Y'sarryn who stood over her, waiting impatiently.

"Well, she, not it, is definitely human and female. The body is in a bad way and there are many wounds and lacerations that have not been treated. See this large wound here, under this cloth on her shoulder. That's starting to suppurate and is badly in need of cleaning. But, there's something else strange about her, uh, I suppose you could call it her, well, her spirit. Something feels off, like, well, I know it sounds strange but like the colours are all wrong or something. Anyway, let's first get the body working right, and then we can focus on the rest of her."

K'trell worked on as the sun climbed overhead, until finally she wiped the sweat off her brow and sank back, exhausted. She gratefully accepted the cool drink that Y'sarryn provided. He'd sat quietly next to her, lending what strength of magic he'd had to the process. She was surprised at the pure, almost pristine quality of his magic, but was too focused on the task at hand to comment. Nasrindo had come in and just sat and watched as the wounds slowly leaked out their poisonous fluids, then he gently leaned forward and wiped up the mess, slowly moving around the body with K'trell and cleaning as she healed. She rested now, exhausted from the healing and recovering slowly.

The men finally left the room once they could tell that K'trell had gained some strength, and after she had glared at them and pointed her finger to the door. Once the men left, she quickly and efficiently stripped the woman and washed her clean, clothing her in some robes Y'sarryn had thoughtfully provided. Looking down on the sleeping face, darkened and ravaged by sun and wind, she could almost imagine her to be one of the tribes-folk. She'd even seen the birth-mark that Y'sarryn had alluded to, comparing it to her own and seeing the similarity. Step-sister! What a thought that was. That this strange individual could some-how be related to her? She shook her head, and then deftly tied Sirroya with the rope that Y'sarryn had thoughtfully provided, and finally stepped outside and joined the men. Y'sarryn knocked his pipe out carefully and turned to K'trell as she emerged.

"Well, how is she? Are you sure that is really, well, is that, could that really be her? She seemed so, well, so wild earlier. That's not the Sirroya I knew at all."

"Yes, Y'sarryn, I believe she is human and not some wraith or undead or anything like that. I just think that there is something not right deep within her. In fact, I think it must be the same harsh magic that I encountered in Darjoon, something she got from the touch of the lizard-people. Somehow it's wrapped itself around her consciousness and is affecting her. I have an idea, although it's possibly not a good one. It's something that Nasrindo did when he encountered Darjoon for the first time after the attack. Do you remember, Nas? You spoke those awful words that you said you could read in front of you, the one's that glowed by themselves?"

"Of course I do, K'trell, I remember it all too well", he shivered, "I also remember the aftermath of what occurred as a result. Besides, I have had no reaction to Sirroya in that way, none at all."

Y'sarryn smiled softly at Nasrindo's unconsciously familiar use of the Healer's name.

"I know, Nas, it's obvious you didn't. But I do know some of that, that disgusting tongue. And although I normally would never, ever want to speak it, I feel it may be the only way to undo what was done. After that, well, I'm afraid we must prepare ourselves for the, what did you call it, the aftermath. Although I don't think this is exactly the same. I can't be sure but Darjoon's odd blend of magic is pretty unique, and she has none of that. She certainly responded to the spell I placed on her, without reacting magically. Also, it seems her magic is more like our's, a blend of Old Lands and Sorcerer's Isle, yes, but nothing more than that. I say ours, although...", she looked at Y'sarryn speculatively, but he briefly shook his head and she could see his eyes warning her so she closed her mouth and said no more about his strangely pure magic.

She looked at each of them in turn, hoping one of them would argue her out of it. The thought of that language crossing her tongue was not one she wanted to contemplate, let alone go in and do. But she just knew in her heart that it was right, it was the only way to bring Sirroya back from this madness that consumed her. Y'sarryn simply nodded his head at her, the concern etched into the lines around his mouth and the set look in his eyes. Nasrindo, being who he was, reached over to her and took her in his arms. She relaxed into his strong, muscular embrace for a moment and shivered slightly, her emotions betraying her thoughts.

"If you are sure, my desert dove", he whispered in her ear, "then do this. But know that I will be at your back with my spear and I will not hesitate to drive it into her heart if you are threatened. You are too precious for me to let anything happen to you, and besides, what would Darjoon do to me if I was to let harm come to you. Hmm, come to think of it, what will he do to me if I was to harm his beloved Sirroya? Ah well, it seems you now carry my fate in your hands along with your own, my love."

She laughed at the last part, feeling the tension leave her. Trust Nasrindo to come up with something so practical. Although he was right, she didn't think anyone would want to give Darjoon that kind of bad news, let alone be the one responsible for it. Her heart fluttered as she thought of how Darjoon would feel, seeing Sirroya alive and well, and she looked up at Nasrindo's face, seeing the reflected love in his eyes. Yes, she had to do this for

Darjoon, she had to bring back his love.

Y'sarryn had insisted they eat the midday meal first, and K'trell was glad of it. She'd needed to recover her strength, and build up her reserves for what was to come. There was no way of knowing if it would work, nor what would happen if it did. She had to be prepared to erect defensive shields in case the worst happened. At least Sirroya did not appear to have anywhere near the level of magic that Darjoon had, although she'd underestimated him at some cost. She didn't want to make the same mistake again.

They'd bound Sirroya tightly and then bound her to the central supports of the cottage. If she took those out, she'd at least bring the cottage down around her, giving them time to react. Nasrindo stood behind K'trell with his spear, just as he'd promised, and even Y'sarryn had taken up his bow and stood prepared with an arrow nocked and ready. K'trell had meditated for some time, rummaging through her memories, including the one where Nasrindo had "released" Darjoon. She thought she had the right words and the right pronunciation, but would only know when she spoke them. Her fear was that if she used the wrong words, then strange, dark magic could result and that would be very, very bad. Her absolute worst fear was that there was an ancient gateway spell that had similar overtones to what she was about to recite. She'd been able to put it from her mind, so she could not confuse it with what she needed, but Turama help them if she got it wrong.

Taking a deep breath, Sirroya recited the dreadful words she believed would bring Sirroya back from where she was lost inside herself. After the first word, the inert body suddenly convulsed, as if an electric shock had gone through it. Then, at the second, it shuddered and strained against the bonds, the eyelids snapping open to reveal whirling blue eyes that occasionally turned back into her head, revealing only the white of the eyes. At the third

word, Sirroya audibly gasped, and stared at K'trell as if
transfixed. The fourth word saw a greenish mist seep out
of Sirroya's mouth, hanging in the air, sinuous and curving
and writhing around her head. At the fifth word, she
suddenly threw back her head and shrieked, the mist
shredding and seemingly fleeing the little cottage. Sirroya
slumped back, eyes closed and didn't move while K'trell
completed the incantation, the words heavy and booming
in the silence after the scream.

Finished at last, the Healer staggered back to be
caught by Nasrindo, while Y'sarryn knelt down next to the
prostrate form of the girl and felt her pulse. He looked up
at the others, a wan smile on his face. The bow held
loosely at his side trembled in the hunter's grasp, the only
sign his nerves had been on edge.

"Well, she's alive and unless I'm mistaken that's a
healthy pulse. Do you think that's dealt with now, Great
Healer?"

K'trell closed her eyes and sent out her magic, then
smiled briefly.

"I can no longer sense the alien presence inside her
and she does seem healthier than before. I think we must
now let nature do what it does best. She will need plenty of
rest, and then some liquid nourishment, some broth
maybe. Why don't you two take her to my room. She can
share it with me and I can keep an eye on her there."

The Healer made her way outside and slumped down
at the table, pouring herself something to drink. The words
still boomed in her head, taunting her and trying to find a
place to rest inside. She bent down, placing her head in her
hands on the table and resisted the words until finally they
faded to a whisper in the corner of her mind and then
were gone. When she lifted her head, the darkness was
already settling in and Nasrindo was sitting quietly
opposite, watching her intently. She gave him a weak
smile, then stretched wearily as she felt the ache in her
back.

"Nas? How long have I been sitting here? My back really hurts. Actually, so does my head."

He looked at her lovingly for a moment before replying, "Actually, my dove, you've been here for hours. I was worried about you, but Y'sarryn said you needed your rest. Something about the magic you used, although he didn't elaborate. Nor did I want him to. It somehow, well it didn't seem right and I have a feeling I don't need to know about it. How are you feeling now?"

"I'm okay, I think. You're right, there is nothing good about that awful language, or that magic, it's just horrible, Nas, absolutely horrible. I don't know how the lizard-men can use it, or where they got it from, I mean it just doesn't make sense. It belongs to an entirely different age, to an entirely different people. The little I've been able to glean, it's, ah, no, sorry, you're right. Let's not talk about it, shall we. Are you willing to go for a walk? I just need some fresh air."

Y'sarryn stood at the door and watched the couple leave. The tall, strong warrior and the agile Healer next to him almost glowed in the growing darkness. He smiled, pleased that Darjoon had found two strong allies. Then he frowned as he thought of the fact that Darjoon was due back tomorrow night, it being the time of the next moonrise. Would he actually make it back? And what would he be like if he did, after being in the company of those crazy people in the Circle?

# 11 INTO THE UNKOWN

Darjoon had almost finished packing and now he looked around the small room that had been his home for such a short time. As much as he was glad to be leaving and going back to his friends, he knew there was so much more that he could learn here. Already, the revelation of what the Dremrel really were had unlocked clues to memories laying dormant inside him, memories that had been placed there during his time in the 'machine' or whatever it had been back in the desert ruins. How much more of that chaotic, jumbled confusion could be unravelled in this place? Even as just a simple mage, it was a glorious opportunity to discover deeper knowledge, both from those around him and from delving into the extensive library that S'klaratim had told him about. Now, barely a Circle member, he had to leave already. He realised ruefully that expecting to learn about portals so quickly had been naive of him, as Y'sarryn and the others had tried to point out. He'd have to leave now, then wait for his opportunity when he returned. He shook his head and grinned ruefully, "Darjoon, you're thinking like a silly youngling, this is not the place for you right now. There is more to do, young raven, than spend time roosting in an unfamiliar tree. Or a dangerous one, even."

S'klaratim entered the room without knocking as usual. Darjoon opened his mouth to scold him, then closed it again as he saw the excited look on his face.

"Well Darjoon, are you ready to be surprised? Wait until you see what I've got in store for you! You think you know about portals, do you? Just you wait! Follow me, but do it quietly and quickly."

The young mage whispered excitedly at the last, then tapped his nose while at the same time trying to put his other finger over his lips. Darjoon had to bite his lip so he didn't laugh out loud at the sight.

"Well, young S'klaratim", he whispered back, "lead on and I will follow you to the very River of Life."

The mage gave him an angry glare at his patronising tone, then composed his face into its usual haughty look and stepped out the room briskly, flinging his words over his shoulder, "I'm not much younger than you, you know!"

Darjoon kicked himself mentally as he followed the young mage down the dark corridor.

"Foot in mouth, Darjoon, foot in mouth", he muttered quietly to himself, then started as S'klaratim shushed him quite loudly.

As they proceeded quietly down the hall, they occasionally darted into alcoves or down other corridors as mages made their way backwards and forwards. But the farther they went into the mountain depths, the quieter it became until eventually they reached a level where no-one was in evidence.

"There are very few of us who ever venture down this far", he whispered theatrically to Darjoon, "Probably because those who do, don't really come back."

The last was followed by a little giggle, and again Darjoon wondered just how unbalanced the young mage really was. Well, if he was truly mad, then Darjoon was following him, so what did that make him? He shook his head and grinned again. The truth is that he was starting to enjoy these adventures a little too much.

They finally stopped opposite a strangely carved door set in an obscure side tunnel. The walls here were not panelled like the others but simply exposed as bare rock and it seemed that they had been created fairly recently.

"No-one seems to know who built this, or when. I know, I know, it does look new, but apparently it's been here longer than the rest of this place. Now Darjoon, you must promise me that you will put me forward for the final tests, yes?"

"S'klaratim, I told you before that I will do it, and I always keep my word. I know have to leave the Circle for now, but before I go anywhere I will speak to Grollak and put you forward. But you must promise me that you will get through them unscathed, okay?"

The young mage sniffed and drew himself up as if to make some pointed remark, then deflated and jumped around like an excited puppy.

"Ooh, the tests, the tests, I'm going to do the tests! Oh, I just knew you would be good for me. I knew your power before anyone else even guessed at it. Just wait until I'm a member and then you can see my true power, Darjoon. Just you wait!"

Darjoon smiled at the happy young mage dancing in front of him.

"I can just imagine, S'klaratim, I can just imagine. I'm sure you'll do very well indeed."

S'klaratim stopped his dancing abruptly and stared at Darjoon, his eyes glowing in the dim corridor, feverishly bright and sparkling with a strange light.

"Yes, yes, I must do very well. Now I must go and prepare, Darjoon. Yes, I need to get myself ready for the tests. But I will see you later, won't I? Before you leave? Yes, I will. I will see you later, Darjoon."

The young mage strode off down the corridor and then over his shoulder yelled out, "Oh just go in through the door! Once you're in there, you'll know what to do."

The footsteps faded down the corridor and Darjoon stopped himself from calling the initiate back. Then, slowly, he eased the door open and slipped inside, only to gasp and look around in wonder. The room's walls were hidden behind luxuriant plant growth, with beautiful vines and tall stems that housed bright, colourful and exotic flowers of all shapes and sizes. There was a heady perfume in the air, and Darjoon breathed it in, intoxicated by scents he'd never smelt before. Long, ornate shelves seemed to be arranged like a maze, housing some exquisite plants, but there were also long, rectangular, glass boxes containing a myriad assortment of strange and wonderful insects, reptiles and long, slithering shapes that were snakes he'd never seen before. Fascinated, Darjoon progressed up and down the aisles in the maze, twisting his head this way and that to try and see everything that was on display. Occasionally, a beautiful, brightly coloured bird would flit just overhead, tantalizingly out of arm's reach. The door opened and closed behind him, but he didn't even notice as he was so captivated by the living colours and fragrances around him. Finally, having traversed the maze, he arrived at what appeared to be a large, golden rectangle embedded in the wall decorated with strange symbols on the outside that he couldn't understand. Casting about, he recognised a white, fat-tailed lizard reclining in a basket opposite the door and positioned underneath a shelf. Remembering what he'd had to do previously to open a door, and smiling at the sight of the fat creature, Darjoon closed his eyes, and then jumped as the lizard started speaking to him.

"Fascinating, isn't it? Ah, I remember when it was only half as full as it is now. Oh yes, it stills thrills me every time I come in here. And that smell, oh, you could bottle it up and sell it, the women would go mad for it, I'm sure."

Darjoon opened his eyes and stared at the lizard, which simply regarded him in affected boredom, staring out of lowered, heavily-lidded green eyes. The inscrutable visage of the wizened reptile did not lend itself to the voice, and he jumped as it spoke again.

"Ah yes, there is so much to see and so much to learn. I wish I had as much time as you seem to have to enjoy this place. I would be down here every day of course, but I have far more important matters to attend to."

Darjoon had watched the lizard carefully this time, and he could swear the lips and tongue did not move at all. He crouched down to get a closer look, then practically shrieked like a girl as a heavy hand came down on his shoulder, followed by a wheezing, elderly mage who crouched down next to him and looked at the lizard too. The mage put out a trembling veined and mottled hand to pat the creature on the head.

"I assure you, young mage, it is quite well, but thank you for taking such a keen interest in my little friend. It is quite happy here, you know, as there are many strange and exotic insects that are simply free to roam, and of course some of them end up roaming their way into her belly. So you see, even though she is tethered, she is still content. Sometimes, the chains we must all inevitably wear are not always bad, in fact, they can be quite good for us. What do you think, Darjoon?"

They both stood up and Darjoon bowed involuntarily. Something about this elderly mage just demanded his respect and there was an innate wisdom and authority that radiated from him. The mage smiled, as if in understanding, and then winked at Darjoon conspiratorially.

"Oh, I know why you are here, you know. Oh yes, I'm quite sure of it. In fact, I have a one hundred percent confidence as to what you are after, am I right?"

Darjoon stared wide-eyed at the old mage. He was fairly sure that if the old man tried anything, he could take him, but he didn't understand. If the Circle knew why he was here, why would it send this old bird? Unless he was a truly powerful mage, in which case it was going to be a shame to destroy this lovely room. They would never take him alive to make him talk. The mage carried on, seemingly blissfully unaware of Darjoon's murderous thoughts and intentions.

"Yes, I think we all come here for the same reason, my boy. Knowledge! They say, knowledge is power, but it is so much more, so much more, don't you agree? You know, you're awfully quiet for someone who is supposed to be very opinionated, at least that's what I'm led to believe. That you're opinionated, not quiet, I mean. In any event, that's what Grollak told me. Oh, listen to me. I know your name and who you are but you know nothing about me. I am, well, I'm, uh, yes, well, my name, yes, I think I know that. Hmm, just hold on a moment, it's, uh, well, it's um, hmm! This is a little embarrassing, really. You see, I have so much knowledge stored up in my poor little old head, that I sometimes forget the mundane things, the things that I don't think are so important, like my name, for instance. Ah, hold on, I wrote it down here somewhere on something in my pockets, let me look. It's here! Oh no, no, that's not it, that was yesterday's dinner, I think, no it's, what? Oh no, that's definitely not it, that's my potion for, well, when you get old, you'll... Oh never mind, here it is. This is my name, it's, wait, let me see, yes, it's Darjoon. There you go, my boy, my name is Darjoon. Eh, what? You look confused? Oh, I see, silly me, no, no, that's your name, isn't it. Ha, ha, oh goodness, what a bother. Well, why don't you just call me the Librarian, after all, it's what I do, you know. And besides, we call, uh, that man, you know, the one in the middle, um, oh yes, Grollak, well, we call him the Centre, so why can't I just be the Librarian then, eh? It works for me, it's so much easier to remember and so much more important than my name. Yes? Hello Darjoon, I am the Librarian."

Darjoon shook his head, then grinned in relief. What

a silly old man. He would've sneaked countless books past him in College.

"Come to think of it, Darjoon, I haven't seen you in the Library before now, you know. After all, it's not as if you have to steal our books, eh? Ha ha, wink, wink, nudge, nudge and all that, yes. Oh no, we offer easy access to our books here. We're not like that silly, stuffy College of yours, well, I suppose I should say, ours. No, no, it's all available here. Knowledge, I mean. Take history, for example. In that silly College they only teach you a limited history, don't they, eh? The 'After' history, for example. Eh, what's that? Speak up, boy, my hearing's not what it was, you know."

"I said", Darjoon said loudly, waking the lizard who'd dozed off, lulled by the old man's voice, "What do you mean by 'After' history?"

"Hmm, yes, the 'After' history. You interested in history, eh? Good for you. Wish all young mages took an interest in history these days. Oh, well, you see, the 'After' history deals with, well, basically with current events and that's hardly interesting, now is it. But if we look at 'Before' history, well now, that's really interesting, eh? What's that? Really young mage, you will have to speak far more clearly than that. Why do you speak in such a funny way?"

"I said", Darjoon was almost shouting now, "Can you explain 'Before' history then?"

"Before what story, I don't know what you mean? Oh, hold on. Drat it, it's in here somewhere."

The old mage produced a short trumpet-shaped piece of brass from his robe and placed the short end in his ear while Darjoon was speaking.

"Ah yes, better. Well alright, alright, young man, there's no need to shout at me, you know. I'm not entirely deaf. Well, at least not yet, anyway, eh? Ha ha! It's quite simple really, our world's history exists in two major parts, the Before and the After. The difference, or fulcrum if you like, is an event we call the 'Accident'. During this Accident, or just 'Before the Accident' if you prefer, this world underwent enormous change. Everything you see in this room, well, it's really all from the Before time. This part of our world, where the raven-born now live was once a glorious paradise, a luxuriant, tropical world filled with exotic plants, birds and animals. Even our beautiful friend sitting here dozing, well, she is from the Before time. She wouldn't survive out there now, oh no, not in that horrible place we now call home. There was a time when we were still in the egg, when little friends like her ran around freely, but then, well I'm afraid partly as a result of our hatching, or maybe because of the Great Raven, trickster that she is, well it all caused or contributed to the Accident. Whatever started the Accident, once it happened it changed our lives and this world forever, you see. Oh yes, once there was even a great forest, larger even than what you see in Spidral today, and then after the Arrival there were two. Once we lived with others, like us, but also so unlike us and together, we were in harmony, but now apart, well, that's when it all fell apart. Once the Darken Hills really were, well, hills and not the hulking great mountain range they became. Oh, so much changed, once we crawled out of the egg."

The old mage sniggered to himself, then stopped and stared at Darjoon for a long moment, as if studying him.

"But now, Darjoon, now it all hangs in the balance again. What was united before, is now lost, but must be united again, somehow, or indeed, all will be lost again, only I fear this time it could be forever. Can you do it, Darjoon, can you unite all of us?", he peered up at Darjoon, then laughed and laughed, wheezing and wiping his rheumy eyes until he finally stopped. Darjoon just stared at him, perplexed. The mage looked at Darjoon, and then waved a hand dismissively.

"Oh, don't mind me, young mage. I read far too many books, apparently. The knowledge inside becomes so heavy, I wonder how I can stand up under the weight of it all, eh? Do you know the feeling? Now, what did I come in here for, let me think? I'm sure there was something I needed to do here, wasn't there? Let me see, oh yes, now I remember. It's that silly lizard at our secret entrance, you know the one, you've met him before, well now that silly boy needs his food. Fortunately, I have a collection of just what he likes, eh? All the juicy insects get caught in my little trap and once he's had some of those, he's happy again. Or wait, is this him here, and maybe she is there? Oh, it's so confusing, I can never remember. We change them around so they don't get too bored, you see. Poor things. Oh well Darjoon, it was nice to meet you, even if you're not a talkative young raven. Not much to say, eh? Well, not all of us know what we know? Not all of us are built the same way, are we, my big boy? Hee, hee, hee."

Suddenly the old man grabbed Darjoon's wrist in a surprisingly strong grip, and as Darjoon gently tried to pull his hand away, the man held tighter and looked intently at him and spoke fiercely, "Darjoon, be very careful about the knowledge you have gained, and even more careful about the knowledge you seek. Look at me, Darjoon, look carefully. Because knowledge can come with a terrible price, young raven. Oh yes, Darjoon, a terrible price, indeed, make sure you count the cost of it. Ah well, no matter, I'm just an old man now. But I'll see you soon, Darjoon, I'll see you sooner than you think, hee, hee, hee."

The old man let Darjoon go, then spun around and walked away from him, meandering back through the maze of shelves. Darjoon waited until he heard the door on the far side open and close.

"What a crazy old man", he muttered, then he turned to the lizard, "Alright, boy, or uh, girl, let's see what you've got. Talkative, he said? How did he think I could get a word in anyway? Silly old fool."

Closing his eyes, he looked through the lizard's eyes,

and smiled as a large, ornate door knob appeared in the middle of the golden panel. Keeping the lizard's view with his own eyes closed, he approached the door and started turning the handle gently, then heard the soft snick of a catch releasing. Some instinct warned him and he ripped his hand off the door knob just as two sharp, circular blades unfurled around it, rising up like the hood of a snake. In moments they subsided, but not before he saw the wicked, gleaming sharp edges through his own eyes. He'd lost the vision from the lizard, but the aftermath of the shiny blades stayed imprinted on his retina. If his hand had remained on the door knob he'd now be looking at his fingers lying on the floor. He shuddered involuntarily. The door had not been opened, but he just had to get into that room. Closing his eyes again, he picked up the lizard's vision and this time simply studied the door knob closely. He noticed that rather than the surrounding edges being worn, there was a dull patch right in the middle of the knob. Gulping, he approached the door and reached out his hand, then withdrew it. Through the lizard's eyes, he could see a small, empty flower pot on a bench nearby. Grabbing that, he approached the door again, this time using the pot to push against the middle of the door knob and hopefully protect his fingers. This time, instead of the soft, snicking sound he'd heard earlier, a grinding of gears and levers heralded the metallic unlocking of what sounded like large bars of metal sliding into or out of their sockets. The door swung open a little and a faint, stale air leaked out. Shaking off the lizard's vision, he carefully stepped through the door, holding the pot as if it were a weapon.

The room was large and round with wooden panelling to the sides and had an intricately laid marble floor. Above him were large panes of glass arranged in a great big circular dome. To his surprise, given how far down in the mountain he must be, he could see blue sky through the glass and even clouds scudding by, blown by the strong mountain winds. To one side of the room he saw a large golden telescope.

"What is this?", he muttered to himself, "There's no map here. This is an observatory, although it's not as large as the one at the College. What use is this? That silly S'klaratim, I knew I should never have trusted him."

Looking around, he could see that apart from a small cabinet on the other side of the room, opposite the telescope, there was no other furniture or anything remotely looking like a map case or a bookshelf. Hissing in exasperation, Darjoon approached the cabinet carefully. Who knew what that might do when tampered with, and just what strange traps awaited the unwary. Studying it fully, he could see no obvious oddities. Sighing as he realised he should have done this by the door, he gently cast out his magic into the room but detected nothing unusual. Realising he was still holding the flower pot, he placed it on top of the cabinet, then gently turned the small handle and opened it. Inside was a large glass jar that seemed to be glowing of its own accord.

Kneeling down, Darjoon peered intently at the jar, then started and jerked back as the glowing thing inside darted straight at him. He chuckled ruefully as he saw it was just a little firefly, somehow caught inside the jar. A faint metallic tinkling noise puzzled him until he realised it came from the little firefly as it bumped up against the glass. Augmenting his vision with a little magic, he peered closely at the little insect and stared in realisation as his jaw dropped.

Rather than the fireflies he was familiar with back in the forest, this one appeared to be made out of metal. Looking closer, he sent out a small tendril of magic, intending to understand and identify the metal it was made of. The insect suddenly began glowing brighter and brighter and a loud humming noise seemed to emanate from beneath him. Darjoon drew back as the insect got even brighter, then realised something above him was changing, somehow the sky and clouds had disappeared and were now replaced by a growing brightness and he squinted as individual pinpricks of light began to appear. Standing up and stepping back from the jar, he tilted his head to look up at the ceiling. The brightness was slowly fading now and what remained made him laugh out loud.

"You clever, clever mages", he exclaimed in awe, "What a beautiful sight."

A map appeared across the dome, covering all of the Old Lands as he knew them as well as what appeared to be other large land masses. A number of bright, coloured lights were scattered across the map, and in the lower corner of the room a chart had appeared and was glowing against the wall, arcane symbols appearing next to colours that matched the points. The symbols meant nothing to him, and he groaned as he realised he had nothing with which to inscribe, no parchment and no pen. Looking back at the map, he could see there were only a few lights on the Glass Isle itself. Desperately he searched for matching colours in the Old Lands, and grinned when he found one blinking on the Plains of Breath. Staring, the grin faded as he realised it was in what must be the same location as the strange cave that Sirroya and himself had stumbled into so long ago.

A lump stuck in his throat as different images of a blue-eyed, smiling woman flickered through his mind. It had seemed like ages since they'd been together, and it was his fault that her bright light had gone out forever. He didn't want to believe she was gone, but what choice did he have. The only evidence of her being alive were the ramblings of a dying old man.

"Come, Darjoon, focus! Now is not the time for recrimination", he told himself, or at least he thought it was his voice. He quickly memorised the symbols next to the colour that identified the portal to the Glass Isle. But would this portal work both ways? Should he find another, perhaps? The rattling of the door interrupted him and he froze in horror. As he lost his magical focus, the map slowly faded above him and so he quickly closed the cabinet door, watching in relief as the sky reappeared almost instantly.

There was nowhere to hide, so running to an empty part of the room, he crouched down and threw out a shield spell that he hoped would conceal him. As it fell in place, the door opened and the Librarian stepped into the room. He looked around, muttering to himself then stopped suddenly as he glanced at the cabinet. Darjoon cursed inwardly as he saw the flower pot he'd placed there. The Librarian looked around the room, then walked over and picked up the pot and giggled briefly. Turning, he simply walked back out and closed the door behind him.

Darjoon breathed in deep gasps, realising he'd been holding his breath the whole time. Waiting what seemed like an eternity, he slipped out the door and made his way back to his room, encountering practically no-one the whole way there. By the time he made it back, he was sweating with anxiety. Grabbing his pack from under the bed, he finished stuffing in the remaining odds and ends then jumped as a voice boomed out behind him.

"Ah, Darjoon, there you are! What's the matter, boy, you look flushed? Have you been using the exercise facilities? Good for you, you looked like you could do with that and I'm glad to see it. You can never be too fit, you know. We might not be fanatical about it here like they are in the College, but it pays to keep in shape. Now I hope you have everything you need, Darjoon? You only have to ask and the Circle will provide for you, it is our way, you know."

Darjoon steeled himself, then asked the mage, "Grollak, thank you for your kindness and hospitality. There is, in fact, something that I hope you can help me with. I have promised S'klaratim that I would put him forward for the final tests, and I would like to do that now."

"Ah, I see, would you indeed. Well yes, I suppose you're right. I don't think there's any sense in putting it off anymore. I'll make the arrangements, Darjoon, if that's what you really want. But just to be clear, there are no guarantees that he will make it through, you understand that, don't you? Are you sure he's ready?"

Darjoon took a quick, deep breath. What he said now would determine S'klaratim's fate. He could be sentencing the young mage to a horrible death, or sentencing the Circle to a renegade, mad mage.

"Yes, Grollak, I'm sure. I appreciate it's only been a short time that I've known him, and it's true that he can be odd at times, but I believe that he will serve us well in the future."

"Hmm, well, I hope for all our sakes you're right, Darjoon. I can't say I share your certainty. Now listen, I won't keep you as I see you've finished packing. You have a safe trip, young mage and I'm sure we'll be seeing each other quite soon. Don't worry, we will contact you in due course, and we'll be watching over you. In the meantime, may the Great Raven fold you in her wings and keep you safe."

Darjoon muttered the reverse blessing to the older mage and then stared as Grollak walked jauntily away. He was beginning to think there might be some truth in the rumours that the Circle mages were all, well, a bit off-centre. There were certainly some strange individuals here. Putting S'klaratim forward had seemed almost too easy. He shouldered his pack, walked out the door and then without encountering S'klaratim or anyone else, emerged into the midday sun shining over the Hills.

The journey from the Darken Hills to Spidral was uneventful, although he was greeted again by the Forest guardians, the two tall trees standing at the path leading into the deep forest. This time, however, he repeated their greeting back to them, something from his memory just slipping into place, and so this time he seemed to have no trouble along the trail, not even hearing voices or feeling anything menacing as had happened before. At least, he didn't wake up knee-deep in a pond or anything unusual. Finally, after some time travelling through the murky, green depths and musing on his time with the Circle, he arrived at the tree-top village just as the moon was rising. Strolling along the familiar suspended walk-way that led into the village while a familiar, small blue bird flitted overhead, he smiled as he saw the ubiquitous figure of Y'sarryn waiting for him under the far tree, hand raised in greeting.

This time however, there was no familiar greeting in his head and as he approached the hunter, he could see there was a pensive look to him. After greeting him as a raven-born, Darjoon tilted his head quizzically and was about to ask what was wrong when before he could say anything, Y'sarryn grabbed him uncharacteristically in a big bear hug.

"Okay, okay", he spluttered, taken aback, "What's gotten into you, Y'sarryn? Are you going soft in your old age, then? I mean, look, you won't believe the weird people I've had to deal with, so don't you start acting strangely too, eh?"

Y'sarryn threw back his head and laughed deeply.

"No, Darjoon, I don't have the madness of the Circle mages, I'm just very glad to see you. It's been, well, an interesting few weeks and I'm afraid a lot has gone on here while you've been gone. I'm just relieved to see you back safe and sound, that's all. In some ways, Darjoon, I, well, I feel like a father to you, you know."

Darjoon swallowed the lump in his throat and then attempted a nonchalant swagger as he walked alongside the tall hunter. He tried to make light of the man's comments.

"Yes, well, you'd have to be raven-born to be my father, now wouldn't you? And as you're obviously just some scrawny Spidralite hunter..."

He yelled as Y'sarryn punched him on the arm, then

raced ahead of him through the moonlit gloom of the forest night. Y'sarryn chased him up and down ladders and walkways, initially enjoying the game, and then desperately trying to catch him before he got to his hut. But Darjoon slowed down as he approached, seeing Nasrindo and K'trell standing waiting for him with their arms folded.

"You know, it still, huh, huh, amazes me", Y'sarryn was puffing as he caught up to him, "For a, huh, huh, big man you, huh, huh, can move surprisingly quickly."

Then he looked up and saw the two waiting as well.

"You know, Darjoon, they weren't at all happy with your leaving. If you hadn't returned tonight, then they would've come after you, no matter what I said. But just remember, it's only out of their love for you that they are so upset."

The pair approached the desert folk and Darjoon looked at them sheepishly.

"Well, look what the truktari dragged in", Y'sarryn tried to lighten the moment.

"Yes, just look! But I hope its claws were sharp and piercing and its teeth were long and strong. So Darjoon, I thought we were in this together? Why did you drag us all the way from the desert if you simply intended to abandon us here in this tree? No, wait, I'm not finished with you yet, I haven't even started", K'trell was visibly shaking in anger.

"You think I gave up my tribe to be your, your, pet or your plaything? You think the fate of the Old Lands is something we can all just thumb our noses at? Just like you do? What, you got bored and decided to go rambling around, when we should be trying to figure out a way to get to the Glass Isle? I can make allowances for how young you are, Darjoon, but isn't it time you grew up? No, I'm still not done yet", she drew in a deep breath as Darjoon made another feeble protest, then suddenly she deflated and her eyes brightened.

Stepping forward she reached towards him and

fiercely pulled him into her embrace.

"Darjoon, I, I don't know what to say. I'm sorry, we, I mean, I, well, we were just concerned for you. And there's something you need to know, something that's happened, Darjoon, the most amazing...", she let go of the now rigid Darjoon and stepped back in surprise, then, seeing his face, she turned to look behind her.

Darjoon stared at the entrance to the hut, too afraid to wipe his eyes although he didn't believe what they were seeing. The blonde hair, the blue-green eyes, even in the early gloom they were clearly visible to him. He stared in awe and despair. It couldn't be true. If it was a vision, then it was an awful vision, maybe a result of all the stress and now the emotion that these people were bringing out in him. His vision blurred as the figure started walking out of the hut and came towards him.

"Darjoon", she said.

TO BE CONTINUED

# ABOUT THE AUTHOR

Growing up in the sugar cane farms of the Natal midlands in South Africa, and later enjoying the wild outdoors of what was then the Eastern Transvaal, Jackson always had a love of open spaces. He now enjoys living in the tamer countryside of southern England. Being an avid reader from a young age, he eagerly devoured J.R.R. Tolkien, C.S. Lewis, Edgar Rice Burroughs, and later Raymond E. Feist, among others. Daydreaming out in the country was always second nature to him and a means of escape from the confines of modern living. This escapism resulted in many untold stories, but now they fight their way free, released into the world as words on a page.